"Well, come on then."

Gigi placed her glass on the bar. "Twirl me around till I tell you to stop."

They left Sarah alone with the boiler-maker from Essex County that was currently wreaking havoc with her nerve-endings. Again, they stood in silence, more awkward now that Gigi had left. She didn't know what to do with her eyes or her hands. How long could she stare at her dwindling drink?

"Dance with me." It was a soft, gentle statement without hint of question.

She looked up. Shadows hit the angles of his face in such a way that the mysterious appearance he'd worn earlier had morphed into a smokiness that billowed to her. The vapor seeped into and through her being.

Hesitation flooded her brain, but her body was a different story. Charges of glee spread through her veins, roaring in beat with the music. There was a war going on inside her, but one faction had all the power and she knew it.

Gulping the last of her drink, she handed him the empty glass and looked him dead in the eye. "Sure."

Praise for M. Kate Quinn

Letters and Lace

by

M. Kate Quinn

The Ronan's Harbor Series

This is a work of fiction. Names, characters, places, and incidents are either the product of the author's imagination or are used fictitiously, and any resemblance to actual persons living or dead, business establishments, events, or locales, is entirely coincidental.

Letters and Lace

COPYRIGHT © 2013 by M. Kate Quinn

Cover Art by *Kim Mendoza*

The Wild Rose Press, Inc.
PO Box 708
Adams Basin, NY 14410-0708
Visit us at www.thewildrosepress.com

Publishing History
First *Last Rose of Summer* Edition, 2013
Print ISBN 978-1-61217-862-2
Digital ISBN 978-1-61217-863-9

The Ronan's Harbor Series
Published in the United States of America

Dedication

To my girlfriends,
my tried and true soulmates and anchors in any storm.
I love you all.

To my six kids,
Joe, Rob, Melanie, Steven, Michael and Keith.
The Brady's have nothing on my bunch.

And to the dearest man who shares my life,
who is my life,
my husband, Harvey.

My cup runneth over...

Chapter One

The air inside the cavernous space was stale, the exact opposite of Sarah Grayson's vision for it.

She surveyed the sunroom of her Jersey shore bed-and-breakfast where scattered square tables supported upturned chairs with brown wooden legs pointing to the ceiling like barren saplings. It was a far cry from the sumptuous scene it would become on June first—a spectacular setting for Hannah, her only child, on her wedding day.

In the quiet of preseason solitude, Sarah was enwrapped in the anticipation of the task ahead. The determination fueling her soul was heady.

Reaching into her pants pocket, she crossed to the back wall. She withdrew the old, tarnished storage room key, inserted it into the lock, and turned the glass knob. With the door open, she was momentarily startled by the assaulting smell of must. She squinted into the dank space that for years had been her bone of contention.

Finally she'd saved enough money to do the conversion. With carpenters due to start work this week, her mind reeled with ideas for the sunroom's added expanse. She eyed the cracked flagstone floor—quaint although too damaged to salvage—and pictured the mess lifting it would create. But, no matter, the result would be worth the distress.

She closed the door behind her, stepping back into the sunroom. The bank of windows along the front wall offered a testament to the gray, drizzly April morning, though she was not dismayed by the cloudy scene. She relished the awaiting transformation to both inside and out of her Cornelia Inn.

There'd be no guests for weeks, giving her time to ready the inn for the season. But the wedding preparations would steal her time. The new sunroom would need window treatments, there was wall art to find. Eagerness tingled over her skin.

The sound of the doorbell jarred her reverie. She went through to the small, square entry hall and opened the front door.

"Norman, hello," she greeted. She was surprised to see the town letter carrier at her door rather than offering his usual quick wave from the sidewalk as he stuffed mailboxes along the roadway.

"Morning, Sarah," he said shyly. His nose was a distinct pink from the chilly early April air. "I, uh, brought you your mail. This one here requires your signature."

She accepted the bundle of envelopes into her hand, sensing trepidation in her long-time acquaintance. "Thank you," she said. "Kind of cold today, huh? Do you have time for a cup of tea, Norman?"

He extended a ballpoint pen to her with a quick jerk of his hand "'Fraid not today, Sarah," he said, his tone contrite.

She signed the receipt. Norman knew something. That was one thing about life in Ronan's Harbor. Everybody got wind of everyone else's news, especially those that hand-delivered it to your doorstep.

After a momentary hesitation, Norman nodded goodbye and turned to leave. His heel caught on the upturned edge of the welcome mat and he stumbled, doing a fancy tap-dance kind of trot to stay upright. His brown leather mail satchel swayed away from his body, slapping back against his side and adding to his precariousness.

Sarah grabbed his arm to assist, but he was heavy and rather than stop his wobbling, she inadvertently joined his footwork, trotting in step—a drunken Ginger Rogers led by a freaky Fred Astaire. She couldn't help but laugh.

Finally, thanks to his grab of the weathered wicker chair near the house's entrance, the dance was over.

"I'm okay," he said swiftly. Now his entire face was as pink as his nose.

"Are you sure?" she asked, sorry that she'd let the giggles get the best of her. "Can I get you something?"

"No," he said, lifting a reassuring hand. "But, you might want to tack that down."

"I certainly will."

One more thing to add to her to-do list.

Sarah closed the door and studied the envelope. The heavy stock was similar to the wedding invitations that they'd just put in the mail. She ran a finger over the raised glossy lettering accompanied by an official-looking stamp of the town municipal authority. *What now?*

She carried the stack into the sunroom where she'd left her tea. Sitting at a little table she slit the logoed envelope with the nail of her index finger and carefully withdrew the page.

Her eyes scanned and rescanned the jargon, her

gaze riveting again to a series of stunning snippets: *Official complaint, halt renovation, required limited use permit for parties on premises of bed-and-breakfasts.*

Her heart pounded in her chest. Why would someone in Ronan's Harbor file a complaint against her plans? Since when was it illegal to host your own child's wedding? What the hell was a "conditional use permit?"

Her face flushed hot. Hadn't her carpenter told her there'd been no need to obtain a building permit?

Out of nowhere, like a ghost from her past, an image of her ex-husband's face popped into her head. She saw Gary's scowl, and could almost hear his chortle at her ignorance.

Hannah's footfalls sounded on the stairs and Sarah quickly slipped the letter back into its envelope, her fingers fumbling in the simple task. She tucked it at the bottom of the stack of mail and for good measure, she plopped her tea cup on top of the bundle. She took a deep, steadying breath.

"There you are," Hannah called from the doorway.

Sarah turned to her daughter, eying the china cup in the girl's hands. "Good morning."

Hannah approached with careful, measured steps, holding her cup with two hands. "I poured some of your latest concoction. That okay?"

Hannah continued across the room, her coltish legs exposed beneath the hem of the plaid boxer shorts she'd slept in.

Sarah's heart blipped with nostalgia. A quick flash of her daughter as a teenager came to mind, all legs and arms, softball uniform full of grass stains, hat visor askew, her yellow lab puppy, Parker, bounding at her heels.

Hannah took a sip from her delicate cup before licking her tongue over her lip. "What do you call this one, Mom?"

"The Wedding Tea," Sarah said. She gave her daughter a sly grin. "You like?"

"Seriously, Mom?" Hannah laughed. "All the things on that to-do list of yours and you went first for dreaming up a tea for the event?"

"Divine, isn't it? Citrus slices, apples, hibiscus, rosehips." Sarah turned her gaze back to the sunroom, ignoring the doubt that laced her daughter's words. She refused to turn her head in the direction of the mail that sat screaming at her from the corner of the table.

"You're sure about tackling all this, right, Mom?" Hannah's voice continued to ring with undeniable uncertainty.

Sarah snapped her head around to meet Hannah's slate-blue gaze. She had her father's eyes and she narrowed them just the way he did. Reflexively, Sarah bristled.

"Your wedding tea is not the *only* item checked off that list of mine, my dear. Believe me; I've got it all under control." She felt her insides twist. At least that's what she'd thought before the damned mail delivery.

Hannah shrugged, cocked her head as she perused the room. "Daddy said—"

A warning surged in Sarah veins. "I'm really not concerned with what your father said."

She sat straight in her chair, her shoulders square. She could almost feel the walls of her Cornelia Inn reach to embrace her. She loved her inn.

Little had she known when Gary had purchased the

inn eighteen years ago—his sole idea to provide Sarah what he termed a "nice little hobby"—that it would become hers alone in the divorce settlement. Nor had she known that the inn would become her salvation.

Now she wondered what it was that her ex had said to Hannah. But, she wouldn't ask and knew she was better off not knowing.

"It's just that, well, you're sure this won't be too much for you, right, Mom? The wedding's around the corner and the guy hasn't even started working on the storage room. You sure it'll be ready in time?"

No. Sarah shook the thought. "Of course." Her tone was convincingly emphatic. "He told me three weeks, tops. His crew will be here on Monday. Don't worry. I'm not."

"Okay, but, I know it's a lot with you just running The Cornelia. Planning my wedding and making sure all this gets done..." Hannah's face scrunched with an effort to conceal her hesitancy, but it still clung to her words like sugar granules.

Sarah waved a nonchalant hand. "The invites are in the mail, remember? It's full steam ahead now. I have no concerns, nor should you. Trust your mother." Sarah didn't verbalize the other part of her thought. *Trust your mother—the way your father never did—to do a good job.*

She could just imagine Gary's reaction to this latest tidbit of news from the town. Oh, he'd love to point the salon-groomed tip of his finger right at her face while laughing his sardonic sound through his dentist-treated blinding, broad smile. How many times over the years had he done just that?

Well, she'd give him no reason now to approach

her with his red, distress-of-constipation-looking pinched face. Or worse, to use his mocking tone that always rang out with his signature put-down—calling her *Sarah Doodle*. No. Above all else, no.

Thankfully, these days she was far from Gary's scrutinizing radar, he being consumed with his new wife and their toddler, of all things. Why Gary had decided to become a father again at fifty still baffled her.

Gary's new little family kept him busy enough to leave Sarah alone these days, but somehow she sensed his persistent I-told-you-so hovering over her head like a canopy of thorns. She figured that certainly justified her delight when she'd learned Gary's colicky bundle of joy was lactose intolerant and had mastered the art of projectile vomiting. Sarah smiled at the thought, then banished it.

"You love this place," Hannah said. Her tone was round, wrapped in appreciation.

Sarah watched her daughter's eyes scan the sunroom. She tried to view it through Hannah's eyes and did her best to ignore the brief doubt that fluttered across her skin. Was it foolish to believe she could actually pull this off? Her gaze found Hannah's. "You love The Cornelia, too. Almost as much as I do."

Hannah laughed. "Nobody could love the old girl as much as you do, Mom. Not after all you've put into it."

At the time of their all-too civilized severance it had taken all the courage she could muster to thumb her nose at Gary's sympathy-laced offer of alimony. She'd looked him in his gray-blue eyes and said, "Keep it."

Afterward every cell in her body had rattled with

fear. She had made sure he'd never known her utter terror at pulling off being a sole innkeeper, viewed it as a dare.

He'd never learned of those early days when she'd dined on spaghetti and had stretched her food budget to its limit with peanut butter and jam on store-brand English muffins. She'd kept mum about all the sleepless nights, the wee hours of the morning spent at her little writing desk pouring over her books unsure of how she'd keep the lights on, and the furnace full of oil.

Now, there was no way she would let that municipal authority letter intimidate her. And, she sure as hell wasn't letting Gary in on it. Nor was there the need to bother Hannah with the complaint. She'd fix it. She had to.

She sipped her tea, letting it warm its way through her, just like her determination that Hannah's wedding would be perfect, a total success attributable to her capable hand.

"Your wedding needs to be here. Right here in this room."

"If you're not worried, then I'm not worried." Hannah furnished a small grin.

"Now, you'd better go on and get ready. Aren't you meeting your fiancé in the City?"

"Oh, my God—Ian." Hannah bolted from the room, padding up the stairs in her fuzzy slippers.

"Hmm…" Sarah said with a smirk. "And, you're wondering how *I* can juggle everything?"

As soon as Hannah had disappeared up the staircase to their small third floor apartment, Sarah grabbed the letter again and reread it. Damn whoever it was that was making a case out of this.

Keeping this from Hannah and anyone else would be no easy feat in Ronan's Harbor. Not with the way news—all kinds, but mostly bad—spread around the little shore town like honey on a hot scone.

Hannah re-appeared, dressed and ready for her trip into the City. She stood in the sunroom's entrance, tall and lean, smart-looking in her pencil skirt and blouse.

"I almost forgot about meeting Ian," Hannah said, her tone rushed. She fiddled with the clasp of her wristwatch. "I've got to run."

"Don't rush. Drive safely," Sarah said, painting a smile on her face. She'd spare Hannah. She'd straighten it out with the town and her daughter wouldn't even have to know. Just a technicality, after all. Easy peasy.

"I'll call you," Hannah's eyes fell to the cluster of envelopes on the table. "Was that the mailman at the door earlier, Mom?"

"Yes," Sarah said, forcing disinterest into her tone. Her hand floated to rest onto the teacup atop the letters.

"Was it Norman Wallace?" Hannah's words were in sing-song and a wide grin broke out across her face. "Since when do we get door-to-door service, Mother?" Her voice filled with implication, her tone light and teasing. "Special delivery for a special lady?"

"Oh, stop it." Sarah waved her off. "Don't you have an appointment to get to?"

"Mr. Wallace has a crush on you, Mom."

Sarah stood from the chair and pulled the envelopes into her grasp. "Don't be silly."

"I think you should invite him to be your guest at the wedding. He can catch the garter." Hannah gave an exaggerated wink.

The image of poor Norman cha-chaing on her front

porch almost made Sarah laugh again. No. She would not be dating the mailman.

"Come on, seriously, Mom. After all your work with the planning of it, wouldn't it be nice to enjoy the festivities with a date?"

"Planning your wedding isn't work, sweetie," Sarah said. It's my pleasure." *And no complaining neighbor or fool town law is going to ruin it.*

"You never have any fun, Mom. You need to, you know, go out a little."

"I do," Sarah said. "As a matter of fact Gigi and I are painting the town red this very evening, going to go stay out to all hours of the night. Be, you know, hussies."

Hannah laughed loud, shaking her pretty head. "Are you two going to Captain's Pier House again tonight? Is that your hot time?"

"Yes," Sarah said, lifting one shoulder against the remark. "It happens to be Ladies Night."

"Oh, wow, sure you can handle a night of Mr. Bailey's three-piece combo playing their version of The Beatles?"

"The City, my darling, the City" Sarah said pointing toward the doorway. "Now go. Give my love to Ian."

****

Alone in the foyer, Sarah's gaze sought the framed oil portrait adorning the wall above the antique credenza. Cornelia Vandermark DeGraff looked out from the frame, dark brown eyes painted expertly to reveal the courage Sarah knew resided inside her inn's namesake.

Cornelia stood before the parlor's fireplace, one

delicate hand clasping an ornate silk fa
widow's frothy, lemon-chiffon-colored g
low beneath her corseted waist, draping w   ～ or
fabric that swooped around to her back—a tailor's
masterpiece scandalously unbefitting a woman who'd
lost her husband, tyrant though he'd been.

Sarah knew well the story behind the regal brunette
with her hair femininely clustered in ringlets atop her
crown and girlish bangs frizzled over her forehead.
Cornelia DeGraff had not been a delicate flower.

The founder of the Ronan's Harbor Garden Club
had been a maverick, unwilling to conform to societal
morés. Sarah knew that pretty prop in her hand had
been less her norm than the pipe she was rumored to
have smoked out on her front porch—much to the
shock of the townsfolk.

What would Cornelia have done about the filed
complaint? She looked the old girl dead in the eye. "We
won't stand for it, will we, Cornelia?"

Sarah retrieved the letter and shoved it into her
jeans pocket. She needed to remember to bring it along
with her tonight to show her best friend. Gigi would
help her come up with a strategy.

She spent the day going over her lists, cross-
checking her calendar, careful not to forget any of the
wedding details appointments or the workmen's
projected scheduling. She marked down Monday
night's meeting at the town hall regarding the
complaint.

No matter how she tried to avoid thinking about it,
the news hung in her head like an infection, throbbing
against her temples, reminding her she had a problem.

It was dusk when Sarah finally put away her

ₚaperwork. As if on automatic pilot she entered her bathroom and ran water to fill the tub. A hot soak usually worked miracles whenever she needed to wash away stress.

How much of my adult life have I spent with pruny skin? Based on the possibility of some saboteur ruining her sunroom plans—and halting Hannah's dream wedding at the inn—Sarah figured she'd have oak tree-like bark for skin before Monday night at seven-thirty.

The phone rang while she soaked. Sarah was careful not to drop the handset into the water where the previous one, as well as her MP-3 player, had met their sudsy demise.

She heard her friend, Gigi's sensuous tone. "Ready for action?"

"Ready," Sarah said, attempting to sound enthused. She closed her eyes, leaning against the inflatable pillow Gigi had given her one Christmas. "Just taking a bath."

"A, you don't sound ready, and B, you only switch from shower to bath when you need to escape something cruddy."

Sarah smiled against the device in her wet hand. A, Gigi often spoke in bullet points, and B, she knew Sarah better than anybody on the planet. So C, there was no sense in giving her friend lip service. She blew out a long breath, chasing some bubbles off her fingertips. "Cruddy's the right word."

"Okay, spill it."

"We'll talk about it later at the Pier House. I got a letter today from town hall. Somebody filed a complaint against me."

"What asshole would do that?" Gigi's normally

12

deep tone changed to her angry rasp. "Are you serious?"

"Yup." Sarah was too tired to discuss it now. The high temperature of the water was making her drowsy.

"Okay, Sarah, look. Whatever it is, we'll handle it. Nobody's pulling that shit and getting away with it. Remember that time the Coopers tried to sue me because their geraniums died after a week?"

A lazy grin grew on Sarah's face as she remembered the disgruntled customers trying to poison townspeople's minds against Bayside Blossoms, her friend's treasured flower shop.

The only poison that had taken hold was the entire box of plant food Gigi discovered the fools had dumped onto their freshly planted bed of geraniums, wiping out the poor plants like a plague. Sarah recalled how she and Gigi had sneaked onto the woman's property after dark to get a soil sample.

Yes, Gigi was right. Nobody pulls that shit and gets away with it.

Sarah sat up straight in the tub. It was time to get out and give her skin the chance to resume what smoothness it had left after forty-six years of bubble therapy.

"You know what, Gigi, you're right. Whoever this complainer is better watch out."

"Tonight we'll make a toast," Gigi said. "To the sorry ass who thinks they can mess with us."

"You got it," Sarah said. "See you later."

She pressed the "off" button and the handset began to slip from her grasp. Frantically, she jerked her hand out from the tub and the handset fell to the floor and skidded across the tile. *Saved, at least, from drowning.*

I'll check the blunt-force trauma later.

She leaned over to the chrome lever at the front of the tub and gave it a full twist. She heard the momentary pop of water startled from its complacency followed by the gurgle as it drained.

By the time Gigi was due to come by for her Sarah had regrouped sufficiently, even when the doubt of her ability to combat the complaint tried to encroach into her brain. She reminded herself that though she wasn't sure how, she would be saving her plans.

She took extra care in her appearance for tonight, deciding to dress with her "as-if" mentality. She didn't pull out the strategy often, but it had its merits—appear *as if* you're full of confidence and there's a good chance the world will believe it.

Tonight in her close-fit black pants and trendy tunic sweater, she had the look of assurance. The silver hoop earrings, the long drippy chain necklace—all of it worked the façade. Sarah straightened her shoulders and air-kissed her painted lips toward the image in the mirror. Confidence, she was loaded with it.

Later, as they drove down Ocean Avenue toward the beach on their way to The Pier House, Gigi bubbled with typical excitement.

"Something awesome's in store for us tonight, Sarah," she said with a broad grin. "I feel it." She scrunched her nose for emphasis.

"If you say so."

Gigi clucked her tongue. "Come on. Loosen up. You look great, by the way."

"Thanks," Sarah said. "So do you."

In contradiction to Sarah's smooth-lined outfit, Gigi's ensemble had been sewn with threads soaked in "wow." There was that familiar flash in Gigi's eyes that matched the electric blue of her billowy blouse. No one needed to tell her she looked great.

Gigi hummed with audible admiration. "Girl, your ex should see you these days."

Sarah's fingers brushed over the soft strands of her un-sprayed hair, a flowing mass of waves that had a mind of its own. She'd abandoned the tedious efforts to straighten the arrogant waves years ago—especially since it had been Gary's idea in the first place.

When the strings of pin lights lining the roof of the small building came into twinkly view, Gigi flipped down the visor above her head and looked into the rectangular vanity mirror, lit now by a small bulb.

"Um, you're driving," Sarah commented.

Gigi, ignoring Sarah's observation, ran well-manicured fingers over her pointed, spiky hair—jet black these days, color choice of the month. Just two months earlier, her short wacky hair had been a deep red—burgundy really—in honor of Valentine's Day.

Sarah's wheat-brown that had been the same all her life. It was true, Sarah supposed, that no two women could appear more unalike. But, it had been love at first sight for the two friends on the day Sarah had walked into her first Garden Club meeting.

Luckily for her, she'd sat right beside Virginia Allen, the proprietor of the town's flower shop. Gigi had handed her a plastic cup and had leaned close. "Have some," she had whispered. "I spiked the hell out of it."

Sarah had taken a tentative sip, immediately tasting the distinct tang of wine—a lot of wine—and it was good.

The woman with the strange hairdo and crazy, dangling feathered earrings had given her a toothy grin. "I'm Gigi," she'd said. "You're not one of these prima donnas. I can tell."

That had been over a decade ago, and since then the two had faced a lot of things; Gigi's scare with a phantom lump in her breast, as well as her painful breakups with on-again-off-again boyfriend, Mickey Nolan. There'd been Sarah's divorce, followed by the anguish of her going solo at the inn.

Gigi pulled her car into one of the lot's parking spaces and the two scurried toward the entrance against the chilly ocean breeze. Music wafted through the flimsily tented patio that jutted from the main building. They hurried through the door and snaked a path to the bar.

"I'd say sixty-forty," Gigi said perusing the people milling about. "Not bad."

Gigi had the habit of assessing the ratio of women versus men at Ladies Nights. Typically, the scales at these Pier House events tipped toward an abundance of middle-aged women, men were a meager showing.

Sarah didn't care. She was out and dressed up, and doing her best to forget about the letter that sat folded in her purse.

Gigi ordered her a cosmopolitan, a pink martini that Sarah didn't normally drink. They hit her too quickly and she didn't like the fuzzy-brained effect. She took a tiny sip, vowing to herself to let the beverage last her the evening.

Gigi eyed the crowd over the rim of her cone-shaped glass. "I see one."

"For God's sake, Gigi, we're not at a pet store.

Stop acting like you're shopping for a puppy."

"Oh, what I see is no puppy. I spotted me a Rottweiler."

Sarah couldn't help but laugh. She followed her friend's gaze to the other side of the room, near Pete Bailey's combo busily crucifying a ballad.

The man was dark. His navy blue oxford was tucked into faded jeans. His dark hair brushed straight back over his head had a few uncooperative strands falling forward. He brought a partially-filled pilsner glass to his mouth and took a sip of dark beer.

In the subdued light Sarah detected the chisel of his facial planes, the angles coming together in a rugged kind of broodiness that looked both appealing and dangerous. She turned to look fully at her friend. Gigi's face was that of a child after finding a package with her name on it on Christmas morning.

"Down girl," Sarah warned, knowing such a comment was about as effective as an eyedropper of water on an inferno.

"Come with me." She walked in the man's direction not even hesitating a beat to be sure Sarah would follow.

They wove through the throng of women dolled up in their evening-out attire. They passed clusters huddled together in giggly conversations, reminding Sarah of a school dance. It was pathetic really, but who was she to say? She was at the dance, too. And she'd come with the Prom Queen.

They hovered near the man, but not too close. Sarah knew the drill. Get in his direct line of vision, let him know you're there, wait for him to approach.

Gigi broke out her usual moves, touching a delicate

hand to her hair, laughing with her head back, running a hand over a thigh to brush away non-existent lint. Sarah didn't understand why her friend bothered. Gigi always got noticed. She exuded pheromones the same way fresh basil filled a room with its aroma. Truly, if pheromones looked like snowflakes, Gigi would be a walking blizzard.

The band took a break, the three local men abandoning their instruments for a stint at the bar. People gathered around them offering compliments on the guys' performances.

The people in Ronan's Harbor were nothing if not supportive of each other. Sarah scrutinized the faces of the people she knew, wondering, *So, which one of them is trying to ruin my life?* The feeling was ugly. These were her people. The idea of one of them filing a complaint against her felt like a personal slap. It stung.

Gigi's target approached, sauntering toward them like a gun-slinger traversing a dirt road in an old western. Sarah hated to admit it, but the guy *was* hot. Smoldering with a subtlety that gave Sarah a little foreign-feeling pang. This kind of twinge had been dormant so long that at first she thought the cosmo had done a job on her already. She looked down at her glass, still three-quarters full.

He stopped when he reached their table, offering a small half-smile. He had a nice mouth and his lopsided grin only served to make it more appealing. Gigi had picked a good one this time, that was for sure.

"I'm Gigi," she said, her voice dropping an octave. She offered a hand, which he took into his own.

"Benny," he said. He turned toward Sarah. "And?"

"Oh," she startled. Usually with Gigi around, men

tended to regard her as a lamppost. "I'm Sarah."

"Nice to meet you both," he said, but his gaze was on Sarah. She tried to pull her eyes from him, but they refused to cooperate.

He held up his empty pilsner. "I'm heading for another one of these. Can I get you ladies a drink?"

Sarah looked down at her glass, then over to Gigi's which was nearly drained.

"I'm good for now, thanks," Sarah said.

"Oh, come on, Sar, drink up, honey." Gigi poked an elbow at her.

The move caused Sarah's hand to jerk spilling the cosmopolitan onto her sweater. A big wet patch appeared, like glaze on a muffin, on one breast of the cotton-synthetic blend.

"Oh my God," Gigi said. "I'm sorry."

Sarah stole a glance at Benny whose eyes had found the wet mound on her chest. A rush of heat flooded her face.

"I, uh…excuse me," she said.

She headed toward the bar with the mission of grabbing some paper towels. She hoped the garment wasn't ruined, but she was more upset by her reaction to Gigi's Rottweiler. Why was she looking at him? Why was *he* looking at her? He made her nervous and the feeling was new, scary.

She reminded herself that Gigi was excited over this newcomer. Truthfully it wasn't every day a guy like this one showed up in Ronan's Harbor.

This Benny person was probably a business man, just passing through. There'd been plenty of those during their visits to Ladies Nights. Guys with wives and kiddies tucked away at home while they perused the local scene, did some flirting, and gave away drinks and empty promises as if they were both free.

Somehow she sensed this Benny didn't fit that mold. His was a far cry from the typical appearance of a transient businessman. This was a cowboy who'd taken a wrong turn at the corral and had landed on the Pier House's doorstep.

So, even if her sweater did reek of cosmo, she'd stick around for Gigi's sake. She vowed to keep her eyes off the wayward cowpoke.

It was Benny that managed to get his hands on a stack of paper towels and extended them to Sarah. She broke her vow in record time.

There was a shiny message of sympathy in his dark eyes. They seized Sarah's gaze, zapping her ability to avert from the lock they had on her. Air was suddenly trapped inside her lungs. He volunteered an easy smile, exposing a crooked eyetooth that for some reason just added to his appeal.

She couldn't remember the last time she'd reacted to a man's physicality. Right now she could actually feel her nipples pressing hard against the scratchy fabric of that ridiculous demi-cupped bra she'd bought on a whim one Saturday at the mall.

It was as though her body had taken on a persona all its own, betraying her practiced aloofness—peeking out from behind the well-placed coating of armor she'd brushed onto her view of men, that shield she'd stayed safely behind for years.

She reminded herself that this was Gigi's Rottweiler. She'd never really entertain making a move toward Benny anyway. Hell, she was just happy knowing she wasn't dead.

Sarah accepted the paper towels and muttered a hushed, "Thank you." Their fingers brushed against each other with a flash of electricity—*two sticks producing enough friction to ignite a flame.* Her own brazen thought jolted her.

She unfolded a towel and pressed it to her sweater. Suddenly the move felt intimate and she didn't need to lift her gaze to feel his stare.

"I'm going to, uh, head to the ladies' room to work on this," she said to Gigi. She motioned to the front of her sweater and instantly hated herself for bringing attention to the area where her body advertised its reaction to Benny like a set of high beams. She dashed off.

In the bright, stark light of the ladies room, Sarah stood in front of the sink and looked into the oval mirror above it. *Look at yourself,* she criticized inwardly. She was a sight. The dark patch over one boob looked like she'd missed a baby's feeding. The nipple stared through the wet fabric that covered it, gawking at her image in the glass. It was good, she decided, that nipples couldn't laugh because this one would be roaring.

She knew trying to rewet the sweater to rinse it of the spilled drink would only make her nipples happier. She opted to stand under the hand dryer—no easy feat considering it had been affixed to the wall at the ideal height for a Smurf. She folded her five-foot-six self as best she could under the force of air. Sadly, nipples liked that too. The sorry truth was now that her armor had been cracked open, her physical reactions seeped out like lava, too hot to stop. She needed to get her ass home and, what? Take another bath? One in ice cubes, maybe?

She rejoined Gigi standing at the bar with Benny, laughing in that flirty way she'd mastered.

"How'd you do?" Gigi asked letting her eyes cast to Sarah's sweater.

"Oh, it's fine," she said with a little laugh that sounded to her own ears like she'd swallowed a feather. "No harm done."

"Here you go, ma'am," Benny said. He reached to the bar's surface and retrieved a new cosmopolitan and handed it to Sarah. Their fingers touched and again a bolt of something new shot through her. He was turning her into a power plant.

"Thank you," she said, focusing her gaze onto the glass and away from his dark eyes.

"Benny was just telling me he's a retired police officer from up north."

"Oh, wow." Her comment was lame, but, all things considered, the fact that the two syllables were coherent was a success.

"Glendale," he said. "You familiar with Essex County?"

"Some." Sarah said. "I grew up in Morris."

"Ah, a Morris girl."

His eyes called her. She ignored them. "Yes."

An awkward silence fell over all of them, Gigi, Benny, Sarah, and her rotten two-timing body—which at the moment was screaming at the ex-cop from Essex County, New Jersey.

"Honey, it's my turn to visit the powder room," Gigi said, pinching the arm of Sarah's sweater into her fingers. "Come with me."

Sarah knew the tone and the message in the pinch.

Gigi wanted a powwow. Following, she didn't miss the implication of her friend's two-handed push of the ladies room door.

Sarah couldn't help but think Gigi was on to her uncontrollable response to Benny. Her face burned with shame. The small, tiled spaced might as well have been a church confessional. She opened her mouth to begin her apology.

"Wait," Gigi said, holding up a hand like a crossing guard.

Sarah clamped her mouth closed and did what she was told. She waited.

"A, you can't fool me," Gigi said.

"I…"

"And B, there's no denying this specimen's so into you it's like he's blasting it on a highway billboard."

"Wait. What?"

"Sarah." Gigi laughed and placed her hands on Sarah's upper arms. She gave them a squeeze. "I'll kill you if you don't seize this moment."

"But, he's your Rottweiler."

"No, I spotted him. But, he's all yours, honey."

"Gigi, I don't have this in me. I'm out tonight to come off the panic attack I'm having over that filed complaint. Really, that's all I can think about."

"Hold up. Tell me what the letter said."

Sarah unzipped her purse, withdrew the folded envelope, and thrust it at Gigi.

Gigi unfolded the letter and scanned it silently. As she did, her mouth dropped more and more open.

Finally, Gigi lifted her gaze from the page and gave Sarah a penetrating stare. "Well, this is bullshit."

"I've established that, yes. Now I need a plan."

Gigi grazed her palm over the points of her coiffure. "Let's take one step at a time."

She lifted the document and waved it in the air like a flag. "I'm coming with you on Monday night to town hall. I want to see with my own eyes which neighbor complained about what you, as the *owner,* plan for *your* inn. Basically, A, I'm aghast that anyone would be so rotten. And, B, I might bring a pea shooter."

"I just want to make my sunroom look nicer, and host my child's wedding."

"No such inn may hold parties of any kind without petitioning for town permission." Gigi looked up from the text and gave the page a slap. "You know this is only happening because some ass made a case out of it. Who'd do this?"

"I can't imagine," Sarah said. "But, I guess I'll find out on Monday night."

"With me right by your side, pal."

Sarah forced a smile. "Okay, but no pea shooters." Sarah tucked the letter back into her purse and tugged the zipper closed with a demonstrative gesture.

"No promises. We'll deal with that when the time comes, Sarah." Gigi motioned her head toward the door. "Right now there's a very interested man out there."

"I don't know. Maybe you're imagining things."

"Am I?" Gigi narrowed her eyes, almost daring Sarah to deny it.

She had no choice but to be honest. After all, they *were* in a veritable confession booth. "What should I do?"

Gigi spun Sarah toward the door. "Go out there and make us proud."

The music had started again with Pete Bailey and his boys banging out a not-too-awful version of an old standard.

Out of nowhere Norman Wallace, the mailman, appeared at their side, eyes beaming at Sarah. He'd abandoned his gray and blue postal getup for a pair of trousers and an Argyle sweater.

"Hi," he said to the group. His gaze returned to her. "Want to dance, Sarah?"

She peered at the make-shift dance floor in the middle of the room. Three couples swayed under dim lighting. She took a long, slow sip of her cosmo, filling her mouth with the tangy substance while she thought up an excuse.

"How about me, there Normie? Will I do?" Gigi drawled.

Sarah swallowed hard nearly gagging on the huge amount of drink she'd just guzzled.

"Um, yeah, sure," Norman said. It was too dark to know for sure, but Sarah guessed he'd flushed like a school girl at the offer. Hopefully the guy had more moves than that little cha-cha he'd displayed on her front porch.

"Well, come on then." Gigi placed her glass on the bar. "Twirl me around till I tell you to stop."

They left Sarah alone with the boiler-maker from Essex County that was currently wreaking havoc with her nerve-endings. Again, they stood in silence, more awkward now that Gigi had left. She didn't know what to do with her eyes or her hands. How long could she stare at her dwindling drink?

"Dance with me." It was a soft, gentle statement without hint of question.

She looked up. Shadows hit the angles of his face in such a way that the mysterious appearance he'd worn earlier had morphed into a smokiness that billowed to her. The vapor seeped into and through her being.

Hesitation flooded her brain, but her body was a different story. Charges of glee spread through her veins, roaring in beat with the music. There was a war going on inside her, but one faction had all the power and she knew it.

Gulping the last of her drink, she handed him the empty glass and looked him dead in the eye. "Sure."

Chapter Two

His arms were strong but she knew they'd be. He smelled good, something earthy and visceral and Sarah was intoxicated by it. Well, that and one-and-a-half cosmos.

Benny moved well, slow and rhythmically. Without words she felt his body communicating with hers, telling it how and when to move, left then right, forward and back. They didn't miss a step as though they were one entity.

Her combination of drunkenness on his scent and the ingested vodka allowed her to relax into the dance. She let herself move freely, easing closer into his arms. This was dangerous. And it was stimulating. For the first time in more years than she could count Sarah was acutely aware of being alive.

Benny pressed his face against the side of hers, temple to temple, one throbbing pulse calling to the other. Sarah lifted her gaze, breaking the contact of their skin. The movement placed her mouth just a breath from his lips. She felt her old self hovering above this new creature she had become tonight. Without a second thought, Sarah acquiesced to the urges whirling within her. Her lips parted as his head bent forward, his mouth pressing onto hers in a kiss she felt to her toes. She didn't even know his last name. She didn't care. *I don't even know who the hell I am!*

****

Benny moved his mouth over hers, enjoying her taste, both sweet and spicy, a mingling dichotomy he guessed personified this Sarah person.

He held her tight, her body melded against his. He felt her warmth and let it bathe him, dull his mind of any other thought than this. There'd be time later for warnings to trickle in, time to rationalize his behavior. But, for now, it was just the two of them, nothing before and nothing after. Just the dance. He curled her hand to his chest and pressed it close.

His first regret arrived when the music ended. The world around them reappeared—the sounds of people talking, the staccato of appreciative, clapping hands. It was time to release his arms and let her go. He didn't want to.

She lifted her head from his shoulder and tendered him a shy smile, her full just-kissed lips closed. Her hazel eyes were filled with smokiness and an expression that went deep. Even at first glance he had seen that they were filled with a kind of knowing—as if all the experiences of her lifetime, and perhaps other lifetimes before, were written right there in the amber in their depths.

Their parting felt awkward, disjointed. As they walked silently back to the bar, the next regret came hard. He knew this had been a bad idea. Very bad.

Sure, he had liked her look the moment he'd laid eyes on her. She and her friend, Gigi, were an attractive pair. He knew immediately that the off-beat looking Gigi had given him "the eye." And, truthfully, he didn't mind her demonstrative flirtation, found her type interesting.

But, there was something about Sarah, the unpretentious woman whose more conservative appearance did not pale in comparison to her friend. Her natural appeal was what drew him to act totally unlike himself, to go against his ironclad resolve.

His brother Sal would laugh like hell if he had seen little brother Benny pretzeled around a virtual stranger in a beat-up little beach bar. Sal would have most likely slapped him on the back, given one of his raucous whoops, and told him to go get lucky.

He watched Sarah as she walked ahead of him, her hips' gentle sway a subtle sight with a not-so-subtle impact to his senses. He looked away.

Benny didn't approach this kind of woman, even when he found them attractive. He'd learned it never ended well. His marriage had been a quick disaster, like an earthquake that rocked a stable place in mere seconds before leaving it in shambles.

In the years that followed, Benny had liked to go it alone. He'd had his share of one-nighters and brief encounters where he and a woman both had no expectations beyond the moment. That had been enough for him. Plenty.

He hadn't even wanted to come to this godforsaken place. This was the price he paid for giving into Sal's cockamamie idea to go in on a flip property at the shore. Mr. Bigshot Captain of Glendale's PD, Sal, was still working, so it became Benny's job to do some clean-up work to the ramshackle house they'd bought. "Pretty it up just enough to unload it," Sal had said.

Wordlessly he and Sarah headed back to their parked drinks at the bar. Gigi and "Normie" greeted them. Benny nodded as though he were listening. What he was actually doing was imploring himself to get the hell out of there before the music started again.

He really needed to close the book on this night *and* this woman. Yet all he could think of was their dance.

****

Sarah was shell-shocked. She furnished polite responses to her friends' conversation, but her mind reeled with images of what had happened on the dance floor.

Her brain teased her with thoughts of her brazen body and how it had smothered everything she believed about herself. It rattled her. She ran her hands over her clothing as though smoothing out wrinkles, but it was really her feeble attempt to cast off the general effect of this stranger named Benny.

Sarah saw that Gigi had switched to diet soda. She grabbed the glass from her and took a big swallow. The cold, fizzy liquid chilled her insides. Hopefully it could quench the damned flame therein.

"Pete's doing quite a job tonight," Gigi said. Sarah knew by the sultry tone that the comment meant more than a mere compliment to the combo's rendition of Sinatra. She and Gigi were in sync enough that Sarah knew the reference was for her daring behavior.

"It's getting late, though, Gigi. Maybe we should head out." Sarah did her best to keep the pleading tone out of her voice. She wanted to get far away from this man that turned her into a hussy—a shameless one.

"So, Benny, what brings you to Ronan's Harbor?" Gigi asked sweetly, ignoring Sarah's request entirely.

"My brother and I bought a little place down on Ocean."

"Oh?" she said with exaggerated interest. "So, you're a permanent import."

"Not exactly," Benny said.

"Fair warning, once you come to Ronan's Harbor, the town and its people get into your blood," Gigi said. "Right, Sarah?"

She smiled at her friend, instead of wringing her neck.

"Norman here has been the mailman in town all his adult life, haven't you Norman?"

"Yes, ma'am. I have the happenings of the whole town with me every day in my leather bag. Everybody's news comes through me, good or bad."

He turned to Sarah. "Sorry, by the way, about your news, Sarah. Word's out you've got some problems but I'm sure you'll work them out."

"Thanks, Norman. I'm sure I will."

"Well, Norman, you might want to come down to town hall for the meeting on Monday," Gigi said. "Together Sarah and I are going to challenge that stupid complaint. You might see a free fireworks display."

She turned her attention to Benny. "Some idiot filed a complaint against Sarah's bed-and-breakfast."

He focused his piercing gaze on Sarah. She felt an urge to elaborate, one of her nervous habits. "All I want to do is make a nice space so I can host my daughter's wedding. I'd like to know why that should be a problem for anybody."

He nodded his angular head, as though he'd quickly assessed her words and found them sound. She guessed it was probably a cop thing. But, whatever prompted his approval didn't matter.

She liked that he saw the validity in her protest.

She liked *him*.

His eyes locked onto hers again, holding them, wooing them.

Her heart raced, her mind reeling with quickly-flashing possibilities for the meaning of the message she read in his dark orbs. It was like peeking in though a darkened doorway. She was too curious to turn away.

Finally, Benny spoke and the spell released. It was only then that Sarah realized she'd been holding her breath. "I should say good night."

It was as if a faucet had been turned to stop the flow of her body's reactions. A crazy sting of disappoint snapped at her.

As if in slow motion she watched Benny's hand misjudge the proximity of the bar's surface. His half-full beer glass tipped at the edge and crashed to the floor. The glass cracked in chunks, the liquid spilling at his feet.

Sarah reached for the paper towels left from the stack she'd used to mop up her own spilled drink. She handed them to Benny and their eyes met again.

"I'm an idiot."

Something in his apologetic sound warmed her, but a warning in her brain blew it cold. *Don't,* her mind cautioned. She knew she'd be a total goner if she succumbed to any sign of vulnerability in the magnetic Rottweiler, a beseeching mix too appealing to shun.

"Don't be silly," Sarah said. She did her best to clear her mind. "I spilled a drink, too, remember?"

He mopped the beer from his pant leg, his shoe, and the floor. His chuckle sounded more like embarrassment.

Stop. She had no words and made no effort to

assist. Dear God, she couldn't touch him again, especially when he was wet.

"Well that settles it, I guess. Time to go," he said.

She swallowed hard. Although she'd been the first to say it, she didn't want to leave and she didn't want him to go either. Her subconscious shouted at her— *Stay! Let's dance.*

He offered a small grin. "Nice meeting you, Sarah." He turned and nodded. "You, too, Gigi." He extended his hand. "Norman."

"I'm sure we'll see you again," Gigi said slyly. "It's a small town."

"Yes," he said. "It is."

****

Before she knew it, Sarah and Gigi were back outside The Pier House heading to Gigi's car. Propelled by the off-shore breeze and the shock of her behavior, Sarah nearly ran.

There'd be time later to fully regret her boldness, but for the moment, just one delicious minute, she relished the feeling. She felt like a daredevil—or as much of one that she'd ever been in her whole life.

However, she could not help but acknowledge the observation that in one short evening a strange man had conjured more emotion in her than anyone ever had. Wanton desire had zoomed through her veins, and her veins liked it.

The truth was Benny had made a quick exit. His body language had changed with his drink's spill. He hadn't asked to see her again and hadn't asked for her number.

She shook her head. And what if he had? Her breath stalled in her chest. She tried to close out all thoughts about him, but her mind was alive with scenarios.

He hadn't stuck around long enough for any real conversation, hadn't revealed a thing about himself. And he knew nothing concrete about her.

Her mind posted a billboard—*What exactly was that?* Sarah's throat was dry and her swallow scratched. It wouldn't take a library shelf's self-help book to convince her she had hit the pinnacle of her stupidity. Sarah Doodle lived and reined.

"Don't." Gigi's voice broke Sarah's reverie.

"Don't what? Vomit?"

"Stop it."

"Gigi, what the hell is wrong with me? This guy shows up out of nowhere and I wrap myself around him on the dance floor and actually *kiss him?* Did you see the way he made a beeline out of the place as if it was on fire?"

Sarah groaned and covered her face with her hands. She smelled the earthiness of his cologne on her skin. Her hands jerked away.

"Well, I did smell some smoke." Gigi flashed a wicked look. "Felt the heat from your flames. And the feeling was mutual, apparently. Hell, you made the poor guy so nervous he spilled his beer all over the place."

"Oh, my God, Gigi, *this* is a tiny little town. Who knows how many people witnessed my display out on that dance floor? I'm mortified. How am I going to face people? Or worse, face *him* if I run into him again?"

"Will you please just relax, girl?" Gigi said. "For crying out loud, so what? You had a nice, fun night out. Who gives a crap if it wasn't your typical *style?* Come on, admit it. *You had fun.*"

Sarah's mouth twisted sideways. Well, her body had had a good time, a blast even. But now, she was left to face its actions. She could still feel Benny's arms around her. His scent was embedded in her pores. A pathetic-sounding whimper escaped her lips.

"Is that acknowledgement?" Gigi asked with a grin.

"Fine, yes. It was fun. Now, please let me go home and wallow."

"Bask. Go home and *bask.*"

Back home, and inside her refuge, Sarah locked the door behind her and leaned against it. She closed her eyes. The musky, sandalwood aroma had followed her in and threatened to stay. She needed to get a grip.

She trotted up the stairs to her apartment with a mission. She peeled her clothes from her body, kicking herself out of the garments like they were repulsive rags. She bunched them in a wad and stuffed it into the dry cleaning bin.

She turned on the shower and let the full force run steamy hot before stepping inside. She lathered herself good using Hannah's fruity body wash. The apple-scented liquid filled her senses with its sweetness, eradicating any hint of *him.*

She toweled off with vigor, her skin pinking. She relaxed into her cottony pajamas, brushed her teeth, and gargled for more seconds than her norm. Her minty mouth had forgotten entirely about that kiss. It was gone.

She slipped into her terry mules and went back downstairs for her nightly regimen. She doused the light in the parlor. She stood for a moment in the darkness, willing the inn's comfort, needing its embrace.

She was tired and eager to flop into her bed. She needed sleep but more, she needed to close the book on this day.

Sarah made her way back to the front door and wrapped her hand around the brass knob, giving it a jiggle. That's when she noticed it.

Something peeked in from under the front door. Instantly, she flipped on the porch light and opened the door. There was no sign of anyone. The only disturbance was what she realized to be an envelope wedged in the rubber flashing.

She tugged it out producing a gash of black across the front of the white envelope. Her name was printed on the front in blue ink, all the letters capitalized. The word "confidential" was jotted at the lower corner, and underlined twice.

Gigi had been gone for less than a half hour. Had someone been watching and waiting for her to be alone? The hairs on her neck pricked at her skin.

She shoved the door closed and locked it, testing the knob again. Then, she bolted up the staircase and locked the door to her apartment behind her as well. She didn't like the feeling of being watched. Her nerves were raw. *What now?*

Chilled, Sarah climbed into bed and pulled the quilt up over herself. She tore open the envelope.

The stationery was a sandy-toned page with pale watercolor seashells decorating its top edge. The message on it was simple, also written in all capped blue ink. *"Please stop the wedding. You'll regret it if you don't."*

It was as though the words flew from the page and ringed themselves around her neck, squeezing her ability to breath. This was going too far.

Whoever protested her plans was now using fear tactics and she simply wouldn't have it. She didn't know much about legalities but this little note sounded like a threat.

She closed the light and tried to sleep but her mind raced. She began a mental list, a habit she'd given up combating a long time ago. Lists made her happy, kept her grounded. At the moment her cozy bed and locally-crafted quilt weren't providing comfort.

She needed an inventory of possible action plans. Call the police in the morning? Maybe. Call Gigi? Definitely. Tell Hannah? Never.

Another list emerged in her head, a cataloging of all the craziness that had begun in a nanosecond of her life and was now snowballing in a convoluted trail.

She tried to let it go, but her mind zeroed in on a taboo direction—to the music of Bailey's combo at the Pier House and the new guy in town whom she'd publicly molested. This night sucked.

An hour later she still hadn't attained sleep. She needed a cup of tea. She wanted the new blend she'd come up with for Hannah's wedding. She yearned to savor the pungent aroma, have it encircle her in the comforting reminder that nothing would stop her renovation of the sunroom and the wedding would happen as planned, *no matter what*.

She padded down the stairs to the main part of the inn, where she'd left the bag of loose tea she'd named "The Wedding Tea."

In the stillness of the inn's kitchen—the big, old

expanse of white porcelain appliances with the butcher-block island set in the center of the room—she prepared the tea. One deep sip hit the spot, calming her immediately.

When the cup was empty, Sarah climbed the stairs again and went up to bed where gratefully sleep eventually arrived.

****

After his run, Benny trudged back to the house. Bracing against the cold April wind, his head angled away from the air that stung his eyes. He climbed the rickety steps, feeling the old wood give with his weight. *Damn it to hell.*

What the hell was he doing here? He snapped on the small living room's overhead light. His eyes caught the stack of cartons piled up in the corner. Four boxes of belongings. That had been all he'd bothered to bring with him when he gave up his apartment in Montclair. Everything else had been disposable.

He kicked the bottom box with a tap of his toe. That was all his worldly worth, four measly boxes of stuff that easily could have been narrowed to two.

He sat on a lumpy, stuffed chair, his body's pressure releasing a scent of dampness that startled his nose. He yanked open the top box and began the search.

That brochure he'd saved from his last trip to Key West was in one of these boxes. Right now he needed to see it, devour every word, believe the day would come soon when he'd be there.

He found sweaters and shirts, a faded bathing suit. He pushed the box aside and grabbed the next, tugging against the hold of the packing tape. Most of it was stuff he'd saved last minute from the Goodwill pile he'd hauled off to the mission.

As he rummaged, his mind fought him. His thoughts boomeranged back to the nice, unsuspecting innkeeper whose life's plans he'd messed with. Anger brewed in his belly. Sal had painted a much different picture of the whole scenario. Benny could kick himself now for not remembering that Sal always twisted things for his own purposes.

He'd toyed with picking up the phone and calling the fine captain, waking him up in the middle of the night just to tell him off once and for all. But, first, where the hell was that pamphlet?

Benny reached for another box, knowing immediately when he heard the contents rattle that in it was the junk that really had no purpose. For the life of him he didn't know why some of the crap had come along for the ride to the shore when it should have been rotting at the bottom of the dumpster of his apartment complex.

He tore it open anyway. He picked up the first thing he saw, a carved wooden box. How long had it been since he'd actually held the compass, the so-called heirloom that his father had willed to him? He snickered to no one.

The memory of that day flooded back to his mind. He and brother Sal sat on stiff-backed chairs in their father's attorney's office for the reading of the will.

The old man's meager assets had been split down the middle with no surprises. At the end of the brief meeting, the lawyer presented each son with a token of remembrance that their father had specified they receive.

He now pictured Sal's gleaming face when he

learned Pop had left him his antique coin collection, a treasure worth a major wad of dough. And, Benny— he'd gotten the tarnished antique brass pocket compass.

He wondered then, and he wondered now, if there had been a subliminal message from the old man when he doled out the memorabilia to his sons? The question hadn't formed in his brain for a long time now. Usually when it had, there'd been a six-pack in his system.

But alone in this foreign place the truth suddenly growled inside of him like hunger. He didn't need a pawnbroker to tell him which son had received the more valuable bequest. And there was just one real interpretation of that shitty fact.

He lifted the object from the faded satin-lined box. It was cold in his palm. He pressed the side button and the cover popped open. The compass face was clear and unmarred despite its age. The north-pointing arrow quaked in his grasp.

Yes, the old man had made it loud and clear. His younger son didn't know where the hell he was going, and never had.

Benny's eye wandered to a gash of turquoise poking out from beneath a couple of useless old photo albums. He knew instantly what it was. He pulled the Key West brochure into his grasp, letting the compass slip back into its box.

He unfolded the glossy paper with a careful, almost reverent gesture. He scanned the photos of silhouetted fishermen, spectacular sunsets, and must-see tourist landmarks. But what appealed most to Benny was the warmth, yet remoteness of the locale.

He savored the italicized page banner that boasted the island as the continental United States' southernmost point. Any further away from his old life and he'd need a boat.

He pulled the compass back into his hand and held it appropriately to his chest. Glancing at the details in the brochure he'd laid open on his lap, he turned the housing and aligned the needle. It would take a while, but he'd get to the place located at latitude twenty-four degrees north and longitude eighty-one degrees west.

For now, one thing was sure. Benny knew exactly where he was headed tomorrow and he wouldn't need a compass for the destination.

Chapter Three

Sarah sat on a wooden stool at Gigi's flower shop workbench. While her friend arranged a spray of yellow roses as part of a sizeable funeral order, Sarah's anonymous note from last night sat open on the table's pocked surface.

"I'm with you one hundred percent," Gigi said as she eyed her project. She looked up. "That little love note's got to be from whatever asshole made the complaint. Somebody *really* wants to stop your plans. You want me to go with you to the police department? I know some of the guys down there."

"I know you do, Miss Popularity," Sarah said. "But, no. I'm heading over now."

"Okay, call me." Gigi added a satin bow embossed with a golden statement of devotion. "Old Mr. Griswold sure loved his wife." She smiled appreciatively at her creation. "She carried yellow roses when they got married more than fifty years ago and he insisted on them now. There's a real message in that simple gesture, huh?"

"Yes." Sarah sighed. There were bigger issues in the world, greater obstacles than what she faced. She let the idea of timeless love between a man and a woman warm her.

She reached for the cryptic piece of stationery. This was no tragedy. This was merely an annoyance that she'd nip today, right now, damn it.

She waved the page in Gigi's direction. "I'm on my way. Hopefully, the police will decide this little *message* is a threat, something illegal—or at least unethical enough to, I don't know, have the township committee take pity on me and let me go ahead with the work and the wedding." She refolded the piece of stationary, carefully placing it back in its envelope.

She got up and turned to leave. "Wish me luck."

A wide grin broke out on Gigi's face. "Go get 'em, sister."

****

Benny Benedetto pulled his Jeep into the Glendale Police Department's visitor lot.

He climbed the familiar steps to the front door and entered the building that had been his employment home for twenty-five years. Nothing had changed. The threadbare chairs in the waiting area, the fake potted palm in the corner in need of a good dusting, the over-crowded cork bulletin board on the wall, were all just as they were when he had been an officer on the little Northern Jersey police force.

He made his way past the front window, waving at the ladies behind the glass, old faces and new faces watching him and exchanging comments he could not and did not care to hear.

With each step down the corridor toward the Captain's Office Benny felt the acid in his stomach churn in defense and self-reproach. Why the hell he agreed to go in on the purchase of that beat-to-shit beach house with his arrogant, sleaze-ball brother was beyond him. But now, *Captain Salvatore Benedetto* was going to hear it but good.

Paula, Sal's secretary, grinned with recognition when Benny walked up to her desk. "A sight for sore eyes," she drawled, tilting her chin. Benny's tension eased a bit at her familiar flirtation, although he wasn't, and never had been, interested.

"Hey, Paula," he said. "He in?"

"He's been expecting you, Benny." Paula patted her starchy hair and gave him an appreciative look.

His older brother sat tall behind the laminate desk as though it were a judge's bench, squaring his broad shoulders in a regal posture. "Benny Boy, how's the beach?" Sal boomed. He motioned for Benny to sit in the vinyl chair positioned opposite his throne.

Benny's eyes drifted to the wall behind Sal, scanning the haphazard display of his matted and framed narcissism. He viewed the engraved plaques from local organizations and diplomas Sal had earned ranging from his academy graduation to his karate certificate.

There was a cluster of framed thank-you letters in all shapes and sizes from local muckety-mucks. A new addition, a framed press piece of Sal receiving some award from a local organization, all smiles for the camera, hung right above his fat head.

"I'm sure you didn't come all the way up here to count my awards." Sal let out a string of chuckles.

The smile fell from Sal's face when Benny did not return a cheery greeting. "What's up, brother?"

"You didn't tell me this woman with the inn just wants to make her sunroom look good so she can have her kid's wedding in it."

"Semantics, little brother." Sal sighed and pinched his mouth into a one-sided bunch. "The fact remains her plans could totally screw us up."

Benny folded his arms across his chest. "How have you come to that conclusion?"

"Her bed-and-breakfast is one of four in Ronan's Harbor."

"Yeah, so?"

"They'd all like nothing better than to get the town ordinance changed so they can all start expanding and throwing parties, adding traffic and congestion to the town. Do I need to spell this out for you, Benny? You want to make dough on this house we bought or not?"

"What's that got to do with anything?"

Sal placed his big hands onto the desk top and rotated his swivel chair a quarter turn. He rose and stepped around the desk's corner and positioned his backside at its' front edge.

"Trust me, Benny. This can't happen. It won't. You got that? I've already put the skids into motion. This B&B, *The Cornelia Inn...*" he paused to snicker mockingly at the name, "is run by a ding-bat that ignored the need to get a permit. It's illegal."

"I still don't get why we should we care, Sal. What's it to us what she does at her establishment?"

"Look, Benny," His face contorted with impatience. "We don't want it because this sleepy little town has to stay just as it is if we're going to sell that house of ours and make the big bucks."

Sal blew out a long breath. "Can you imagine if all of the inns decided to start having big bashes? How many nice, American families are going to want a beach cottage in a noisy, over-crowded honky-tonk town? Huh, Benny? How many?"

Benny swallowed his urge to argue the point. The

only thing that mattered to him right now was getting the shack ready for sale. The sooner he would be rid of any ties to his shyster brother and headed to Key West, the better.

"What exactly have you 'put in motion'?" Benny said, not caring that his voice rang with accusation. He knew what lurked inside the bullish egotist. "This isn't anything shady, is it Sal? Because if it is—"

"Benny, Benny, Benny." Sal laughed like a politician in a polyester suit. "Up and up. It's all good. Just trying to look after our interests, pal. I contacted a buddy of mine down there and put a bug in his ear. Our luck is that the owner didn't have any permits for either the work or the event she's planning. Basically she's screwed."

Sal pointed a fat finger at Benny. "I've started it. Now you finish it. Got that? Stop this broad. We'll paint and tidy up our little place and sell. Then I won't care what the hell they do in Ronan's Harbor. I need to count on you."

Sal sounded just like their father. The old man had boomed his commands at them as they grew up. Sal had been his pathetic yes-man, Benny the odd guy out. So frickin' what? He'd never pleased his father up until his dying day. And to his big brother he'd just been a screw-up, a poor excuse for the great Benedetto name in the police world.

The image of Sarah's face last night in the bar was unrelenting. *Doesn't it just figure,* he thought, *that the one time I decided to pay attention to a nice lady like her that it turns out I've already treated her like shit?* This was one for the record books, even for him.

So, yeah, Sal could count on him this one last time.

There was nothing more important than severing this fool alliance with Sal. If that meant *proving* to this Sarah that he was a jerk, that was just par for Benny. If nixing the inn's plans meant selling, moving on, and putting the stupid little town in his rearview mirror, then, sure, he was on board, full-throttle.

He pushed the image of Sarah from his thoughts. It was a blessing in disguise, really. The last thing he needed was involvement with a woman. In the long run he'd have disappointed her anyway. Hell, he already had. *Who needs it?*

"Benny, you with me on this?"

"Yeah, I'm with you."

****

As she pulled into the municipal building's lot, Sarah's cell phone sounded, flashing Hannah's number in the display. Sarah flipped the device open.

"Hi, Mom," Hannah said.

Her voice was so sweet and unassuming. It made Sarah even more aggravated that she had to jump through these hoops. She breathed in, then out, and did her best to relax in her own skin. "Hi, Honey. How was your weekend?"

"We met with some of Ian's work friends for dinner on Saturday. Yesterday we just kind of had a lazy day."

"How's work?"

"Fine." Hannah's tone changed as abruptly as a shifted gear. Temping at a law firm in the City was not what her daughter wanted for the long term, and the job had gone on for over a year.

Her degree was in anthropology, although her father had steered her to dual-major for a more practical business degree. As much as Sarah consoled her daughter during the job crunch, and rationalized the blessing of attaining the temp spot, the poor kid's career dream had choked to accelerate.

She heard Hannah's long breath on the other end. "I was just checking in. Everything good?"

"Oh, sure, wonderful actually." Sarah clamped her mouth shut before she spewed herself into sounding suspicious. "Busy, though. I've got to run."

"How's the work going in the sunroom? Have they broken through the wall yet?"

"Uh, no…" Sarah bit her lip. "There's been a little delay. The carpenter's not coming this week."

"Mom…" Panic coated Hannah's tone. "There isn't a lot of time."

"Don't worry, Hannah. It'll be fine." *Will it? It has to be fine.*

"Ian's going away this weekend on business again, so I'll come home and spend it with you. Okay?"

"Great," Sarah said. "See you then."

She entered the brick municipal building with fueled determination. She wanted this mess cleaned up before Hannah came for the weekend. And she could blissfully get back to normal.

She held the anonymous note in her hand at the ready. The receptionist ushered her into a sitting area where she waited for an available officer.

Soon a young man with a shiny badge and black glossy shoes came out from a doorway, offering his hand. "Mrs. Grayson? I'm Officer Carr. How can I help you today?"

"I have something I'd like to discuss with you."

She showed him the letter and watched as he

studied it. He was young, probably a rookie. She silently hoped he was an overly zealous newbie who would do something big, like arrest the person who complained against her, cuff them good and haul them off to the slammer.

"I found that shoved under my front door last night."

"Any idea who did this, and why?" He turned the paper over, scanned the back, and then looked at the front again.

She shrugged. "I don't know. There's currently a complaint against my plans to do some improvements and host my daughter's wedding at my inn. I own The Cornelia on Tidewater Way. I have to appear Monday night at the town meeting. All I can think of is that maybe it was whoever made the complaint."

She watched his face. It was an unreadable plane. She had hoped this would fire him up. "Who else would want to threaten me?" she added like a poke to kindling.

"Well, Mrs. Grayson, I'm not sure this is technically a threat per se, but how about your daughter?"

"Hannah? Why would she…"

"No, not Hannah herself, but I was thinking maybe someone in her circle of acquaintances? Ex-lover? Disgruntled ex-girlfriend of the groom?"

"No," Sarah was emphatic. "There's no one like that."

"What does Hannah say about this?"

"I'm not telling her. She's got much too much to deal with. No. I'm not going to her with such absurdity."

Officer Carr let out a long sigh, took out a small spiral-bound pad and a pen. He flipped the cover of the pad, perched his pen, and tapped his thumb on the retractor button. "Was anything disturbed at your residence?"

"No."

"Be sure to contact us if you receive another one of these. I'll just make a copy, start a file. Meanwhile, if you can think of anything else, be sure to give us a call. Spell your name, please, and leave me your number."

She watched him jot down her information then close the cover on his pad. He looked up and gave her a quick smile.

"That's it?" she asked.

"For now."

Chapter Four

On Monday evening Sarah and Gigi sat in the back of the room at town hall. The parsons' benches gave Sarah the feeling that they were in church rather than a court room, which was fine considering she was praying.

She tried to read the faces of the township committee members as they sat in high-backed padded chairs behind the large rectangular table at the head of the room. None of them, not even her friend, Mayor John Reynolds, looked her way.

John called the meeting to order. Gigi patted Sarah's knee and gave an encouraging little smile. "We'll fix this," she whispered.

Sarah scanned the room. She recognized everyone, or at least the ones she could see. She knew the clerk, Tim Conover, his wife Betty was a co-member with Sarah of the Ronan's Harbor Garden Club.

The Zoning Officer wasn't someone she knew by name but his starchy face was familiar. Sarah had seen him, slight and skinny with hunched bony shoulders, at the bank and at the post office. Plenty of times she'd spied him walking his fuzzy Brillo pad of a dog along the roadside, letting the little guy pee on everybody's plants. She bristled. Maybe she'd give him a citation, like a citizen's arrest or something, for illegal piddle.

The rhetoric faded in and out of Sarah's attention

like a radio broadcast with poor reception. Her mind reeled with what she wanted to say while snippets of conversation about replacement snow fences and new stop signs on Main Street filtered into her ear.

She'd practiced how she wanted to defend her plans. She'd rehearsed it over and over in front of her grandmother's cheval mirror. But now all her thoughts jumbled into one clog of nothing.

"Mrs. Grayson," the Zoning Officer said, snapping her to full attention. "We're here in regard to your land use at Four Tidewater Way, the bed-and-breakfast known as The Cornelia Inn."

"Yes," she said, the word bursting out like a gunshot in a tunnel.

"Sarah," the mayor interjected, his face stoic but his eyes kind. "It's come to our attention that you're doing some construction at your establishment, yet we have no building permit on file. A detailed report with the specifics of your project is required to obtain a permit."

He looked down at the paperwork in front of him. "Additionally, we'll need you to initiate the conditional use process for your inn for holding catered events. In order to do so, you'll need to fill out the proper paperwork and file with initial payment. Mr. Pallis here can provide you the forms."

"John...Mr. Mayor." Sarah stood up from her bench, keeping her attention on him and not Pallis, the zoning guy. "It's just a matter of tearing down a store room wall to add space to my sun porch. I just want to hold my daughter's wedding at my residence. Why do I need to go through all of this? It's a bit extreme, don't you think?"

"Please re-examine the town regulations regarding inns such as yours. It clearly states that no parties of any kind will be permitted on the premises," Mr. Pallis interjected. "And no one may perform construction in Ronan's Harbor without first obtaining written consent." He clucked his tongue. "We must all follow the same rules, Mrs. Grayson."

She felt the heat of blood rushing to her cheeks. *Calm down there, Barney Fife.* "Well I think it's abominable that someone would lodge such a complaint." She stood straighter.

"The bottom line, Mrs. Grayson, is that you have side-stepped proper channels. A town member bringing it to our attention is not the issue."

Gigi stood now, pressing close to Sarah, their shoulders melded like two comrades in a foxhole.

"How long does this process take?" Sarah asked.

"Minimum three to four months, perhaps as many as five,"

"The wedding is June first. That's two months away." Panic squeezed her vocal chords making her sound like a cartoon mouse to her own ears. "The invitations have already been mailed. What am I supposed to do now?" She cleared her throat.

"I suggest you petition immediately and perhaps consider an alternate location," Mr. Pallis said. His head angled at a challenging slant, giving Sarah the thought that it wouldn't take much to slap the sphere right off its long scrawny post.

"Sarah," John Reynolds said. "If you have any further questions, please feel free to contact me."

And just like that the meeting ended and Sarah watched dazedly as a clerk came out of the wings with a black garbage bag in her hands and fussed about, filling it with empty Styrofoam cups and napkins used by the councilmen.

Another clerk approached her with paperwork, asked for a signature, and dashed off with a promise to give her a copy.

The men stood from their chairs and talked among themselves in hushed tones, all impervious to the fact that they'd just dropped a bomb on her life.

She turned her gaze to Gigi. "So that's that?"

"My pea shooter's in the car," Gigi said.

The clerk returned with paperwork, offered a conciliatory "thank you," and strode away. Sarah folded the papers and shoved them into her purse.

Shuffling through the crowd of exiting attendees, Sarah eyed the room. When the bottleneck dissipated she saw him—Benny Benedetto stood alone in the aisle in a black windbreaker with his hands shoved into the pockets of his jeans. His eyes bored into hers.

The hairs on the back of her neck came to attention, and she reached to rake fingernails over the surface. She willed her body to "knock it off." This was not the time to delve into her encounter on the dance floor.

"Your Rottweiler is here," Gigi said under her breath.

She pulled from his gaze and shook her head. "Let's get out of here."

"Are you kidding? Think about it, Sarah. Why the hell would a guy brand new to town come to one of these boring town meetings? He wanted to see you."

"That's ridiculous." Doubt coated her words and she couldn't help but let her eyes flutter back his way.

Was that true? The bright lighting didn't detract from her memory of him. He was still appealing, cute in a broody kind of way.

Gigi nudged Sarah again. "At least maybe tonight won't be a total waste. Go talk to him."

"For crying out loud, Gigi, my world is crumbling. Let's just get out of here."

"Only if you look at me and tell me you are really not interested."

"I'm not."

"Look at me."

Sarah met Gigi's gaze and couldn't keep the smile from forming on her lips. "Okay, we'll just say 'hello.'"

They did a ridiculous-feeling sideways stride along the pew-like benches toward where he stood. She felt his gaze on her skin.

"Hello." Her heart throbbed like a time bomb.

"Hi, Sarah," he said. His voice was low. Well, maybe not low, but far from exuberant.

This is a mistake, her mind warned.

He gave Gigi a nod accompanied by a slight smile. "Gigi."

"Hey there."

"What, uh, brings you out tonight?" Sarah could almost feel Gigi's mental thumbs-up approval.

Benny shrugged a big, toned shoulder. "Keeping up on town doings."

Silence hung in the air, thick and choking like smoke. Sarah's mind reeled with absurd comments she'd never say. *Remember being wrapped around me on a dance floor the other night? See these lips you kissed? Want to do it again?*

She had to get the heck out of there. Her body had

taken over her mind and she had the stark thought that the man was not even interested. Embarrassment coated her like varnish.

"Well, it was nice seeing you again. Good night, ladies." He proceeded to move into the line of departing attendees.

Sarah pulled her eyes over to Gigi. "I'm an idiot."

"No, he is."

Sarah's heart hiccupped. Her mouth pinched into a tight pucker, one that felt perfect for shooting peas.

****

Sarah and Gigi drove back to The Cornelia together, sitting in the front seat of Sarah's car as animated as crash test dummies.

Finally, Gigi spoke. "You better not be beating yourself up over there."

Sarah asked sarcastically, "What specifically about this night are you referring? My bombing with the town over the complaint, or my pathetic approach to a guy clearly anxious *not* to speak to me?"

"Don't. You'll fix the town's issue and so what about the guy. He's probably gay."

Sarah didn't share Gigi's confidence. The town problem was far from solved, and she guessed that it would be quite a while before she'd allow her guard to waver again when it came to men. Of one thing she did feel confident: No way, no how was Benny Benedetto gay.

A car was parked in her wide driveway and she groaned with recognition. *What the hell is Gary doing here?*

"Look. It's Captain Viagra," Gigi announced as if it was a good thing.

Sarah smiled despite his presence. She loved Gigi's nickname for her ex-husband. "Perfect end to a perfect night. Just perfect."

"Want me to go in with you?"

"No, Gary I can handle."

"Looks like Pippi Longstocking's with him."

Gigi knew Gary's shiny new wife's name was Piper and not Pippi. It was her way of easing Sarah's tension.

Sarah was grateful. "Don't leave; wait till I get rid of him."

"Wasn't planning on it," Gigi said. "We for sure need a drink after this fun-filled evening."

As soon as Sarah opened her car door, Gary emerged from his ridiculously oversized SUV. He hopped to the ground from its lofty carriage as though he were young and spry. His pained grunt gave him away. She smirked.

"What's going on, Sarah?" he asked, leaning back against his vehicle. He shook his head at her, his face a shadowy scowl in the glow of her outdoor lighting.

"What do you mean *going on*?"

"John Reynolds called me."

Well that explains John's mood at the meeting. "It's nothing, Gary. I'm handling it."

"You are, huh? Didn't I tell you it was too much to take on Hannah's wedding? Seriously, Sarah you're your own worst enemy."

I can think of a worse one, Captain Viagra. She sighed like a bored southern belle "It's not your concern."

"It most certainly is. Hannah's my daughter, too." Even in the dim light she could see the vein in his forehead bulge to the surface like a blue snaking highway on her GPS screen. "I proposed that we have the wedding at my club. It would have been so elegant, but you and your hairbrained ideas…"

Sarah turned her gaze to the truck's interior. Piper had unbuckled her seatbelt and knelt on her seat, reaching back to the bolstered child in her seat. Toddler Tina looked pissed at the stuffed toy her mother dangled at her.

"Your family's waiting, Gary. You should go." She turned away from him, determined not to look back.

"You call me if you get in more hot water, Sarah Doodle."

She made like she hadn't heard the all-too-familiar condescending nickname; wishing, if fact, that she really hadn't.

****

They shared a bottle of chardonnay in Sarah's apartment. Sarah pulled a bag of chips from the pantry, plied it open. "Here, help me eat these so I don't O.D. on them."

Gigi reached into the bag and withdrew a cluster of the delicate golden slices. "Anything for you, pal."

"So, okay, what happens if there isn't enough time?" Sarah asked between her crunching mouthfuls. "What am I supposed to do with sixty people on June first?"

"Well, I'm sure Captain Viagra has a solution."

"Yeah, but over my dead body…"

Sarah buzzed through a sequence of chips like a beaver jawing on a log. "I could try talking to Mrs. Mayor, Gretchen Reynolds, at the Garden Club meeting on Friday. Maybe she can lean on her husband."

"It's worth a try. Maybe you can find out who initiated the complaint and you can approach them and see if they'll relent."

"Well, after thinking about it, I'm not sure if I want to confront somebody crazy enough to slip late-night anonymous notes under my door. It's just freaky." She shrugged. "Anyway, how would I find out who it was?"

"Ask John Reynolds."

She snickered. "He'd tell Gary that info before he'd tell me." She had an idea. "You think it's on the paperwork they gave me tonight?"

She didn't wait for Gigi to respond. Instead she found her purse where she'd flung it on the kitchen chair and fished inside for the folded documents.

She brought them back to where Gigi sat licking her finger clean of chip salt. Sarah unfolded the papers and turned on a table lamp. She scanned the verbiage.

"Does it say?" Gigi asked.

"It's refers to the complainant." Her eyes rushed over the text. In a box at the bottom was a hand-written three-line summary of the meeting's outcome. In essence, it was a polite way of conveying she had to do their bidding or there'd be no improvement to her inn. And no wedding, either.

She looked further. At the bottom left was John Reynolds's signature as well as Zoning Officer Nicholas Pallis's. On the bottom right just below where she'd scratched her name onto the designated line there was one more signature, a name etched above the line marked "Complainant." Her mouth clamped tight.

"What?" Gigi said. "Why do you look like that?"

"The name's here all right."

"Who is it?"

"Benjamin Benedetto."

"Are you kidding me?" Gigi darted over to look at the paper. "Well, holy shit."

Sarah's heart fell in her chest like a rock thrown from a cliff. For the life of her she couldn't wrap her brain around the emotion. Whatever it was, it was fierce and hurtful.

"Hey," Gigi said, starting to pace. "We can use this to our advantage." She stopped and turned to stare at Sarah. Her eyes were wide with anticipation. "This guy, asshole that he is, probably still has the hots for you."

"You're nuts," Sarah spat. "He was toying with me that night at the Pier House. Got his jollies. He's a sicko."

"No, Sarah." She held up a hand. "Hear me out. But just as a sidebar, I love how pissed you sound. Usually you try to see the rainbow side of everything."

"There are no rainbows in the sewer, my friend."

"Listen. I say tomorrow you doll yourself up a little, go over to his place and cozy up to him, appeal to his brain, the one below his belt. You can make nice-nice and get him to withdraw the complaint." Gigi lifted her hands into the air like she'd just discovered the nose on her face.

"Oh, I intend to pay a little visit to the man at Sixty Ocean tomorrow, before I go file the damned applications. But there will be nothing *nice-nice* about it."

Chapter Five

Sarah drank her morning coffee while pacing around the kitchen. She didn't care what it took, she'd handle this. It was one thing for Benny to formally complain about the wedding for whatever business it was of his. It was entirely another matter to shove a mysterious message under her door in the dark of night.

She spilled the rest of her coffee into the sink, rinsing it away with a forceful spray of water, enjoying the weapon-like feel of the nozzle's trigger in her hand.

She knew if she showed up at his door and barked at him like the rabid dog she felt like, it might make matters worse. About that much, Gigi had been right. She needed to finesse the situation, use a soft approach, appeal to his kinder side. She clucked her tongue. That was assuming, of course, that he had one.

She decided to bring him muffins. She opened a box of bran muffin mix she had in the cupboard and dumped it into a bowl. Following the directions, she added the egg, water, and corn oil. She put the pan in the oven and dashed to get dressed.

As she lined a plate with the moist little buns it made her smile to think that maybe he'd get the subliminal message that an offering of fiber balls might relieve what he seemed to be full of.

Sarah carried the foil-covered dish with one hand on top to shield against the ocean breeze. She walked down the avenue toward his house wondering why she'd never really taken notice of the place before.

Sitting back from the street, it was a small, squat little structure with weathered brown cedar shakes. Next to the Morrison's refurbished three-story stunner the Benedetto man's house looked like an outbuilding.

She opened the front, loudly-squeaking gate. Crumbs of rust peppered her fingers. She shoved it closed behind her with her hip. She stepped up onto the cement porch and rapped on the aluminum storm door's frame.

As she waited her eyes scanned the small yard. The sandy patch was decorated with a small weathered wooden lighthouse bearing a rectangular plaque boasting "Welcome" in bold lettering. *Ha.*

The inside wooden front door opened. And there he stood, speechless, staring at her through the glass of the outer door.

Her ignorant body had an immediate reaction, as if to say *I remember you.* She squared her shoulders. There was no reasoning with a chemical reaction.

"I hope I'm not disturbing you," she said curtly, yet politely.

She had all she could do to keep her eyes focused on the small scar on his forehead. Any other part of his face was too dangerous to take in. The eyes were a killer, to say nothing of the man's mouth.

Wordlessly, he opened the door, bracing it with his thick, sculpted arm. "Come in."

She carefully stepped across the threshold, heart quickening. Maybe *he* was crazy. Images of scary newspaper headlines flashed in her mind. She hovered close to the door.

The aroma of some delicious-smelling confection, something with cinnamon and sugar, wafted in the air. It had not occurred to her that perhaps there was a Mrs. Benedetto. Dear God, had she really made a total fool of herself with a married man?

"I'm sorry, are you in the middle of something?" She looked at the far wall toward what she assumed was the kitchen.

"Nah, I was just fooling around in the kitchen. Sarah, listen, I…"

"You're a baker?" she blurted, unable to mask her surprise. Somehow she couldn't imagine this guy knowing his way around a kitchen. A wrestling ring, maybe. A dance floor, God yeah.

"Something wrong with that?" His hands rested on his hips, but she saw an unnerving tease in his eyes.

"No," she said, laughing a silly little sound. She silently admonished herself. She needed to knock that off. "Not at all. I guess it's just, I don't know, not what I'd expect."

"What's that you have?" His head motioned toward her covered plate.

"I brought you some muffins."

She jutted the dish toward him and he took it, his face a big fat question mark. "Why, may I ask are you bringing me muffins?"

"To be neighborly."

"I see."

"Actually, I thought we could discuss the letter."

"Sarah, first let me say…"

"No." Her voice was louder and more emphatic than she'd intended. She wouldn't give him a chance to explain anything. She didn't want his excuses. She wanted him to undo his damage.

And, in case he was about to bring up the night at the Pier House, she'd nip that before he got started. That little nightmare would never resurface.

She took a breath. "Benny, I thought maybe if you withdrew the complaint the town might drop it and…"

He shook his head. "I can't do that."

"Excuse me?"

"I cannot undo this, Sarah. I gave my brother my word. And, after all, it is a town law." His low voice sounded pained.

Sarah didn't care. She wanted to throttle him. Damn him for coming to this town and upsetting her world in more ways than she'd allow herself to tally.

"Okay," she said, her jaw aching from the tight clench. "Just so you know I've gone to the police about *this*." She pulled out the letter she'd found under her front door.

"What's that?"

A sarcastic laugh popped from her lips. "Your stupid little note. It doesn't scare me, and I resent you sneaking up to my door at night to leave it there."

"I don't know what you're talking about, but I think we'd better end this conversation before one of us says something they'll regret."

Oh, she had regrets already, plenty of them. Sarah unfolded the page, read the message out loud, and then glared at him. "Are you trying to tell me you didn't write this?"

"That's right."

"So, somebody else just happened to warn me to stop the wedding at the same time you and your complaint came to my attention? You expect me to believe that?"

"You're free to believe whatever you want." He shrugged his shoulders. "But, I did not put that note at your door."

A buzzer sounded and he turned toward the kitchen. "That's my strudel."

His strudel? She shook away the image of this goon in an apron. "Well, I believe you wrote this *and* that you delivered it as a scare tactic. I also believe the police will determine this to be a threat."

He gave a quick look over his shoulder. "Being a retired police officer, I know what a threat is, and whether it is or isn't happens to be none of my business. I didn't write it. Now, if you'll excuse me…"

"Yeah, I know…your strudel. You haven't heard the last from me, Mr. Benedetto."

"Sarah…"

She stormed out the door.

****

Benny charged to the kitchen to turn off the timer's buzzing sound searing his brain. He opened the oven door and saw that the edges of his confection had browned too much, one side was nearly black. *Damn it to hell.* He grabbed the old burn-stained oven mitts from the counter and withdrew the strudel, placing it on top of a cracked trivet.

He didn't know this oven's temperament, or the accuracy of its thermostat. It took experience to determine an oven's heat setting level. With any luck, he'd kiss this old relic goodbye long before he'd figure it out.

He tugged off the mitts and threw them down. So now somebody was leaving notes at Sarah's door? Who and, better yet, why? *Stop,* he implored silently reminding himself that his badge was tucked away in one of his storage cartons.

He hated the situation he'd put Sarah in. But, that little note she found was another problem entirely. His gut told him it spelled trouble. But this trouble didn't concern him, even if it was Sarah Grayson.

His gut told him Sarah was a genuinely nice lady— too nice for the likes of him, that was for sure. He should have remembered that before he'd asked her to dance that night at the bar, let alone gone and kissed her.

He touched a knife tip into the ruined end of the strudel. Black flakes of dough rained onto the counter. He figured roughly eight minutes less next time he baked a strudel in the old oven. That should do it.

He could deal with a temperamental oven much easier than he could deal with the opposite sex. When it came to women he'd always messed it up. Brief encounters—no strings, no hurt feelings—were the best way for him to go. It made life a whole hell of a lot easier that way.

He touched a fingertip to the darkened dough. His skin sizzled on a dab of hot apple liquid. *Shit.*

He ran the sore fingertip under the cold tap water spray for a long time waiting for the sting to settle down.

What does it matter, really, that I've made an enemy of Sarah Grayson?

Their having any kind of connection didn't fit into his life plan. He'd been momentarily swayed by her, something he didn't understand. It would have been easy if it had just been his typical primal need reaction surfacing. But, there was something beyond that with this woman.

No flash, no subliminal cat call. Sarah Grayson had wooed his interest, had given him a single moment of what? Hope? Belief in possibilities?

Christ, maybe Sal was right. He'd gone soft. He needed to leave Sarah and her secretive note the hell alone, stop the cop in himself from pondering scenarios of who'd stoop to that ploy.

Benny shut the faucet off and dried his hand on a checked, threadbare towel. His fingertip pulsed. This wasn't going away yet.

Chapter Six

"Wait. Back up." Gigi held a long-stemmed red rose in mid-air and halted her stem clipping as though she'd suddenly been frozen solid. "Did you say 'strudel'?"

"Yeah," Sarah said, tapping her fingers on the flower shop's work table. "I hope he burned it."

Gigi resumed her task, snipping the ends off the thorny stalks then gently slipping the delicate blooms among the others in the vase. She tilted her head, surveying the progress. "So, what next, Sarah?"

"Fight the bastard." She shrugged. "I filed all the paperwork today."

Gigi continued her arranging, adding sprigs of fern, tufts of powdery baby's breath, all the while tilting her head from side to side, assessing the balance of her project. But what she was really doing was revving up, getting ready to make a bold statement.

Sarah felt what was coming next—knew her friend like she knew herself—and she didn't have to wait long.

"I still think you should woo the son-of-a-bitch. Maybe ask him out for a drink."

"Seriously, Gigi, must you think *bed* whenever there's an available man in the vicinity? Even a crazy one?"

Gigi gave a little shrug and put on the pouty face

that got her everywhere with everyone. "I didn't say 'bed' him, sweetie." She turned and gave Sarah a sloe-eyed glance. "We can't help it if he'll *think* you're going to bed him."

"There's a name for that, Gigi, and it's not pretty. No thanks."

This was nothing new. Gigi had been through more men since her divorce than Sarah could count; which she'd never do for fear of fueling her concern.

Now it was Sarah's turn to tilt her head. She eyed Gigi fussing about with her greenery, her pretty features set on the task. Why, oh why, did this talented, beautiful, smart woman resort to the gathering of conquests like buds in a vase?

Gigi went to the ribbon rack. "You're using the mommy voice."

"I'll tell you what. Let's not go anywhere near this guy. After this is all settled, if you want, *you* can go for it—since you're so anxious. Screw him to the wall for all I care."

Gigi let out a loud crack of laughter. "I seriously love when you talk dirty."

"Can't you, like, take up stamp collecting or something?"

Her friend laughed again and shook her head as if Sarah was the crazy one. She cut a long strand of red ribbon with one clean slice from her scissors.

****

Sarah put the accordion file away in the bottom drawer of her dresser—under the skimpy camisoles she'd never wear but Gigi still insisted on buying her for birthdays. She thought again of her friend and shook her head.

She couldn't decide if Gigi had an overwhelming sense of herself, or not enough of one. Either way, it was worrisome.

Sarah gazed into the standing antique mirror surveying her own look. *Not bad. Not good, either.* True, lately she'd lost her urge for the treadmill and her hand weights sat in a wicker basket near the closet. But she was active. She was healthy and all her clothes still fit. Well, most of them.

She leaned in close to her image to get a better look at her face; to survey what she already knew was there. The tiny lines around her plain brown eyes seemed to multiply day by day, vying to outnumber the freckles that peppered her cheeks and the bridge of her nose. Well, that would fix her for detesting those freckles all her life. Now they were the preferred blemish.

She patted her nondescript brown hair. It was frizzed today, unruly, the way it always looked now that she had stopped the tedious treatments involved with forcing the smooth silkiness that Gary had preferred.

He would cluck his tongue at this image, she thought. Truthfully, everything about the way she appeared now was a contradiction to her former spouse's standards for her. She was the antithesis of her old self.

And she was starting to like this person looking out at her. After all, this was her. It was this woman that would tackle this new, horrible set of problems. She turned off the light and shut the door.

The wedding caterer called to go over menu plans and Sarah made arrangements to meet with them when Hannah arrived on Saturday. So what if the town wasn't on board with the wedding. *Plans as usual*, she decided. *Act as if.*

Norman Wallace delivered the mail to her door again and gave her one of his sheepish grins. "Hello, there, Sarah. How are you today?"

Norman was a nice enough guy, kind of sweet. Hannah's teasing words filtered into her thoughts. Was it true that Norman was interested in her? She tried to imagine it.

In a flash she saw a scene in her head of herself in Norman's arms dancing at Hannah's wedding, the way she had danced with Benny. The idea made her shudder.

It had been a long time since she felt that whirly stir inside her body when in close proximity to an appealing, available man. But, she sure as hell knew when the feeling was absent. Leave it to her to pick a crazy one—hell-bent on ruining her life.

"Weather's holding out, huh?" Norman said.

"What?" she startled back to attention. "Yes, no rain in the forecast."

She saw the tender look in his eyes again and, frankly, it shamed her that his affect was borderline appall. "Norman, I'm sorry, but I don't have time to offer you tea today. Busy with Hannah's wedding plans, you know."

"Is that going to, you know, be okay?" he asked tentatively.

"Of course." Her insides folded in on themselves. Were people jabbering about this? Would word make its way to Hannah's ears?

"Down at Gilbert's the guys were talking," Norman said. "You know how that goes. Anything worth mentioning in this little town goes right to the barber shop."

"Well, that's not good," she said, her jaw clenched. "I don't want Hannah to know anything about that silly permit problem. You understand?"

She heard the mommy voice coming from her own lips. She swallowed hard. "Norman, I'm sorry. It's just that I don't want people buzzing about this. It'll be remedied soon enough."

"Okay, Sarah," Norman said and offered a prideful smile. "I'll defend you."

Oh boy.

When Norman was gone she sat down with pen and paper and began a new to-do list. She needed to keep her mind focused on the wedding and let go of the idea that the permit might not come through. That was not an option.

She barely heard the soft rap at the front door. If it was Norman coming back to *defend her* she might have to start drinking during the day. She opened the door.

Benny stood at the threshold with her dish in his grasp. His face was contorted into a scowl like someone had wound him too tight. He thrust the dish in her direction. "Your dish."

She accepted it into her hands.

"Did you make those muffins?"

"Um, sort of. It was a box mix."

"Oh. Well, they were a little dry. If you'd made them from scratch I'd have advised you to add more liquid to the recipe. I like apple sauce. It adds more moisture without more fat."

She was in the Twilight Zone, she knew that now. This crazy man was channeling Julia Child. Everything about him was suddenly pissing her off. She wanted him gone from her presence, wanted him off her front porch. This gourmet needed to gallop on out of her way.

"If there's nothing else then…" She slowly inched the door closed. "Thank you for returning my plate."

"Sarah…wait."

To her own surprise, she let her hand fall from the doorknob.

"The cops came to my door."

"I see."

"They questioned me about that little note you received. I know you didn't believe me when I told you I'm not the one that put it under your door."

"That's right." She kept her tone and gaze steady and emphatic. Inside she was pure jelly.

"Well, they did. Have they reported back to you?"

"Not yet." She felt her face flush at his scrutiny. She momentarily closed her eyes. *You hate this guy. You hate this guy.*

"Actually they think it might be some sort of prank. From someone you know."

"People I know don't do things like that, Benny."

"I'm just relaying their opinion."

He surprised her by smiling. It was a lopsided curve of his mouth.

Benny continued, "Want my expert opinion?"

"Does it involve apple sauce?"

"Not this time." Both sides of his mouth matched now. A full jack-o-lantern grin was plastered on his face. "My advice is to ignore it. Don't give it any credence and it'll just go away."

"I'll take that under advisement. I'll use that

73

strategy with all my annoyances, beginning now. If you'll excuse me…good day, Benny."

He hesitated for the briefest of moments, his eyes piercing, stilling her breath. *Please go.*

The air expelled from her chest when Benny turned way. She watched him retreat—his muscular body navigated the stairs with ease and his ordinary, non-designer jeans hugged his legs—before closing the door.

Sarah startled at her observation and its contradiction to her common sense. All the time that she'd failed to notice *anything* physical about a man, and now eyeballing faded denim stretched across the butt of this nuisance gave her a lightning-like jab of electricity.

This was a problem.

****

By the time Hannah arrived for the weekend, Sarah had her game face on. She had wrestled herself free of the effects of Benny's physicality and did her best to put aside her worries about the wedding and the cryptic note.

She knew that when the weekend was over, she'd focus on proving who wrote the anonymous little tidbit. Damn the local PD for advising her to ignore the note, "chalk it up to a prankster" was how they'd put it when they'd called. Double damn Benny for starting this mess and agreeing with their advice, and worse, for looking pretty darned good in faded Levi's.

Sarah and Gigi sat at the large island in The Cornelia's kitchen, photographs of flower arrangements fanned out in front of them. Hannah burst into the room, hands outstretched, her face a mask of distress.

"Pumpkin, don't scrunch your forehead you'll get premature wrinkles," Gigi said.

"Daddy wants Tina to be my flower girl!" She plopped herself onto a counter stool, groaning as if her foot was caught in the jaws of a bear trap. "Seriously."

Sarah shared a quick glance with Gigi. "Hannah, let me pour you some tea."

"I don't want tea, Mother." She was like a grouchy twelve-year-old, the stubborn child that still managed to surface from time to time.

Sarah made her tea anyway.

"Why should I have to have Tina in my wedding? She's only three. You know what a pain that's going to be?"

"It's your wedding, honey bun," Gigi soothed. "If you don't want a toddler in your wedding party, that's up to you. Besides she's so young. Is this kid even housebroken yet?"

"Um, Gigi, dear, that would be potty-trained, not housebroken." Sarah was now convinced that she might have two cranky adolescents on her hands. "Tina's not a beagle."

"I know, but still…" Hannah piped in. "You haven't had to spend any time with her. She's a spoiled brat. Daddy and Piper let her get away with everything. It's ridiculous."

"Here, drink this." Sarah placed the mug of tea in front of Hannah, ignoring the theatrics.

"Maybe you can *discuss* this with your father. You know, tell him your concerns."

"Nope." She sipped her tea. "He won't listen. Whatever Piper and Tina want is gold. I'm doomed."

Sarah hated that Hannah felt like the outsider when

it came to Gary and his new family. It shouldn't be like that. Hannah should have equal say in matters that concerned her.

But the last thing Sarah could do was to tell her daughter to put her foot down and deny the request. Experience told her it would start an argument that would only escalate and might never end.

Besides, she needed Gary to stay the hell out of *her* way—especially now that there was this little matter of someone trying to sabotage the wedding event. No. She'd keep her opinion out of it.

"Hannah, maybe you can appeal to Piper. At least ask her to be extra watchful of Tina that day."

"Or, maybe get the kid a leash." Gigi closed her mouth abruptly when Sarah shot her a narrowed glare.

"Okay, not a leash, per se," Gigi said. "But, you know they have those things that look like a leash. You see kids tugging at the end of them in the mall. You could get a satin one, maybe."

"Hannah, I suggest you talk with Piper." Sarah said. "She'll make sure Tina behaves."

"Oh, like that'll happen. The kid's a prima donna, Mom."

She placed her elbows on the table and leaned forward, fixing her eyes onto Sarah. "I want my wedding day to be perfect. I mean, my career's nowhere. At least I can have a beautiful, flawless wedding day. Is that so much to ask? Can you understand that, Mom?"

Sarah's heart skipped with a thud. Yes, she understood. And, she'd make sure that's just what Hannah got.

"Let's go over the centerpiece ideas." Gigi

rearranged the fanned photos on the table top. "Then I've got to get back to the shop."

Sarah could tell her daughter's heart wasn't in the effort. Hannah sat slumped over the pictures while Gigi and Sarah gushed over them. It was maddening. Sarah had the errant thought that if this little bride was going to behave like a teenager, maybe she'd send her to her room like the good old days.

They decided on low, square vases brimming with hydrangea blossoms—arrangements that promised to add just the right touch to the splendid day.

Sarah walked Gigi to the door and when they were sufficiently out of Hannah's hearing Gigi leaned close. She whispered, "So, what's our little girl like at the dentist?"

Sarah grinned. "I can't believe this Tina thing has her so upset. I mean, if it means that much to her she should put her foot down with Gary."

"You mean just like you used to?" Gigi's well-trimmed left eyebrow lifted in a sarcastic arc.

"Point taken, friend," Sarah said. "Now, go. Leave me here with this cranky creature."

She found Hannah still sitting in the kitchen, a defeated, blank look on her pretty face.

"Let's go over the caterer's information before she gets here, shall we?" Sarah said. She went to the desk, tucked into the room's alcove, and pulled out her wedding file. She brought it back to the island and opened the cover.

"Okay, good idea," Hannah said. Her voice was subdued, her tone lackluster. "I'm sorry, Mom. I'm acting atrocious."

"Honey, is something else bothering you, you

know, besides Dad's insistence on Tina being the flower girl?"

"No. Yes. I don't know."

Sarah closed the file folder. "Okay, kid. Talk to me."

"It's just that this whole thing feels like it's gotten torn out from under me or something. I mean, one minute I'm engaged and everybody's all happy and proud and now all I do is stress over the event. This isn't fun anymore."

Hannah's eyes brimmed with threatening tears. Her mouth pulled itself up at one corner—the signature expression she'd used all her life when refusing to succumb to crying.

Worry, like ice water in her veins, shot through Sarah. "Are you having second thoughts about marrying Ian?"

"What?" Hannah straightened her posture. "No. Are you kidding me? No."

"Okay, what then?"

"I don't know." Hannah raked a hand through her long hair. "Maybe it's just this thing with Daddy and his push for Tina's participation in the ceremony. I'm tired of him telling me what to do. I mean, does it ever end, Mom? How did you stand it all those years?"

Good question. Sarah thought back to a time when she herself had fought for her beliefs. It always ended in her acquiescence. She'd been a jellyfish when it came to Gary Grayson. His approval was so coveted that she'd just give in and do things his way.

She touched her wild, shaggy hair. *Not anymore.* "Look, Hannah, your father—"

"I know, I know. He means well. I get that. As we

speak, he's meeting up with Ian in Chicago. They're both there on business, but they're planning on taking some time to get in nine holes of golf. Ian's excited. He loves Dad."

"It's nice that your men get along," Sarah offered. The words tasted stale on her tongue.

Of course Gary liked Ian. He'd all but hand-picked the young businessman to be his son-in-law. Sarah recalled when Gary had first mentioned Ian to Hannah during a dinner function at the club; she'd refused to meet him. It had been out of spite, of course. Yet, how sweet the approval of a strict, discerning father.

Sarah's chest ached as she eyed her only child. She seemed so young sitting there with her face scrunched up and her mouth pouted. Hell, she was only twenty-three. That was considered young these days for the walk down the aisle.

Sure, Sarah had married even younger, but that was then. Was Hannah jumping into this whole wedding thing sooner than she really should?

Sarah said cautiously, "You have to decide what's important to you."

Hannah gave her mother a little smile. Sarah knew the one—the brave smile. The one that said she'd be fine.

"Let's go over the menu," Hannah said, reaching across the island and giving the file folder a flip open. "The catering people will be here at four."

Emily Melrose arrived right on time. By then Sarah and Hannah had pretty much come up with their preference list, although their selections would not be final until after the tasting event. It was scheduled for the coming weekend when Ian would be available to help decide on selections.

Emily, a wisp of a woman with intense dark eyes, flipped through her appointment book. "We're hosting the tasting on Saturday, as you know, Hannah. I need a final head count. You initially said four attendees, is that right?"

"Make it six," Hannah said, with a quick roll of her eyes. She turned to her mother. "Daddy wants Piper to come, so of course, my three-year-old stepsister Tina will be there."

"That's fine," Sarah said brightly. That took an effort on her part, considering she couldn't fathom how the rail-thin Piper, who clearly didn't eat, was going to give input on food.

"I guess," Hannah said. "So, six of us. That okay?"

"Okay?" Emily said with clearly enough enthusiasm for all of them. She placed a hand on top of Hannah's. "The more the merrier. We want everyone happy."

"Wonderful," Sarah said. "We're looking forward to it."

"Bring your appetites!" Emily added.

After Emily left and all the food-talk had spoken to their bellies, Sarah and Hannah made a quick dinner of scrambled eggs and home-fried potatoes. A find in the refrigerator's crisper yielded a green pepper and an onion which they chopped up and added to their concoction. Not bothering with setting the table, they perched themselves at the island and sipped a crisp Chablis with their meal.

"So, just to recap"—Hannah twirled her goblet by its stem, casting a languid gaze on the undulating liquid in the bowl of the glass—"next Saturday we go to The

Melrose at three. All six of us. Thank God Ian's parents aren't in town or we'd need a friggin' bus."

"It'll be fun," Sarah said. "You'll see."

Deciding a lazy night was in order, they chose to watch a movie while propped against a cluster of pillows on Sarah's bed. Over the years this had become a mother-daughter ritual.

A spy thriller, the movie required more attention than they had to offer. Halfway through Hannah conked out. The sight of her daughter in repose, angelic face innocent and blissful, made Sarah's heart swell.

She pulled a soft, nubby throw up over the girl and switched off the television. Closing her bedroom door softly behind her, Sarah maneuvered the staircase to the main floor of the inn to turn off the lights and double-check the door locks.

As she approached the front door she spotted the tab of a familiar-looking paper poking in from under it. Emotion zinged through her; but this time instead of a burst of fear, the feeling was a distinct surge of rage. She yanked open the door and tugged out the envelope.

The paper was the same, as was the capitalized printing. To no surprise, inside was one sheet of identical stationary. *"Meet me at the Pier House 9:00 PM on Monday night. I'll explain everything. But come alone."*

Her body quaked and she couldn't stay still. Someone had sneaked onto her porch again tonight. The intrusion and her privacy's violation fueled her anger. If these damned notes really had nothing to do with Benny Benedetto, then who the hell was responsible? This had to stop. Now.

She grabbed her windbreaker from the hall closet

before peering down at her feet. Her cotton socks would never do for a sprint down the avenue. She stifled an urge to swear aloud.

She needed to go back upstairs to retrieve her sneakers. That would require finesse in order to not awaken Hannah. There was no way she could explain a late-night walk to her daughter or risk causing her to question the motive. But she was going, damn it.

Sarah gingerly ascended the stairs, pausing at each step. Her windbreaker would not cooperate. With each movement the scratchy fabric sounded with a loud zip-zip. She knew removing the jacket while she was halfway up the stairs would be too noisy, yet she needed shoes.

She had a new idea. She descended the stairs she'd already climbed, her arms extended out from her body like wings to remedy the fabric-on-fabric racket.

Dashing back to the coat closet, she crouched onto her hands and knees, feeling her way in the dark interior of the space. At this point she didn't even want to turn on a light, the darkness suddenly becoming a blanket of security.

Her fingers found the wicker basket of work clothes she used when gardening. She found her rubber boots.

Sarah donned the pink floral galoshes, slipped her pink-handled trowel into her jacket pocket to use as a weapon if she needed it, and squeaked and zip-zipped her way to the front door. She opened the door carefully and slipped outside.

Making her way down Tidewater to Ocean Avenue, she clomped like a Clydesdale. She was totally unsure of where she was going. All she knew was that she had to do something. She wasn't going to just sit home and "ignore" these letters like the PD had advised.

She thought of Benny Benedetto and his arrogant assurance that the town police were right in dismissing the problem. She'd do this on her own. Somewhere in this dark night was a person who'd put a second letter under her door and, damn it, she was going to find them.

Chapter Seven

Sarah made her way to the boardwalk. Her windbreaker billowed out from her frame like a kite, doing little to keep her body warm.

She spied the glow of lights dotting the row of homes, thinking all the people in their little town were nestled and cozy and feeling safe. Meanwhile somebody kept sticking notes at her door.

The wooden walkway sounded like a hollow drumbeat under her boot-clad footfalls. Up several yards ahead she caught a glimpse of a figure in shadow walking rapidly away from her. Before allowing herself to mull the idea, Sarah reached a hand into her jacket pocket and withdrew the trowel then broke into a clippety-clopping jog, her heart pounding.

The figure stopped and turned toward her and she slowed her pace. Suddenly every episode of every cop show she'd ever watched flashed through her mind. What did the pretty female television detectives do in such circumstances, usually right before a commercial break?

Common sense told her to run like hell away from this dark place and this lone figure. But her feet had turned to lead and she stood affixed to the boards.

The figure approached her and she sucked in a cold, misty breath. She wielded her weapon, the little shovel's point aimed right at the stranger.

One more step in her direction revealed his face as it came into view under the beachfront lantern's beam. She could not speak. It was Benny. Even as he came closer she remained mute.

"Going gardening?" he asked.

"What?" She regarded the tool in her hand. "No. What are you doing out here all alone at night?"

"I was just going to ask you the same thing." He pointed to her galoshes. "Expecting rain?"

She was pissed now. "I just grabbed whatever I could find so I didn't waste time. I'm going to find out who's putting notes under my door. Enough is enough."

"Notes?"

"Yes, notes, plural. Another one tonight. Interesting, Benny, that you're out here. And you appeared to be walking really fast, almost running really. Running away from something?"

He blew out a long breath of air. "I jog regularly. Really, Sarah, I have nothing to do with either of your notes."

"Well, I guess I'll find out on Monday night, won't I?"

"Why Monday night?"

She pulled the note out from her pocket and jutted it in his direction. He took it from her and held the paper under the glow of the street lamp.

"Okay, first of all, I didn't write this." He lifted his gaze. "But I do think you should mention it to the police. Just so they know. And, whatever you do, do not go to the Pier House to meet this clown."

Sarah snapped the paper out of his grasp and shoved it back in her pocket. "I've already tried the police, remember? Now I'm going to do it my way. I am going to the Pier House to have it out with whoever this is."

"I strongly suggest you don't."

"I'm going."

"At least don't go alone, Sarah, for God's sake."

"I'm not scared." She was lying. All of a sudden, she *was* scared. But, she wouldn't let that stop her.

"And what are you planning to do if this guy tries to pull something? Are you going to plant flowers on him?" He pointed to her trowel.

She turned to leave. "Good night, Benny."

"It's not wise to—"

She clomped away, the sound of her rubber boots drowning his words.

****

Back in the cottage, Benny went straight to the kitchen and pulled a large bowl out of a cabinet. He lined the counter with his needs, rubber spatula, whisk, the clacking set of stainless steel measuring spoons, the glass measuring cup.

Banana bread. That was what he needed to do— bake something. He eyed the browning, freckled bananas dangling limply on their hook. The little brown dots reminded him of the sprinkling of freckles across Sarah's nose. *Christ man, stop.*

He peeled the fruit, freeing it of its skin, then began to work. Pulverizing the bananas with the potato masher felt good. His heavy hand turned the fruit into pulp. With each thrust of the implement, he began to feel better, more relaxed.

Damn that screwball woman. It wasn't his problem if she got herself killed being an idiot. His time to worry about such things was behind him. It had been the one thing he detested most when he was on the force—morons trying to do his job. How many well-intentioned civilians wound up in the emergency ward, or worse? He couldn't count. *Shit-for-brains, all of them.*

A half a stick of butter melted ten seconds in the microwave slipped easily off the dish into the mixing bowl. He cracked two eggs against the rim, torpedoing the shells into the trash can several feet away. He measured the sugar, leveling the cupful with the flat edge of the spatula, and then whisked the ingredients with gusto.

This chick was asking to get her ass kicked. Screaming for it, really. Was it any of his concern if that was just what she got? He whipped his hand around and around, applying pressure to his effort, whirling the batter precariously close to the rim.

When the project was complete he slid it into the oven, set twenty-five degrees lower than the recipe called for based on his too-brown strudel from the other morning. He set the timer.

He put all the dishes into the sink, almost enjoying the clatter it made. With the faucet at full throttle he filled the marred porcelain vessel with sudsy water. He poured himself a cup of stale coffee, nuked it in the microwave and burned his lip while tasting to see if it was too hot. It was.

Damn it to hell. The image of Sarah Grayson, wacky rain boots on her feet, shielding herself with a piece-of-shit little tin shovel meant to dig holes for flower seeds planted itself in his brain, took root.

He gulped his coffee, still too hot and numbing. He waited for the oven timer to go off, knowing way before the banana bread was golden and springy that he was doomed.

He had to follow Sarah Grayson to the Pier House on Monday night. *Damn it to hell.*

Chapter Eight

The Pier House bustled with patrons, the seating on the back deck nearly at capacity. Sarah and Gigi followed the young hostess to a table at the far end of the veranda. They were seated beside a vinyl window inset of the canvas tenting used to shield the space. Luckily, their table was positioned near a propane heater that bathed them in a blast of warmth.

"Cozy," Gigi said, eyeing the limited space between tables. "Can't believe there's nothing available inside on a Monday night. There should be this many men here on Ladies Night."

"There's an NCAA tournament game on tonight. Lots of Villanova fans in Ronan's Harbor," Sarah mused. "Look, the bar out here is packed too. All guys staring up at the TV's."

"I did notice the guys at the bar," Gigi said, raising a coy shoulder.

"Down girl. Without a basketball in your hands, you're as good as invisible."

"Fear not," she said skimming the laminated menu, her voice nonchalant. "I'm already smitten."

Sarah felt a tug inside her chest. She remembered her offhand comment in the flower shop that Gigi could go after Benny when this mess was over. "Please don't say you're referring to Mr. Benedetto."

"Go after your sloppy seconds? No thanks." Gigi

laughed, but then stifled herself when the waitress appeared.

They ordered red wine and burgers. The moment the waitress trotted off, Sarah leaned in. "Well?"

"Calm down, Sarah. It's Mickey Nolan." Gigi sighed like a teenager. "It's always been Mickey Nolan."

The wine arrived in time for Sarah to take a swig and swallow the words that fought to escape her mouth. *Not him again,* still rang in her ears though.

Sarah didn't trust Mickey and she didn't believe his promises about his never-ending separation from his wife nearing its end in court. How many times had the guy made an excuse about why there'd been a delay in the divorce?

Each time Gigi fought against her feelings, did her best to get angry, and pushed him away until he had a firm court date. And each time he floated back into her life riding on sugary promises that never panned out.

"Make that go away," Gigi said, pointing a finger at Sarah's face.

"What?" Sarah asked.

"You're not talking, but you're wearing the mommy face. Don't. This time he means it, Sar. His divorce is definitely going to happen."

Sarah tried to undo her expression but she could feel it on her face like too much pancake makeup. She leaned one elbow on the table and rested her chin in her hand. "And you believe him this time because?"

"Because he's taking me to Vegas."

Sarah sat up. "Why?"

"To celebrate, of course. As soon as the judge signs on the dotted line, we're booking the trip. Mickey likes the hotel with the canals running through it."

Sarah opened her mouth to speak, but thankfully their dinners arrived brimming and hot in red plastic baskets. She took a big bite of her burger, filling her mouth.

"So," Gigi said, swallowing then taking a sip of her wine. "When this mystery person shows up at nine, what's the plan? Am I sticking around? You want me to go up to the bar and just wait while you talk to him?"

"Maybe," Sarah said. "But, stay nearby. You know, just in case."

She checked her watch then surveyed the view outside the window. The beach was dark, but enough light from the lanterns along the beachfront boardwalk lit a portion of the white sand and she could see people strolling along the boardwalk, mostly two-by-two.

A lone jogger trotted past the slow moving duos and it brought to mind her running into Benny on the boardwalk. The way his mouth had screwed sideways at the sight of her in those gardener's boots gave her a twinge of something even now. Was it anger? Humiliation? She shook it from her mind while sipping her wine.

"Scoping out the joint, Colombo?" Gigi asked.

Sarah turned her attention to her friend. "Ha ha. No. Just looking out at the walkers."

"Isn't that the kid Hannah used to date in high school?" Gigi pointed to the little storefront positioned several yards from where they sat.

Sarah craned her neck to get a good look. Indeed, it was Jeremy Hudson, carrying a large cardboard box into his little store. There were several other cartons stacked by the front door. "Business must be doing pretty well," she mused. "His parents would be glad to know their little store is thriving. Nice people."

"You know I've never been inside the place. What does he sell besides suntan lotion anyway?"

"All kinds of sundries, beach chairs and toys, stuff like that. It's been a while since I've been inside The Beachcomber myself." Sarah thought back to when Jeremy's father's arthritis had gotten so bad that his parents made the decision to move to Arizona. "His mother used to have a whole souvenir section with shore-themed merchandise. She dabbled in crafts, I think. Greeting cards, too. You know a typical variety store."

"Who's that?" Gigi asked motioning her head.

Sarah viewed a pretty young woman, tiny-framed but apparently agile as she hoisted a carton from the stack outside the shop's door.

"No clue."

Gigi cocked her head. "Maybe Moon Doggie's got himself a new Gidget," she said referring to the old nicknames she had given to Jeremy and Hannah back when they were young, inseparable, and often at the beach.

"Everybody deserves to be happy," Sarah smiled. She had always liked Jeremy.

"Like Mickey and me." Gigi's face was bathed in anticipation of Sarah's agreement coupled with an emphatic nod.

When it didn't come, she sighed and checked her watch. "By the way, Sar, it's five after nine. I think you've been stood up."

"Whoever it is will be here," Sarah said. "I mean, nobody goes through this kind of effort to just chicken out."

The sound of a siren in the distance jarred their attention. Flashing red and blue lights danced along the white canvas wall, causing the deck's patrons to rise from their seats and huddle by the vinyl windows.

Sarah viewed the bar where many of the stools stood empty, the customers having abandoned their televised basketball game for a look at whatever was going on outside. A solitary patron was still seated in the farthest corner of the bar, almost hidden in shadow. But, one good look caused the hairs on the back of her neck to jab taut. *Benny Benedetto.*

Waitresses buzzed nearby with speculation but her main focus remained on the man at the bar. "Son-of-a-bitch," she hissed under her breath, causing Gigi's head to snap back in her direction.

"What?"

"I'll be right back." Sarah rose, her chair scraping loudly on the floor boards. "Our friend Mr. Benedetto is at the bar."

Gigi peered around her uplifted shoulder in the direction of the counter. "Well, well..." It was a sultry sing-song.

Sarah quickly navigated the maze of tables as though racing a clock on a game show. She could tell he had seen her. He had pivoted in his seat and sat facing her now as she approached. The first thing her eyes locked onto was the denim clad thigh jutted out as if on display, the faded fabric firm against his leg. *For crying out loud, doesn't he own anything besides jeans?*

"May I ask you what you're doing?" Her hand flew to her hip.

"Having a beer and watching the game."

"And spying on me?"

"Where's your note writer?"

"I don't know, Benny." She cocked her head to the side. "Am I talking to him right now?"

He sipped from his mug before placing it back square on a coaster. She ignored the way his lips closed in on themselves briefly as a postscript to his liquid indulgence. At least she willed herself to focus anyway.

"Well?" she said, glossing her tone with venom.

"I refuse to respond to such an asinine question." He took a deep breath and let it expend. She ignored the rise and fall of his chest, refusing to remember its rock-hard feel against her torso.

"Avoidance doesn't mean not-guilty." She hated the breathiness of her tone. She cleared her throat, hoping her memory of that other night at the Pier House would follow suit.

"I didn't write those notes, Sarah. But, I do think you're crazy for deciding to meet whoever it is. At least you brought your friend along."

The bartender approached and swiped a damp towel over the wooden surface. "Can I get you something?" he asked Sarah.

"What are you drinking?" Benny offered. He turned to the bartender. "Whatever she and her friend are drinking, it's on me."

"Nothing, thank you," she said to the man behind the counter. She lifted her chin to Benny. "Just tell me what you're doing here if you didn't write the notes."

"Enjoying the action on the court." He motioned his head toward the television suspended from the ceiling. Then his dark eyes zeroed in on hers. "And making sure you don't get yourself hurt."

She swallowed hard and silently cursed her eyes for enjoying their feast.

"I see you've abandoned your gardening gear."

His little smirky smile deserved a pinch, and her fingers twitched with the urge. But she knew better than to touch him. Any more.

Benny threw several bills onto the bar, took a quick sip of his beer. "I'm going to check out whatever's going on out there." He pointed in the direction of the huddled onlookers crowded at the clear plastic windows along the back wall.

Just then a waiter approached carrying a tray of dishes and glasses. "Have any updates, Mack?" Benny asked him.

"They're saying two guys mugged somebody, took his wallet, and roughed him up, too. The ambulance just pulled up." The waiter shook his head. "And, the season hasn't even started yet."

Something about the ambulance's presence struck a new nerve and Sarah began to wonder if the incident might have something to do with the non-showing of her appointment.

She and Benny exchanged the briefest glance, as quick as a blink, but in that instant she saw the same question reflected in his dark eyes.

He said nothing, however, and turned his attention to the task of zipping his jacket. "My guess is that since nobody showed up tonight the police were right about those notes. Just a prank."

Her hunch was that Benny believed his own words about as much as she did, and she had an urge to challenge him. But he was gone.

Chapter Nine

"Come on," Sarah said as she returned to the table. She opened her purse and dug out some bills from her wallet.

"How much?" Gigi asked, grabbing her purse.

"Tonight's my treat, Gigi. After all, I dragged you out here to be my co-sleuth."

"Well, Cagney, Lacey here thanks you." Gigi slipped her purse strap over her shoulder. "Where are we headed?"

"The beach."

"I'm with you," she said. "So, what'd your buddy have to say?"

"He's an ass, and please do not refer to him as *my buddy.*" Sarah closed her payment into the waiter's vinyl bill holder. "He claims he was here to make sure we didn't get into trouble."

"Really? Hmm…that's kind of sweet," Gigi said with a smile. Her mouth immediately lost its curve as though it had been slapped away. "What? You don't think that was kind of gallant for a cop to just come out to keep an eye on your little mystery meeting?"

"No, I do not," Sarah said. "He's a *retired* cop, by the way, and he should mind his own business."

Gigi responded with a brief shake of her head. The two made their way toward the commotion on the boardwalk.

By the time they reached the crowd of people standing by the storefronts, the ambulance had driven off down a side street. Two police vehicles were still parked in the head-in parking spaces by the beach entrance.

A small group of standers-by talked with two officers while other spectators continued to stare. Benny was among the crowd, standing front and center, arms folded across his chest. His intent gaze reminded Sarah of a sports coach on the sidelines of a playoff game.

"Look at him," she said, motioning her head. "Is he serious? Why doesn't he just go home and bake some more strudel?"

Gigi laughed. "You're sounding less and less fond of this guy."

"Bingo."

"It's almost like you've forgotten that hot kiss on the dance floor. Accent on 'almost.'"

"Gigi, I swear…"

Sarah couldn't help watching Benny though. He unfolded his arms and approached the officers with assured steps—the sheriff in an old western. He engaged them in conversation and Sarah could read the authority written all over his gestures, even from this distance. After a few minutes he walked away, heading down the boardwalk toward his cottage.

"Much as I hate to do this…" Sarah watched Benny's figure retreat down the walkway. She tugged Gigi's arm. "Come on. I've got to see if he found out anything."

They scurried past those still milling along the macadam, nearly breaking into a jog to catch up to

Benny. "Wait up," she called.

He stopped and turned in their direction.

Up close, in the lamplight, his face shone blank and expressionless. Was it the cop in him providing the poker face? It was really unnerving. Suddenly Sarah wished she hadn't followed after him.

"I, uh, just wondered if they said anything about what happened." She did her best to keep her voice casual.

He didn't speak; his face still deadpan.

"You know, I mean, could what happened at the beach have anything to do with the person who left the notes at my door?"

"They'll check into it."

"You mentioned my notes?" It felt like an intrusion, but wasn't that why she had run after him in the first place—to find out if he had some insight? He was screwing up her thought process, as if it needed any more frazzling.

"They didn't seem concerned." He shrugged. He sounded terse and impatient.

Sarah felt a heated flush come to her cheeks. But the damned notes were her issue, not his—and if he'd stuck his nose into her business she deserved whatever information he'd attained.

"Who was it they took away in the ambulance?" She kept her tone steady in spite of her growing frustration.

He inclined his head toward the shoreline. "One of the punks from the beach. He and one of his buddies decided to double-team some guy and steal his wallet."

He snickered. "Only they didn't know the guy they attacked has a karate black belt. He went at them like a ninja. Seems he kicked the one little thief in the forehead with the heel of his shoe, sending him to the hospital for stitches."

"Well, that's good; at least, they didn't get away with the man's belongings." Gigi said.

"Yeah, they did," Benny said. "The second kid took off."

"God, I hope they find him," Gigi said.

"He's on foot. They'll nab him." Benny sounded sure.

"Ronan's Harbor's such a nice, safe town. I hope this isn't a sign of things to come," Gigi said.

"You and me both," Benny said. "Properties will be worth squat if word gets around that riff-raff is moving in on the place."

He turned his gaze to Sarah. "Goodnight, ladies. Take care."

Benny walked away leaving Sarah and Gigi in their silence.

A male voice came out of nowhere. "And it's only April."

Sarah turned to find Jeremy Hudson at her side, just as tall and lanky as he'd been in high school. His hair was burnished gold, much darker than when he'd been a fixture at The Cornelia night and day during his and Hannah's teen summers. She guessed that the former towhead, now being a store owner, didn't get much time to enjoy the outdoors where the sunshine would bleach his shaggy head.

"Jeremy," she smiled, "how are you?"

He leaned down and gave her a quick kiss on the cheek. "Fine, Mrs. Grayson. Hi, Mrs. Allen. What's the scoop?" He motioned his head toward the nearby policemen.

"We heard two young guys mugged a man."

Jeremy shook his head. "Punks."

"Ronan's Harbor didn't used to have punks," Gigi lamented.

"Hopefully it's just an occasional odd occurrence," Sarah said.

He pulled his mouth down at the corners. "Even an occasional problem is too many problems."

Sarah nodded. "By the way, how are your parents, Jeremy?"

His face softened, his boyish good looks evident even in the subdued night light. "Dad's health isn't great. The emphysema's more tolerable out west, but it's still debilitating. Mom's good. She's made a few friends, works part-time in a library."

"Please say hello when you talk with them."

"Will do. How's Hannah?"

"She's great, getting married soon."

"I heard. Please tell her I asked after her."

The moment felt awkward. Sarah couldn't tell if it was solely her own feelings bathing her emotions. Jeremy and Hannah's breakup had been tough on both of them; and if truth be told, on her, too.

They were two nice kids that had needed to move on, she to college, he to taking over The Beachcomber. Theirs had been a love too young and mistimed to go the distance.

Halting her thoughts, she asked, "How's business?"

"Doing well." His mouth turned into a proud grin. "You haven't been inside since I took over. Why don't you come in and take a look?"

Obligingly they followed Jeremy into his little store, the lights low except for a bright hue emitting from a backroom doorway.

"It's past closing time, but we're here unpacking a shipment that arrived late today." Jeremy shook his head, placing his hands on his hips. "I don't trust the boxes to stay out there overnight. Not these days."

Just then a figure appeared in the doorway to the back of the store—the same young woman Sarah had seen earlier, diminutive and spry, with a cardboard box braced at her hip. Her eyes brightened when she saw them and her lips curved into a polite smile. She waved what looked like a box cutter in the air. "Am I opening everything tonight, Jer?"

Jeremy checked his watch. "It's getting late, Mara. Why don't you go on home? We can inventory the merch tomorrow. But come here a second, I want to introduce you."

She approached and Jeremy made the introductions by laughingly referring to Mara as his "right hand man." But, Sarah didn't miss the warm, appreciative look Mara's eyes cast when she gazed up at Jeremy.

He turned to Sarah, stretching his arms wide. "Well, how do you like the place?"

"It's great, Jeremy. You've made some nice changes. I like the cabinets." She pointed to a couple of pieces of old white-washed furniture positioned strategically in the store, each used for the display of merchandise. "Nice touch."

"Her idea." Jeremy pointed a thumb at his beaming *right hand man.*

This Mara seemed like a lovely girl, and if the two were a couple, it made Sarah's heart glad. She'd always liked the boy—kind and soft-spoken, earthy and unpretentious; very unlike Hannah's new love, Ian. She stole another glance at Mara. The raven-haired, brown-eyed beauty was physically the polar opposite of her flaxen-haired, pale-skinned, obviously Austrian-featured daughter.

Gigi had wandered down an aisle and was browsing a rack of greeting cards, chuckling at the messages.

Sarah navigated past the display of suntan lotions and sunburn remedies. She eyed the shore-themed items arranged on the shelving, taking in packages of balsa pine airplanes, nylon kites, and colorful plastic buckets with shovels.

Near the cards, on a separate shelf her eyes riveted onto a stack of stationary. She felt a sharp jab at the sight of the same beach-patterned paper that the mysterious notes had been written on. She grabbed a package.

"Gigi," she whispered hotly. "Look." She shoved the stationary at her friend.

"Hey, isn't that…?"

"Yes, it is." She turned around to find Jeremy at the front counter going over some paperwork with Mara.

"Did you need something, Mrs. Grayson?" he asked.

"This seashell stationary…" She waved the package toward him as she maneuvered closer to the counter. "Have you sold any of this lately, say in the last two weeks or so?"

"Not sure," he said turning to Mara. "Why? Do you need more than one package?"

"Uh, no." She gave a little laugh. Embarrassed at his misconception that she intended to purchase the stationary, she laid the package on the counter, deciding to buy it. "This one will be fine."

"Mara here can ring you up."

Mara waved a wand over the price tag while Sarah reached into her purse for her wallet.

"I do the inventory and the ordering," she said casually. She accepted the five-dollar bill that Sarah extended her way and slipped it into the cash drawer.

While she counted out coins for Sarah's change, she continued. "We had three packages of that specific pattern a few days ago. I guess I need to reorder it. Funny how merchandise can just sit there for months and then out of nowhere one item becomes the customer favorite. Want us to let you know when the new stock comes in?"

Mara handed the change to Sarah before slipping the package into a thin paper bag.

"No thank you." Sarah took the bag from Mara. "This is more than enough."

"It's funny how you can never tell what's going to move off the shelves. Crazy, right?" The girl smiled.

"Yes," Sarah said. "Crazy."

****

Sarah and Gigi headed back to The Cornelia Inn, their shoulders hunched up against the breeze kicking up from the ocean. Sarah's head spun with the events of the evening, questions pelted her brain like grains of sand in a windstorm.

"Sarah, don't get yourself spooked by any of this, okay? I mean that stationary's probably available everywhere."

"I know," Sarah breathed audibly. "But the fact remains that I've got two anonymous notes and the clock's ticking toward the wedding."

"Do you think it's true that Ronan's Harbor is headed in a direction we don't like? I mean, could what Benny said happen around here?" Gigi asked.

"No." She stopped her pace, planted her feet firmly. Gigi stopped beside her. "Listen to me. Pay no attention to whatever Benny says. I don't. He's only interested in selling and moving on." She began to walk again and Gigi followed suit.

When they reached the inn Gigi jumped in her car, tapped her horn in goodbye, and drove off. Sarah let herself in and bolted the door behind her.

The old mariner's clock on the mantel sounded the stroke of eleven. It was time for bed, but she itched to pull out her reservation log. She had avoided it long enough.

Now that Benny had so graciously planted the seed that the town could suffer if it took on a new flavor, she had to see in black and white what the season promised for The Cornelia.

She sat at the big kitchen's island with a cup of her chamomile in front of her. The light above her bathed the ledger's open pages. She ran a finger down the list of names already booked. She didn't have to look up last year's figures to know the lineup was sparse.

Because of the wedding, she'd blocked out all of May and the first week of June, but that shouldn't pose much of a problem. Her season didn't usually kick in until Memorial Day and the summers had been steady in recent years. With spurts of visitors during the winter months, private group bookings, as well as Valentine's

Day, her income had progressed over time to a doable level.

She pulled out the file of those she'd mailed reminder cards to, her regulars. No response yet from the Harringtons, or the Kinnecoms. They'd been diehards over the years. The Nardos always came with their whole tribe for a family reunion. They'd all been faithful and they'd usually all been booked by this time of year.

The tea was getting cool, but the flavor was a welcome to her senses. She drank the whole cup. She decided that in the morning she'd make a few phone calls to her loyal visitors to see if their reservations had simply slipped their minds. Though, what if the economy had put too big a damper on folks' vacation budgets? Or what if that damned Benny's concern was more of a prophecy? What would become of the town, her inn? What would she do?

Sarah rinsed the teacup and closed her ledger. At the base of the stairs, she let her gaze appreciatively sweep over the tidy foyer. She placed her hand on the glossy finial, her fingers gently gliding over the beautifully detailed carving. Slowly she climbed the staircase. She was tired, though sleep would not come easily. That much she knew.

****

Damn it to hell, I can't sleep. Benny yanked back the sheet and leapt from his bed. Why should he be the only one in this plan to deal with the locals' shenanigans? What he should do, what he really wanted to do, was call Sal, wake *him* up from his slumber. Mr. Police Captain hated that.

It was after one in the morning. Something nagged

at him, and he couldn't put his finger on it. Could that altercation on the beach actually have anything to do with the clown writing those notes to Sarah?

He tried to shrug it off, went into the bathroom, and snapped on the light. He filled a cup with water and chugged it. His face in the mirror looked pretty bad— squinty eyes and frown lines cutting deeper than usual.

Wasn't this supposed to be his time to relax, enjoy the ocean, and all that stuff? Instead he was up in the middle of the night and freezing in his skivvies while he tried to figure out what the hell was gnawing at him. *This is bullshit.*

He snapped off the light. Heading back to bed, he tripped over one of his sneakers. He righted his stance and gave the shoe a sharp kick. And that's when it hit him. *Damn it to hell.*

Chapter Ten

Sarah's doorbell rang just before nine in the morning. Luckily, she'd showered, but she was still in her robe, her hair a damp tangle.

Benny stood in her doorway, a foil-wrapped, shiny brick shape in his hands. She stifled a groan. She couldn't deal with him this early, particularly after little sleep.

"Morning," he said.

"Good morning." Her tentative response was deliberately laced with a what-do-you-want flavor.

"Can I come in a sec?"

She shouldn't let him in. He was nothing but a problem to her, in more ways than one. She considered slamming the door in his face. As she contemplated doing so, his aftershave wafted in through the door and made itself at home. The spicy scent wound itself around her and held her close like two bodies in a dance. *Not now,* she scolded herself inwardly.

She eyed the foil-covered block in his hands; saw his thumb rubbing gently over the glossy wrapper. Her throat scratched when she swallowed. She clasped the lapels of her robe nice and close and held them there.

"Just for a minute," she heard herself say before opening the door wide enough for him to enter.

He handed the foil-covered parcel to her. "Banana bread."

She just stared at the gift and then let herself look Benny in the eye. There was an intensity in those dark, shiny eyes; something smoldering, something unfinished, perhaps. Whatever it was compelled her and she didn't like it. Yet, she continued to hold his gaze. She felt her nipples spring alive like a disloyal pair of daylilies. Not good.

"There's something I'd like to talk to you about," he said, eyeballs all intense and penetrating.

It floored her when the offer of a cup of tea spilled from her lips.

His facial expression eased and he nodded, offering a half smile. "Sure."

She sliced the banana bread, the texture moist and dense. A succulent spicy aroma met her nose. For crying out loud, Benny *and* his baked goods were smelling up her house.

She made two cups of rich black tea, and placed them on the table. Benny sat quietly, watching her every move with his cop-sharp eyes. She skipped her usual dash of sugar, sipping the dark, strong tea, needing it to keep her alert.

"No nuts."

"How's that?" she asked.

He motioned to the slices she'd arranged on a dish. "I usually add walnuts, but I didn't have any."

She couldn't help but laugh. It was such a dichotomy to think of this guy whipping up confections in his kitchen. Baking was usually an extension of love, an inner warm need. She stole a glance at him. Benny coupled with that description seemed absurd. Sitting with him and sharing a spot of tea seemed pretty damned absurd in itself.

"So, Benny, what was it you wanted to talk to me about?"

"Last night's incident."

"Okay, I'm listening." She broke off a corner of the bread. It tasted good, understatedly sweet, but she didn't tell him so.

"The guy that was accosted."

"What about him?"

"I've never seen him before, but that doesn't mean anything," Benny shrugged a shoulder. "Who would I know in this town, right? But, you and Gigi didn't recognize him either I'm guessing?"

Sarah shook her head. "No. Why would that be important?"

"Well, you know how the officer I spoke to said the guy kicked his leather shoe at the kid they transported to the hospital?"

"Yes, I remember."

"His statement was that he'd just been minding his own business, taking a late stroll on the sand. He was in a business suit and wearing dress shoes. Who takes a walk along the beach like that?"

It didn't make much sense now that Benny painted the picture. Yet, maybe the guy just *felt like it*. To each his own. "Odd, I guess." She shrugged. "Maybe he just didn't care about ruining his shoeshine. Not sure I'm following your point."

"I talked with a couple of the locals this morning at Gilbert's Barber Shop. Everybody's buzzing over there. Nobody knows who this guy is. Apparently he had no car—he must have either gotten dropped off, or took the train or a cab. But, what's his story?"

Sarah took a good look at Benny's hair. The black

waves did not appear to have recently seen the business end of a barber's razor. So, what had he been doing at the barbershop this morning? Had he already figured out that the little establishment was the hub of Ronan's Harbor gossip? If so, what was he after?

She took a breath, let it out. "Benny, are you thinking this has something to do with the notes I've gotten? Is that why you're here now?"

He raked his fingers through his dark mass of hair, waves of ebony folding over his fingertips. "It's worth a second look. Trust me; this is the last thing I want to get involved in. But, I came here this morning to mention this to you. You might want to go back down to the town hall and chat with the officer from last night."

Now worry rushed through her veins, charging into her body. *If this big toughie has concerns, well shit, mine are intensified now.*

But, what was in it for him? "I don't understand why you came here, Benny. I'd think you'd be all for somebody *else* sabotaging me."

He ran a hand through his hair again, casting his eyes downward as he did. He raised his face to meet her eyes. "I feel like I have to."

"But why?" Her heart stammered in her chest. Why was he affecting her?

"Look, I was a cop for twenty-five years." His statement was casual, but his eyes shone with something that stirred her. "If someone came to me in those days with a tip or an idea, I appreciated it. That's why I think you should head down to talk with the local PD," he said. He took a deliberate breath. "But, it's your call."

How on earth was she supposed to trust this guy's

advice? Her head spun. His intentions have been nothing but self-serving. So why was she entertaining his suggestion? Better yet, why the hell had she even let him in?

"It'll be worth it just to, you know, ease our minds."

Ease *our* minds? *When did Benny and I form a partnership in this?*

All she wanted was to host a gorgeous, memorable wedding for her daughter. Now here she was with two big fat secrets she needed to keep from Hannah; anonymous warnings randomly appearing under her door and a trouble-making ex-cop looking to join forces.

And this guy reeked of spice and sex and enough charisma to twist her nerves into an intricate braid. Her ex, Gary, would laugh like a hyena if he knew what was happening. Who wouldn't?

Benny looked at her with anticipation in his eyes.

The phone rang, startling Sarah. She went to the counter and picked up the handset. "Hello?"

"Mrs. Grayson, this is Officer Carr calling. We've recovered the wallet from the victim of the beach incident. We'd like you to stop down here at the police station with those notes you received, if you will. Anytime today is fine."

"Can I ask why? Is there a connection with the incident and whoever's written the notes?" She turned to Benny who was looking at her with dark, shiny, questioning eyes.

"We're checking into everything, Mrs. Grayson. We'll talk when you come down. I'll be here until four."

She hung up the phone and faced Benny. *Now what? Can this be good news or bad? Or will it turn out to be a big fat nothing?* "I guess you heard. The police want me to bring the notes down."

She looked down at her robe. "I need to get dressed." She walked Benny toward the front door.

"Sarah, I'm thinking of going down to town hall with you."

"What? Why?"

He shrugged as if it was news to him, too. "I might be able to help."

"If you want to help me at town hall, Benny, withdraw your complaint."

****

Something was up. Sarah was more and more convinced of this as the seconds ticked by in the police station's small interior office. She sat in a worn vinyl chair facing a small laminate desk. A jumble of paper snips and little notes taped onto the sides of the computer screen fanned like fringe.

Finally, Officer Carr entered the room, quickly positioning himself behind the desk. "Thank you for coming."

Sarah's clasped hands on her lap squeezed tightly. The idea of Benny joining her shot into her head. What the hell was wrong with her? Why was she suddenly wishing he was there?

She liked it better when the whole world had been telling her to ignore the notes because they were just a prank.

Although there was no smile in his eyes, Officer Carr's mouth flashed an elastic grin.

"May I see the notes again, Mrs. Grayson?"

Sarah handed him the two envelopes. He flipped open a file folder on the desk and compared the originals to the copies he'd made. Silence hung in the air like fog. Sarah found it tough to breathe.

He lifted his gaze to meet her eyes. "The mugging victim's wallet, as well as his jacket, was recovered in a beach trash receptacle less than a half hour down the main drag, near Normandy."

"Well, that's good, at least—that they found his belongings so quickly," Sarah offered.

"Minus the money, of course, but his credentials were all in place. The reason I wanted to speak with you"—Carr paused, making Sarah's heart stall—"is we located a hand-written list of local realty lots in his jacket pocket. The list is titled "Prospective Properties." The Cornelia Inn is on that list.

"What?"

"What piqued our interest, however, was the paper this list is written on. It's the same shell-patterned stationary as those notes you received."

"That's ridiculous." She startled herself with her sharp tone. "The Cornelia's not for sale."

The officer gave his shoulders a nonchalant lift. "People prospect all the time. No crime in that. But the same stationary? In all probability it's a coincidence. But, we're going to be thorough and send it out for analysis. It doesn't appear to be the same handwriting, but we'd like to have somebody knowledgeable tell us that for sure."

"Okay."

"We'll send the notes up to Bricktown. They have a guy there that can give us an analysis. Shouldn't take more than a couple of days."

Officer Carr stood and reached across the desk, offering his hand. "We'll contact you as soon as we get the report. Trust me; I'm sure this is just a formality. Really."

"But it was the *same* stationary," Sarah added.

"That particular brand of stationary is probably available everywhere from Sandy Hook right on down the shore. It's probably in national distribution as well. He could have picked it up anywhere."

"It does seem a close coincidence to me."

He smiled. "Let's wait for the expert's opinion."

Outside, Sarah blinked at the sunshine in her eyes. Her mind couldn't process what was going on. *Was* this just a formality? Should she be concerned that this guy was in some way dangerous?

"Hi."

She came to attention. Benny leaned, arms folded, against a black Jeep. Suddenly the fear brewing in her system changed to frustration. She stormed toward him.

"Are you kidding me?"

He straightened his stance. "How'd it go?"

"It's not your concern."

"Are they at least looking into the guy?"

She blew out a long breath. Her mind was scrambled. Had the officer said anything specific about the man other than the fact that he'd put her inn on some list? Should she have brought someone along to ask the right questions? She eyed Benny.

"The guy had a list in his wallet with my inn on it. The list was written on the same stationary as the notes."

"Same handwriting?"

"They don't think so."

He swore under his breath and raked his hair. "Have they done an analysis?"

"They're sending out for that. They should get the results in a couple of days, and they'll call me then."

"Okay, that's good. So, what about the guy? What'd they tell you about him?"

She shrugged. "Not much. Only that he's not a criminal for compiling a list of prospective shore properties."

"But who is he?"

"They didn't say."

"Sarah, you should know who this is in case he's the guy leaving notes at your door."

She took a deep breath. No matter what he'd done to screw up her life, Benny Benedetto was right about this. "I'm going back in there," she said.

"Let me come with you."

"No-o," she said, groan-like. "I don't need your input."

"I won't talk, okay? I promise. I'll just come along."

She turned on her heel and walked back across the parking lot with Benny, silent as promised, at her side.

She asked the woman at the desk for Officer Carr. He appeared quickly through the door to the front hallway approaching where she and a quiet Benny stood. *Thank goodness*—another moment in the heaviness of their silent companionship and she'd have screamed.

"Thank you for meeting with me again, Officer Carr," she said with deliberate confidence. "I have a question. This man whose handwriting you're sending to get analyzed—can you give me some information on him?"

Officer Carr flashed a look at Benny. Sarah knew he was thinking Benny had put her up to the inquiry. She straightened her stance, trying to appear taller. "I'd feel better knowing his name, in case he tries to contact me or something."

"His name is Clyde Stone. He's from Verona, up in Essex County. He's staying down at the Pelican Motel in Ortley. He's been scouting for a place to buy along the Barnegat Peninsula."

He glanced between Benny and Sarah. "As I said, Mrs. Grayson, so far he's not suspected of anything. Our sending your notes out for analysis is simply part of being thorough."

"Anything on him?" Benny asked.

Sarah shot him a warning look, doing her best to communicate, *You said you wouldn't talk.*

He gave her an annoying yet apologetic smile—just endearing enough that she bit her lip not to react.

Officer Carr shook his head. "Clean." He took a breath as he stretched his mouth over his teeth. "There's nothing on him."

"Have you questioned him?" Benny asked.

Sarah felt her teeth clamp down even harder on her lower lip and she hoped she wouldn't draw blood. She'd tell Benny to shut up if he weren't actually asking good questions.

"Yes." The officer's voice sounded clipped now, laced with indignation. "Of course."

"What did you find out about the punks from the beach?" Benny asked.

"The injured perpetrator's been released from the hospital. He and his accomplice live down in Atlantic

County. They were up here visiting the one's girlfriend when they decided to go find some trouble."

The officer looked at his watch, blowing out a breath. He directed his attention to Sarah. "Most likely there's no correlation between Mr. Stone's and your notes. We're just covering all our bases." Another stretchy lip-pull came and went on his face. "We'll contact you soon."

"That's it for now?" Sarah asked.

Benny cleared his throat. "Officer, let me ask you one more question. What's your take on the fact that this guy was walking alone on a beach at night, wearing a suit and dress shoes? It's not likely he was looking for prospective properties, dressed like a banker, in the dark."

"He'd been in Ronan's Harbor for dinner. He claims he wanted to walk off a large prime rib dinner. We verified he ate at The Lamplight." He looked at Sarah again. "We'll contact you if there're any changes."

She and Benny left the building with resumed silence between them. With the way her head was swimming she couldn't even muster annoyance at him. Could this Clyde Stone guy be the one who'd written the notes? He was staying in a nearby town. Should she worry?

When they came to Benny's vehicle in the parking lot, Benny stopped and turned to face her.

"Now, just keep your eyes open. If you get any more notes make sure you tell me...I mean, *them*."

She groaned. "You know something, I don't know what's worse, these notes or your sorry-assed formal complaint against me. Why am I even talking to you?

You're the enemy."

The pinch in his forehead gave his countenance a genuine look. It didn't matter.

Sarah's mind zoomed. There was no need to continue a conversation, or even any contact, with Benny. All he was, really, was a roadblock—a big kink in her plans.

The notes she'd received were not his problem, and yet it seemed that he wanted to make them his concern. His hanging around was just more trouble she didn't need.

"So long, Benny," she said. She heard the ring of disappointment in her own voice and for the life of her she didn't know why.

"I'm *not* the enemy, Sarah." Benny's voice was subdued. "The complaint was simply a way to protect my family's investment."

A directive to turn away and head home roared in her head. Instead, she stared at him.

"Sarah, my brother and I were concerned about the effect of over-congestion…"

"I know, the effect on your *investment.*" Now she felt a renewed blast of energy. "This town is not an investment to me, Benny. It's not just some pit stop on a map. Ronan's Harbor and The Cornelia Inn have been my home for a long time."

Conviction coursed through her veins. "I'm proud to be a part of Ronan's Harbor's history. I'm sure you don't know that *Ronan* is Dutch for 'little seal.' Back in the seventeen hundreds when settlers landed here they were awed by the frequent appearance of seals basking on a sedge out off the coast. That muddy slip of land, that time's since washed away, reminded them of home, a little Dutch island called Rona. And this became their new home."

"Sarah…"

"And, *my* inn…" She paused to take a breath. She was on a roll, her adrenaline a runaway train on a distinct track. "The history of The Cornelia Inn goes back to those early days. It was owned by the DeGraff's. Cornelia DeGraff was a matriarch in this town. It's an honor to carry on the legacy of her homestead."

She bit back the urge to scream. "So you see, your concern for your stupid little flip property gets no sympathy from me. Your idiotic complaint has rocked my life and, more importantly, my daughter's future. If my existence gets in the way of your profit margin, well that's just tough shit."

She turned on a heel and left, her heart beating in her throat and her temples. It was more than anger drumming inside her. She couldn't define it; but whatever it was, the feeling took her breath away. A sob threatened with a sharp ache in her throat.

She heard quick footfalls approaching, felt a hand on her arm, the touch sending a zoom to her senses. She stopped short. Against all alarm buttons signaling her thoughts, she turned to face him.

Benny's eyes were searching, penetrating her gaze with urgency. He took a last step in her direction and her nerve endings poked, taut like protracted claws. Her whole body stiffened, bracing like a barricade.

Now, of all times, the only thing she could think of was that dance and the kiss that followed. Her eyes found his lips and she remembered how they tasted, how they felt pressed to hers.

She closed her eyes. *Don't,* she commanded silently. But, behind her lids, her mind's eye could see the image of their entwined closeness as they'd swayed to the music. She even heard the melody, the soft notes of the tune that had enveloped them and made them part of the song.

"I had no idea…" His voice was pained.

"Why did you ask me to dance?" It blurted from her lips too quickly to suppress.

"What?"

"That night at the Pier House. You led me on." She felt her breath catch, her heart thunder. Her need for the answer swelled in her chest.

"I didn't know who you were then, Sarah. You have to know that."

"Maybe not at first you didn't. Okay, maybe I'll buy that. But, later when I told you…" She paused to quell the sudden emotion that rushed to her throat. It angered her that the memory conjured such feelings. Foolish tears stung her eyes.

"I regret my actions." His mouth formed a thin line on his face, concealing the fullness of his lips, hiding the crookedness of the one eyetooth. "I regret a lot of things."

If they were not here at this crazy juncture, if these were not their circumstances, Sarah felt somewhere inside that the situation would be different between them. Her body tingled with that instinct. But, this was *here and now.* The reality of that slapped her with an open hand.

"I think you need to just leave me alone," It was a ragged whisper, a plea. She allowed herself to look him in the eye, raised her chin as acceptance to her own challenge.

He paused, breathed deeply, and let the air expel from his chest. And, then…that's what he did. Benny walked away from her, toward his truck.

Chapter Eleven

Back at the house, Benny dialed his brother's office line. Shirley, Sal's secretary, greeted him warmly. She'd been with the precinct forever, having assisted the previous two captains before Salvatore. "Benny, how the heck are you?" she bellowed into the phone.

"I'm good, Shirl. Sal around?"

"You got lucky," she said cheerfully. "He's in the office today. Driving me nuts, if you want to know the truth." She laughed into his ear.

Sal was his usual official-sounding self and his words were clipped. "What's up, Benny? This an update on the bed-and-breakfast?"

"My first question is about a guy in your neck of the woods. The local police tell me there's nothing on him, but just wondering if you'd ask around."

"With all my free time, you mean?" Sal snickered into the phone. "I'm not the retired one, little brother. What's going on? Somebody causing you grief?"

"The name's Clyde Stone. Lives in Verona. He was involved in an altercation on the beach here in town and…"

"Christ, Benny. Don't tell me that shit," Sal snarled. "That stuff is suicide for a vacation town. Word goes around that there's crime brewing and nobody wants in."

After a long, silent pause, Sal continued in a calmer but authoritative voice. "We just need to hang on for a little while, till the market changes. Then we can kiss Ronan's Harbor goodbye and laugh all the way to the bank."

The image of Sarah's face popped into Benny's head. The sad look in her eyes, the worry flecked in them. He closed his eyes, pinched his thumb and index finger in the space between his eyebrows and kneaded the tense muscle there. Yet, the image of Sarah's face was still there in his mind.

What kind of grown-up woman still has freckles on her nose anyway? Makes her look like a kid, or something. Don't they have some goo they use to cover them up?

The way she had looked at him, and all that anger in her voice, normally would have just pissed him off. But, it hadn't. He felt like shit now, thanks to her.

This wasn't like him, and all he had to blame it on at the moment were those damned freckles. And *that's* what pissed him off.

"Can you just see if anybody knows this guy?" Benny asked. "His permanent home is in the town next to yours. Shit, Sal, it's no big deal. Ask one of your guys."

"What do you mean 'permanent home'?"

"He's looking for property down here in Ronan's Harbor."

"Christ."

"I'm almost hesitant to call him the victim after he kicked the crap out of one of the perps. The locals recovered his belongings and found a list. The Cornelia Inn's on it. The cops aren't particularly concerned

123

though. They say people are always looking at beach property, for sale or not."

"So, who gives a crap? What's it got to do with us? Forget about it, Benny."

"Sarah's gotten a couple of anonymous notes telling her to stop her daughter's wedding. She's kind of spooked about it. Maybe this Stone guy's the culprit."

"Okay, brother, first of all, you're calling this chick by her first name now. Stay the frig away from her. Don't go soft on me, Benny. And drop this crap about this what's-his-name idiot that got robbed. You want to make some dough on this shack or not?"

Benny blew out a whoosh of air.

"Do I need to come down there, Benny? Christ, don't be a pansy." He started to laugh. If Benny didn't know better he'd swear it was his old man on the other end of the line with the sardonic sounding chortle.

A memory of his father crowded his brain and began to tumble free. He'd been just a kid, nine maybe, on that Easter Sunday.

The whole family had been seated around the dining room table—Uncle Tony and his clan, Uncle Angelo there in his blue uniform, scheduled for duty that evening, and Benny's grandfather, Dominick Senior. The men had gotten boisterous by the end of Maria's elaborate meal. It happened all the time, a houseful of cops was just too much for everybody.

Benny had delivered the dessert to the table. He'd helped his mother make her famous, flakey, triple-layered coconut cake—her masterpiece. Even at that tender age he'd felt a thrill in creating baked goods. He loved the smell that overtook the house, the delicious aromas that defined their home.

On that long-ago holiday, his father had taken one look at his son carrying that cake and had started his typical shit, ramped up, of course, for the sake of the company at the table.

"Maria, are you kidding me with this?" he boomed to his wife. "You're making the boy into a pansy. Christ, you fittin' him for an apron, for God's sake?"

"Hey boy, where's your apron?" his Uncle Tony had teased, causing a round of laughter around the table. His family members shook their heads as if Benny had shown up in the room naked.

His old man shook his head in disgust. "We got to make a man out of you, Junior, no son of mine is going to be a pansy."

Benny had felt the glass pedestal wobble in his grasp. He jerked his hands in an attempt to right the tilting cake, the movement a misjudgment that caused the white frothy dessert to topple onto the table, coconut first. More laughter overtook the room. He hadn't known what to do—clean up the mess, or run and hide. His brain froze with just one certainty. He was no pansy.

Long after the talk had changed to some other topic, the loud chortles had rung in Benny's ears. The brash mocking sounds that had pelted him then were mimicked now by the noise coming at him from the phone in his grasp—time's bitter echo.

"Answer me, Benny."

His brother's bark snapped him back to the moment. He closed his eyes against any more thoughts.

"For God's sake, Sal. Fine, I'll drop it. All right?"

****

Sarah sat in the folding chair at the Garden Club's meeting, nibbling a cookie provided by the month's hospitality volunteer, Betty Conover.

Betty, a sturdy woman with short and tidy, no-nonsense-styled hair sat in the seat beside Sarah. "How do you like the macaroons?" she asked.

Truthfully, the cookies were over-baked and brittle. Sarah offered a little nod and took another bite, crunching much louder than a macaroon ought to.

Betty leaned in close, gave Sarah a little jab with her elbow. "My husband's told me about your little dilemma."

Sarah swallowed the dry cookie and took a sip from her paper cup of lemonade. How to handle it? The last thing she wanted to do was to be overheard by the other members of the group and have it become a big discussion that would burn up the Ronan's Harbor phone lines.

She shrugged. "Kind of sucks. I'm hoping Hannah doesn't learn of it."

"I yelled at Tim, just so you know," Betty said, straightening her posture. "What's the big deal if you want to host your daughter's reception? It's preposterous to cause you worry."

A surge of gratitude washed over her. "Thank you, Betty."

"Hey"—she tapped Sarah's shoulder and winked an eye—"don't mess with my Garden Club buddies."

After the club's usual discussions of budget numbers and plans for their annual garden tour, the ladies mingled in the living room of their current president, Gretchen Reynolds.

Gretchen, the mayor's wife, was an animated

woman with an infectious way of garnering center stage. She was the first to bring up the brawling incident at the beach. This started a chain of commentary with a cacophony of opinion whirling around the room like a dust devil.

Sarah didn't blame anyone for their concern. The residents of Ronan's Harbor were a protective group, especially the ladies of the Garden Club. Their roots were firmly planted in this little town.

Sarah couldn't help but smile again at Betty Conover's reaction to her "little dilemma," as she had put it, and be touched by the particularly tight embrace Gretchen had given her after the meeting ended.

The group's kinship energized Sarah and gave her a renewed determination to stand her ground, to not be bullied or intimidated by anyone. That included Benny Benedetto. It felt good to remember that.

****

The next morning Sarah spent time at Bayside Blossoms finalizing the wedding's flowers. Gigi, of course, had it all under control. At least that was one thing about which Sarah could relax.

Her friend was still agog about Mickey Dolan and was completely sure that this time he meant it when he said his divorce was going to happen. Sarah wasn't as convinced.

Gigi shrugged off Sarah's words of caution. "Sarah, honey, no offense, but your opinion of men is kind of skewed, thanks to Captain Viagra being such a dog."

It was true that Gary had soured her on trusting men. But Gigi's interest in Mickey had disappointed her friend one time too many. Sarah was a protective creature, and that was just how she felt these days—from her best friend's heart, to Hannah's wedding day, and right down to her beloved inn. Being the keeper of all that mattered was exhausting.

"I'm a big girl," Gigi said, her voice soft and tender. "You can cross me off your worry list. Let's talk about something happy. Is our girl bursting with excitement?"

"No," Sarah said. "It's weird. She's been edgy, kind of cranky."

"Maybe all the details are getting to her."

"Most of the reception's details are worked out—as far as she knows anyway. It's more than that. I think it's got something to do with her career plans. That temping gig is not really what she wants to do."

Sarah sighed. "Maybe it is just pre-wedding jitters."

"I agree," Gigi said. "Brides get like that. She'll relax once the day arrives. After their honeymoon she can sink her teeth into the career plans. Right?"

"Absolutely," Sarah said. She hoped Gigi was right.

****

It was nearly lunchtime as Sarah headed back home. She turned the bend, passing the overgrown hedge in front of the Farleys' cottage. The carpenter's white cargo van was parked in front of her inn. Harvey Scriber sat on the top step of The Cornelia rooting the contents of a plastic cooler.

"Hi Harvey," she began cautiously. She'd spoken to him right after receiving the complaint and asked him to hold off on the work. She hadn't felt it necessary to elaborate, feigning the inn's schedule as the reason.

Harvey looked up with his boyish face, his mouth a quirky smile. He munched a green grape. "My schedule freed up and I thought we'd get a head start, if that's okay. Glad to finally get this show on the road." He motioned with his thumb toward the front door. "Richie's inside cleaning up. Don't mind the mess in there. I did my best to cover the furniture with drop cloths. But you know how sheetrock dust is. It goes everywhere."

"Wait, Harvey, you weren't, uh, supposed to start yet. Um, how'd you guys get in?"

"You gave me a key, remember? Hey Hannah looks great, by the way. Going to make a pretty bride."

"Hannah?"

"Yeah, she's inside."

What was Hannah doing here in the middle of the week?

"Wait till you see how knocking the wall down to the store room has really opened up the space."

Sarah maneuvered up the steps. This was not good. There was that little matter of the permit. Now what was she supposed to do? Have them reconstruct the damned wall?

"Harvey, um, I'll be right back." First she needed to find out what Hannah was doing home, then she'd deal with this.

He popped another grape into his mouth, closing his lips over it. "Like I said, it's still a mess but you'll get the idea of what it's going to look like."

The front door opened and Harvey's coworker, Richie, appeared, bare-footed with his pant legs rolled up knee high. His normally friendly face was a knot of dismay.

"Problemo, Harvey. There's a major leak along the back wall. Rotted the floorboards. The crawl space is a flooded mess."

The three of them hurried inside to the sunroom. Sarah carefully sidestepped the draped drop cloths hanging from the furniture. Along one side of the sunroom was a pile of things the workmen had removed from the storage room topped haphazardly with another large cloth.

Hannah stood in the center of the room in her trim business skirt and short-sleeved cotton sweater, her hands pressed to her slender hips. Sarah's heart quickened.

"Hannah, honey, is everything all right?"

Hannah pointed to the disheveled scene. "Apparently not."

Before she could reply Harvey's voice boomed with warning. "Oh boy, Sarah, this'll take some doing."

He and Richie crouched on hands and knees, peering into the open hatch of the crawl space beneath the sunroom. Richie punctuated Harvey's words with a little whistle.

Sarah approached the mess with scrutiny's eye. A large patch of the old, cracked flagstone had been removed from the floor and the crumbling tiles had been randomly stacked to the side. The raw flooring beneath was warped in spots. Black stains marbled the grains of the wood.

"Can you get this done in time?" Sarah was terrified of the answer.

Harvey cocked his head, sucking air in through his teeth. "We'll do our best, but we're going to have to put in some overtime. I'll need to draw up a new estimate."

A new estimate meant a new cost. As it was, Sarah knew the allotment of renovation money had been absorbed by the initial work plan. There was no way she could afford the added expense, as necessary as it was. And then there was still the fact that the town hadn't approved any work yet.

She needed to come up with something fast. Time was running out. Fear seeped into her bones, so like the dampness that had taken over the entire sun porch.

She turned to Hannah whose eyes fixated on the troublesome scene. She rotated one ankle on a pointed heel.

Sarah eyed Hannah's foot as it circled back and forth like she was screwing it into the rotted floor. She wondered what the penalty would be for ignoring an official town complaint. Would they come and haul her off in handcuffs?

"Whatever it takes, Harvey," she heard herself say before her mind had the chance to process the words. "We just need to get this done."

"Will do," he said. "As I said, I'll need to come up with some new numbers and such, but for now how about you ladies leave us to work our magic." He furnished a reassuring smile.

Sarah gave Hannah a gentle push. "Come on. Let's go upstairs."

Once in the apartment kitchen she commenced preparing lunch for the two of them. She didn't know if Hannah was hungry, and she sure as hell wasn't, but the need to be busy propelled her effort.

The crunch of the rotary can opener's teeth to the metal of the tuna can was the only sound between them. Finally, in a hollow voice, Hannah spoke. "When were you going to tell me?"

Sarah stopped turning the knob on the opener. She'd sensed Hannah's mood earlier, been aware of her rigid stance, and knew by the telltale sign of her screwed mouth that she'd been gnawing the inside of her mouth. A tuna salad sandwich wasn't going to erase any of it.

"Okay," Hannah continued. "So, if you're still not going to say it, let *me* tell *you*." Her voice was bitter now and it jarred Sarah.

"Tell me what, honey?"

"The town's put a hold on my wedding plans because it's *illegal* to host a catered event at an inn. You've applied for a permit for the chaos going on downstairs because that somehow didn't happen in the first place."

Hannah shook her head, her look incredulous. "So don't ask me why they're demolishing the place already and, let's see, what else? Oh, the chances of my wedding reception being here at The Cornelia are about as good as my believing those guys downstairs can get all that shit done before June first. Have I got it right, Mom?"

Sarah's mind reeled. At least Hannah hadn't said anything about the notes. Hopefully, she was still unaware of those.

The look in her daughter's eyes was so much worse than rotted floorboards and a flooded basement. A giant lump lodged itself in Sarah's throat. "Sweetie…" The dropped can opener clinked loudly against the glass bowl. She stepped around the counter.

"No, Mom, don't." Hannah held up a hand, her pretty face pinched by a scowl. "Why do you do this,

Mother? Why can't you just level with me?"

She began to pace. "I'm not fragile; you don't need to keep me in some kind of cocoon, protected from reality. I'm a grownup." Hannah swallowed a sob that Sarah heard forming in her throat.

She instantly reached for her daughter.

Hannah jerked away. The tears springing into her eyes only seemed to enrage the girl further. The air whooshed from her lips. "Daddy told me everything this morning. I was still on the train on my way into work when he called.

Hannah swatted at the tears on her cheek. "And don't look at me like that. Daddy wasn't trying to rat on you, Mother. He was just asking me if you'd gotten the *permit yet."*

Sarah watched Hannah's chest rise and fall as she took a deep breath. "So, naturally, since I *know nothing*, I said *what permit?"* She flung her hands into the air, riled again. "I got right on the next train home, called the office, and told them I was sick. Because, guess what? I am. I'm sick. And with that disaster downstairs, I might vomit right here and now."

Defiance crept into Sarah's bloodstream. This was enough. "Can I talk now?"

Hannah, even in her rant, knew by the sound of the "mommy voice" that it was her turn to shut her trap.

"Thank you," Sarah said to her silent, brooding daughter. She looked so much like a ten-year-old, it wasn't funny. "I thought it best to not bother you with this detail."

"Oh, okay. So this is what you call *a detail?"*

"No," Sarah held up a hand against the snide words. "It's my turn. This is not the *disaster* you think it is. It's a glitch. You understand? I've taken care of it. I believe the permit will come through in time and Harvey and Richie will get that room looking great right on schedule."

She almost believed her own words. "Let's not make too big a deal out of this, Hannah. It looks awful right now, I agree. But it'll come together."

Hannah did not respond, but her slate-toned eyes were shrouded in doubt.

"And, maybe your father didn't *mean* to cause an issue, but if he really wanted to find out about the permit why didn't he just call me?"

Hannah pulled out a kitchen chair and plopped onto it like a bag of potatoes. She leaned her elbows onto the table, raking her hands through her nicely groomed hair and making a mess out of it. "There's no way everything will be ready, Mom, even if you got the permit today. Ian and I should have just run away and gotten married."

Sarah moved back to her tuna. She added some chopped celery and a little onion. "Look, let's just have our lunch and then we'll go over our lists. We'll tackle what's still undone and do as much as possible today, how's that?"

"Mom, we can't just pretend this isn't the major problem that it is. Level with me. Level with yourself."

Sarah put a sandwich on a plate, cut it lengthwise and placed it in front of Hannah. She poured iced tea into two tall glasses.

Sarah took a long pull of the cold liquid. "I just wanted to spare you from this kind of worry. I wanted to handle this by myself, make it perfect for you."

Hannah reached across the counter and touched

Sarah's hand. "I'm sorry I yelled at you," Hannah said. "I know you were just trying to spare me. But, this is my problem, too. I should have known."

"I know," Sarah said. "I'm sorry, Hannah. Sometimes I forget you're an adult, a resilient woman. My protecting you from your own situation wasn't fair. That's the truth of it, honey."

Hannah lifted appealing eyes and produced an anemic smile. "Thank you, Mom. And, I know I've been edgy. So, I can see why you'd think I couldn't handle the news." Her smile broadened. "You can say it. I've been bitchy."

Sarah smiled and demonstrated with two fingers pinched together. "Little bit. But, you're forgiven, bridezilla."

Hannah bit into her sandwich and chewed silently. Her head tilted to the side as though in deep thought. "You know," she said finally. "I think Daddy would love it if I just said 'screw it' and decided to have the wedding at his club. Ian even said as much."

"He did?" Sarah didn't know why but she took that bit of news as a slight.

"You know Ian. He's obsessed with Daddy. But, really I think he just wants everything to go smoothly. No *glitches.*"

"We'll tackle the glitches—together. How's that?"

"You promise there's nothing else you're keeping from me? Like, there's no other jack about to jump out of a box?"

Sarah's cell phone ringing stunned her nearly as much as Hannah's question. As she said "Hello" into the device she could not help but think of the anonymous notes. Did she owe Hannah this information as well? What good would it do her to know about them?

****

Benny decided to walk to the grocer for more baking soda and vanilla. A walk to town would do him good. He wasn't kidding himself by taking Tidewater Way to downtown; the quickest route to George's Grocery was down Main. Yet he found himself on the sidewalk approaching The Cornelia Inn.

The white van parked in front had its back doors splayed open. A carpenter-looking man unloaded some building materials. Benny watched him carry a bucket in one hand and a fold of drop cloths balanced in the crook of his other arm before disappearing through the inn's front doorway.

Benny's insides knotted. *Damn it to hell.* Apparently Sarah Grayson meant it when she'd threatened to go ahead with the renovation sans permission, and have the damned wedding at her inn anyway.

The memory of Sal's disapproving voice beat the hell out of Benny's eardrums. Wouldn't Sal just love to learn that he couldn't uphold a measly complaint?

Benny picked up his pace, headed through the gate, and up the brick walk. He navigated the stairs and stepped cautiously through the gaping front door. "Hello," he called, looking around.

To the right, beyond the entry hall, the open French doors to the sunroom beckoned him. Tarps and crap were all over the place. Two workmen amidst the mess made a racket, clucking at each other like a pair of hens.

"Excuse me," he ventured. The canvas-clad Angry

136

Birds turned in his direction, silenced themselves and gave him a little wave. Two sets of eyes stared at him.

"I, uh, was looking for Sarah."

"She's upstairs in her apartment," the taller one said pointing to the stairway back near the entrance.

Tentatively Benny meandered into the sunroom and cast his eyes around the disarray. "This looks like quite a project."

The shorter guy scratched his head. "Yeah, didn't count on a flooded crawlspace warping floorboards and molding up the sheetrock."

The other one shook his head. "We'll be here day and night getting this ready for the wedding. Her daughter's getting married in, what, like five weeks?"

Benny fists formed into tight knots. He detested having to blow the whistle on this lady's plans. He wanted to call Sal and have him come do his own dirty work.

Oh, he could just hear the caustic accusations that would spew from his brother's fat mouth. He filled his lungs with air, let it expel through his mouth.

He was no coward but he sure as hell felt like an idiot for getting himself involved. He'd agreed to see this through and his only solace was the eventual sale of the damned little shack on Ocean Boulevard.

The craving to erase the memory of this town and everybody in it flourished in him like a well-watered weed. Hell, lately the desire had grown to full-blown need. He *needed* the distance from Sarah and what she evoked in him.

"Can you find Sarah for me?" he asked, halting his reverie. "I need to talk with her."

137

Chapter Twelve

"That was Harvey," Sarah said, placing her phone's handset back in its cradle. "He said somebody's here to see me. Come on, kid, let's go downstairs. After we see who this is, we'll go over our wedding lists again. Okay?"

She and Hannah descended the staircase and the first glance at his dark mass of hair told her it was Benny. Her chest clenched. She forced herself to keep in mind that Hannah was there with her and any debate over the permit issue might send her already head-spinning bride-child into orbit.

Shit. She hoped Benny wasn't there to discuss the notes. God only knew what Hannah would do with *that* news.

"Benny, hi." She spoke cheerfully for the benefit of her self-professed edgy daughter. She could tell he was surprised by her pleasant-sounding smoke screen.

Gruffly, he asked, "Do you have a minute?"

She broadened her dry-toothed grin and introduced him to Hannah.

"Ah," he said, "the bride." The pinch melted from his face, morphing into affable warmth. His eyes shone with that polished-onyx glint that spoke to Sarah's nerve endings—the deeply embedded ones. *No,* she silently warned. *No.*

"Yes." Hannah motioned her head in the direction

of the sunroom. "Hopefully."

"Honey, why don't you go in and check on things? Benny, would you like something to drink? How about a cup of tea?"

She saw the protest forming on his lips. Sarah shot him her best look of necessity. Confusion painted his face but his shoulders relaxed and he offered a tentative nod.

He followed her down the hallway to the inn's kitchen. The moment they were in the room with the door swinging behind them Sarah spun around to face him.

She whispered hotly, "Benny, whatever this is about, please don't discuss the permit or the notes in front of Hannah. First of all she doesn't know a thing about those. And I've convinced her that the whole permit thing is not going to mean the end of our plans."

He raked his hair with an abrupt dash of his hand. "Looks like you convinced yourself, too."

"The carpenters began work unwittingly. I hadn't had a chance to discuss the permit issue with them. They had their own key and showed up while I was out. I'll handle the situation. Is that all?"

He blew out a long breath. "I know it sucks, Sarah, but the law's the law. You can't have the wedding here. Your daughter's going to have to know sometime."

Sarah tightened with an angry surge that yearned to fly from her hands, reach out and shake him silly. "Do you get your jollies making people miserable?"

"Just a talent, I guess." It sounded more like a confession than sarcasm.

Hannah burst through the door carrying a large cardboard box, the bottom warped and stained dark from moisture.

Sarah cast Benny a warning look, although his eyes did not return any sign of acknowledgement.

"Mom, look what the guys found in the crawl space!" Hannah placed the floppy-bottomed box on top of the island. She reached both hands in and withdrew a familiar old stuffed dog—the plush replica of the Seeing Eye puppy she had raised as a teenager. "Look, it's Parker," she exclaimed.

Suddenly, Hannah sounded like her old self. Gone were the anxious demeanor and the dour look that had become her signature these days. She hugged the musty-smelling toy to her body and gave it a squeeze. "You smell, Parker." She scolded as if the object had willfully chosen his mustiness. "Anything we can do about it, Mom? The tag says to spot wash."

"Try baking soda," Benny muttered.

Both women turned in his direction. "Sprinkle baking soda on the dog and let it sit overnight, preferably outdoors. Then tomorrow vacuum it with the attachment thing you use to do your furniture."

Hannah grinned at him. "Well, Mr. Benedetto, you're a life saver."

"Benny," he said. "My father was Mr. Benedetto."

"Thank you, Benny," she said sweetly before flashing Sarah an appreciative glance.

Sarah found the baking soda in the cabinet. She handed it to Hannah doing her best to keep the irony from the front of her mind. The truth was not only was this guy *not* a life saver, he was a wannabe wedding killer.

After Hannah took the stuffed Parker outside to begin her task Sarah turned abruptly toward Benny. She kept her voice low and it came rasped. "Did you come here just to monitor the goings-on at my inn?"

"I think you should concern yourself that the work going on in the sunroom could cause you a problem, Sarah. Unless, of course, you've decided you're above the law."

Adrenaline blasted through her system. She took a step closer, lifting her chin at him. "What if it does? Going to have me arrested?"

"Maybe locking you up would do you some good," he shot back.

"What's that supposed to mean?"

"That way maybe you can stay clear of that mystery correspondent of yours and let the police do their job."

Venom bubbled up from her depths landing in her throat as a bitter-tasting retort. The sound of the back door stifled her protest.

Hannah entered, and it was as though a ring announcer had rung his bell at the end of a round. The warring parties retreated to their own corners, Benny to a stool at the island, Sarah to the stove to put on tea.

She banged the teapot onto a burner with a heavy hand. The only way she'd find herself behind bars was if she gave in to the urge to clobber him, which she might.

"Sentimental toy, huh?" he asked.

His kind comment stilled her as she listened. She sneaked a peek out the corner of her eye.

"Yes," Hannah replied. Her face was warm with nostalgia. "Years ago I raised a puppy as a community service project to be a service dog. His name was Parker. I was nuts about that dog."

In spite of her mood, Sarah felt her lips soften into a curve. She was glad to be facing away from Benny so he wouldn't see. The memory of that sweet golden lab following Hannah around, learning her diligent commands came flooding back.

They had had such a bond. A swell of pride filled her chest at the memory of Hannah's brave goodbye to the beloved Parker when it had come time to relinquish him to his duty.

She poured steaming hot tea into cups. Bracing herself, she turned in his direction and jutted a cup at Benny.

He accepted the offering while gazing at her openly. "Thank you."

Their eyes locked and Sarah bristled at the evident challenge in his dark orbs. "Don't burn your lip."

His mouth quirked up at one side and his eyes flashed with amusement. "Thanks for the warning." He turned his attention to Hannah.

"It must have been tough to give the dog up, huh?"

"I knew going in that that's how it would end." Hannah gave a melancholy shrug. "Hard as it was, it's what I had to do."

She glanced out through the backdoor's window. "I'm going to pin old Parker onto the clothesline to air out." She retreated through the door. "Thank God it's a sunny day," she said as it closed behind her.

As soon as Hannah was out of sight, Benny began, "Sarah, listen—"

"Nope," Sarah said, crossing her arms. "Not listening. You've screwed things up enough for me. Don't burden my daughter with your official complaints. Unless there's something else you've come here to complain about, maybe it's time you left."

The backdoor swung open again, silencing their exchange. Hannah was not alone this time. Gigi strode in, booming in her exuberance. "What's this, a party? Cripes, you're all drinking tea?" She plopped onto a stool beside Benny. "That's no party. We need wine."

Sarah blew out a whoosh of air. She loved Gigi like a sister but today her timing couldn't be worse. How was she supposed to chase Benny away before he did any more damage?

"Well, hello, you," she drawled at Benny.

Benny nodded at her. "Hi."

Gigi rubbed her hands together. "Okay, Sarah, let's uncork a party."

Sarah tried to flash her friend a distinct red flag look.

"Come on. I have a toast."

Sarah rolled her eyes but went to the fridge for the bottle of chardonnay. She suddenly felt like having a glass. She pulled goblets out of the cabinet.

"Let's see what we have to nibble on down here." Hannah rummaged through the cabinets. "Nothing. I'll run upstairs and get some snacks from the apartment." She trotted through the door.

Sarah poured herself a good dose of the white wine. *Might as well,* she thought. She was fairly certain they didn't serve wine in the slammer.

"What a surprise to see you two here like this," Gigi directed at Benny. "I mean, I don't usually invite *my* adversaries in for wine in the afternoon."

Benny pushed away his tea cup and lifted his wine glass to his lips. Sarah silently admitted they were rather appealing lips. *A shame that such a nice mouth spews such bullshit.*

"He's going to be leaving any minute," Sarah said, her voice firm. He had the gall to lift his glass as though toasting her words.

Hannah reentered again carrying a box of crackers and a block of cheese. She arranged the items onto a couple of plates before grabbing a short stack of napkins and putting it all on the island.

Gigi grabbed a cracker and popped it into her mouth with a loud crunch. "Party time!" She eyed the misshapen box on the counter. "What's all that?"

"Memories," Hannah said. She peered into the carton as if it was a treasure chest.

She pulled out her high school notebook. The blue fabric cover was mottled with ink scribbles of hearts and the initials of her and Jeremy Hudson. She flipped open the cover and turned the pages. "Social Studies notes." She wrinkled her nose. "Why the heck would I save these?"

She put the binder back in the box and sucked in her breath. She withdrew an old, black lacquer-painted jewelry box with Japanese flowers on the lid. Sarah recognized it immediately. Years ago it had been a gift from Jeremy.

Hannah gave the little knob of one of the drawers a gentle pull but the face came off in her hand. "Oh man, this thing's rotted."

Surprising Sarah again, Benny stood from his counter stool and stepped closer to Hannah. He took the small drawer face carefully into his hand. "You can fix this," he said. "Wood glue."

Hannah looked at him with appreciative eyes. "Boy, am I lucky you stopped by today."

Sarah smiled. What she was thinking was, *want to bet?*

Hannah perused the interior of the jewelry box, carefully opening the other compartments. "Oh my God."

"What is it, honey?" Sarah came close.

Hannah withdrew a petite oval pendant hanging from a thin, silver chain. Sarah remembered the necklace. It had been Hannah's high school graduation gift from Jeremy—the token of a promise between two kids too young to really know about lifelong promises.

"Opal," Benny said looking over. "October your birth month?"

Hannah nodded without looking away from the object. "The eleventh."

"My wife's birthday was in October, that's how I knew."

For some reason it surprised Sarah to learn of his marriage. The past tense of his statement could mean a couple of scenarios. *Was he a widower? Divorced? Better yet, who cares?* She shook the thoughts from her head.

Hannah held the necklace up to her chest, looking at her reflection in the black door of the microwave oven. She stared at her image for a long moment. "Riding on a rainbow," she mused with a wistful smile.

She looked up at her mother. "Remember?"

Sarah nodded, feeling an odd pull in her chest.

Hannah gazed at Benny and Gigi. "The legend of the opal is that God created opals after riding down to earth on a rainbow." She collapsed the chain into her palm and touched a delicate finger to the stone. "Superstition says that opals lead the wearer to true love." She laughed a hollow sound. "And here it sits in a crumbling box warped by a flooded basement."

"Well, that explains it, then." Benny's mouth twisted sardonically. "I gave my wife an opal for some occasion and very soon after she left me for another man." He brought his wine glass to his mouth and took a pull.

Placing an elbow on the counter surface, Gigi said, "Well, I don't know about you people, but I'm hoping there's a guy on this planet who'll think of something that sweet for me." She bit into a cracker punctuating her statement with a loud crunch. "Just saying."

A quiet came over Hannah as she gently placed the old jewel chest into the carton. She gathered and replaced the other items she'd removed, closing the flaccid flaps back over them. She pulled the box into her arms and headed toward the kitchen door, pushing it open with her backside. "I think I'll take this stuff upstairs for now." And she was gone.

Without the focus of Hannah's finds, the three of them sat in silence for what Sarah felt was a long, awkward minute. She felt Gigi's eyes burning at her with question.

Unable to stand it, she finally spoke. "Thank you for not mentioning the permit in front of her," Sarah said softly. "She's got enough to deal with right now."

Benny blew out a long breath. "I understand the predicament this puts you in, Sarah, but look at it this way—keeping things as they are around here is for the betterment of the town. Can't you just hold the wedding someplace else? Then everybody would be satisfied."

Everybody? She felt her blood stir again. *Like hell.* "With just a few weeks left before the event? Benny, look don't even try to dignify your selfish act by using the excuse that Ronan's Harbor would benefit from my not having the wedding here. I don't care a hoot about your rationale for the complaint and I couldn't care less about whether you and your brother reap big bucks on the house you bought."

She felt the heat in her face. "If we want to discuss what's best for Ronan's Harbor, I vote that you sell your house and get the hell out. Leave me and everyone else around here alone."

He offered no response but stood from his seat, his mouth set in a tight line. Something unrecognizable smoldered in his eyes. It was not anger, but it was intense and it made her heart quicken.

Heat flushed her face with something new and her mouth went dry. Such harsh words were foreign to her tongue and they tasted like bile.

Benny ceremoniously placed his wine glass onto the counter. He offered Gigi, who sat silent and staring, a short nod. He then turned to Sarah. "I'll let myself out."

He walked through the swinging door which slapped back and forth behind him in what looked like a wave goodbye.

Sarah locked onto Gigi's big, round eyes.

"Guess you told him." Gigi's words were a near whisper, her tone as hollow as the sudden feeling of emptiness that sat in Sarah's chest.

Sarah gulped the remainder of the wine in her glass. "Damn him," she said before charging out of the room.

She caught Benny on the front porch. "Benny," she said, breathless from something beyond the short sprint down the hallway from the kitchen.

He turned to her, staring with those big, dark eyes. His mouth curved into a humorless lopsided smile. "You're right, you know…" He shoved his hands into the pockets of his jeans.

Her lips parted to speak, but the words were gnawed away by the solemnity in his eyes.

"I have no business being in this town, let alone messing with its inhabitants." His words were flat and emotionless, but they sent a charge through her.

Heat flushed her face. Finally, she said, "This is a nightmare we don't deserve." She swallowed hard. "And, God only knows what those notes I've gotten are about."

She took a breath to loosen the taut muscles binding her chest like a straight jacket. "But I'm sorry I said what I did. It was unfair and unkind. My nerves are frazzled, but that's no excuse."

His mouth curved into a sad facsimile of a smile. "You're a nice lady, Sarah Grayson. The last thing you need to do is apologize to me." And he turned to leave.

Her eyes followed him as he retreated down the stairs and made his way along the brick sidewalk. It was only after he was out of sight that she realized she had clenched a hand to her sweater, making a tight fist of wool over her heart.

****

Benny skipped the trip to the market and headed in the opposite direction. He thought of Ann Marie and saw the image in his mind of the way she'd looked on the day she had left him. She had had that same angry exasperation on her face, the same ragged sound of bitterness in her voice that had just come from Sarah.

He had never really blamed Ann Marie. Her bitterness had grown from a disappointment Benny couldn't fix. Ann Marie had wanted children. Hell, he had, too.

Shooting blanks is what his brother had said as a result of the gruesome testing he'd had to endure. *Slow swimmers* is what the doctor had said in his lingo for a layman. Whatever the vernacular, the truth was that there would be no kids for Benny and Ann Marie.

That sorry news had only intensified whatever had been wrong with the two of them, and he knew there'd been plenty. But it had become unbearable when they'd discovered that for eternity all they'd ever have was each other. It didn't take Ann Marie long to get the hell out of Dodge.

He thought of the Christmas card he'd spied one year on the fridge in Sal and Bernadine's kitchen. It had been more than an odd feeling seeing his former wife and her new husband, two kids and a dog, peering into a lens. One click forever captured their happy life.

He charged up the steps of the cottage and went inside. He sat alone in the living room for a while, staring at nothing, thinking of everything. He closed his eyes, breathed in and breathed out.

He released his tight lids. Focusing his eyes, it was like seeing the room for the first time. It was a small, square box of a space. The wood floor was marred with scratches, a perfect match for the lumpy walls. He looked up at the ceiling where the light fixture that no longer worked still clung to the surface, rusty patches dotting its rim. Even the damned electrical wiring needed upgrading.

He viewed the furnishings that had come with the

house, the nubby plaid sofa, chipped veneer side tables, cheap glass lamps with stained shades.

Nothing about this place spoke of care. Not like Sarah's Cornelia Inn. He remembered the way the she had spoken of her roots in the home, of the old lady she'd named it after.

He shook his head. He guessed nobody had ever loved this little dump. He smiled mirthlessly. It was no wonder that it was his name on the deed.

Benny stretched his arms over his head and craned his neck to relieve the tension that had taken residence. He had a call to make.

Chapter Thirteen

"Okay, friend o'mine," Gigi intoned when Sarah re-entered the kitchen. She waved her empty wine glass at her. "Pour us some more truth serum and let's have a little talk."

Sarah went to the refrigerator and yanked open the door. She pulled the wine bottle out by its neck and brought it over to the island, firmly placing the bottle down with her fingers still wound around it.

"Easy, tiger, this isn't a ship that needs christening." Gigi reached across the island and took the bottle from Sarah's grasp. She poured a half glass for each of them. "Sit," she said.

Sarah collapsed onto a stool across from Gigi, her arms dangling at her sides.

"Drink," Gigi said.

Sarah looked at her, but didn't move. "I hate him."

Gigi didn't respond, but instead eyed Sarah over the rim of her wine glass.

Sarah said it louder. "I hate him." She dangled the wine glass in front of her, rotating her wrist to make the golden liquid dance in its bowl. "You wanted the truth. And there it is."

"Uh-huh."

She took a swig of the cool wine. But the fragrant blend did not erase the thoughts swimming around in her head. Benny Benedetto had done something to her that no man had ever done before. He'd gotten her mad enough to yell.

All the things that she'd gone through with Gary—all the times he'd made a fool of her, the way he belittled her in front of people and in private—in all that time she'd never once, not one single time, yelled at him.

And now this interloper had turned her into a banshee. That had to be hate. She sipped again.

"The man certainly stirs *something* in you, that's for sure."

"Don't think your innuendo escapes me," Sarah said. She was finally feeling the effect of the wine she'd ingested. She realized she could breathe fully again. "But it's ludicrous to say the least. Have you forgotten that he's trying to sabotage Hannah's wedding for his own selfish purposes? Well, I haven't."

"Better tell that to your pheromones."

Sarah stared at her spiky-haired friend as she sat there puckering her pretty, smirky, over-lipsticked mouth. There was no rationalizing this with Gigi. That much she knew.

Her side-kick was a hopeless believer in fairy tales. Currently her latest delusion was that the infamous Mickey Dolan was back on his shining, white steed, ready to whisk her away to happily ever after. In their case, apparently that meant Las Vegas.

"Aren't we drinking in the afternoon because you have a toast to make?" Sarah took a sip, silently toasting her segue away from Benny Benedetto.

"Well, yes, actually. Mickey's coming over tonight to 'discuss our future.'" Gigi clapped her hands. "He's going to propose."

"Gigi." Sarah couldn't help using her mommy voice. Her best friend often seemed in need of parenting. "Take it easy. Don't jump to conclusions."

"He was going to get our tickets today, he's already booked the hotel and,"—she poked a finger in the air for emphasis—"I found a receipt in his pocket from a jewelry store at the Monmouth Mall." She leaned in conspiratorially. "A *fancy* jeweler."

"Okay, I'll speak in your language. A, you don't know that means he purchased a ring, and B, why are you rummaging through his pockets?"

Gigi shrugged a coy shoulder. "A girl has to stay informed, that's all. The receipt doesn't say the item was a ring, granted, but hell you just saw that opal necklace Hannah pulled out of that box. No ring would outshine the sentiment in something like that. Maybe Mickey's got some of that same romance inside those sexy bones of his. I don't care what the bauble is. I'll love it and I'll know what it means."

"But…"

"No." Gigi held a hand to her chest. "Sarah, honey, look. I'm going with my feelings on this. I have to listen to what's in here no matter what. Honest to God, you should do the same."

"Gigi," Sarah said, not caring that she sounded skeptical. The hope in her friend's eyes stopped her litany. She tendered a conciliatory smile. "If this will make you happy I hope that's just how tonight goes."

Gigi jumped up and dashed around the island like a schoolgirl, throwing her arms around Sarah. "I love you." She squeezed hard then pulled out of the embrace. "I have to run. I've scheduled a manicure, you know, just in case it *is* a ring," she gushed. "Which I think it is. I just do."

She grabbed her purse, slung the strap over her shoulder and headed for the door. With her hand on the doorknob she gave Sarah a winning smile. "Wish me luck."

Sarah blew her a kiss and Gigi caught it and held it to her heart.

****

Sarah cleaned up the kitchen. Thoughts of the day's events careened around in her head despite her attempts to concentrate on the rote task of rinsing suds from the wine glasses and tea mugs.

She hoped Gigi was doing the right thing in going off with Mickey Dolan to Vegas. But, again, she realized she knew next to nothing about men, and even less about relationships. Not to mention pheromones and the havoc they caused.

She checked on Harvey and Richie. They were still at it, sawing off subflooring in a warped area. Again, they assured her they would make every effort to complete the project in what Harvey termed a "jiffy."

Before it went an inch further, it was time for Sarah to tell them the facts. Her stomach ached with the heaviness of the truth she'd swallowed earlier. "Harvey, hold up."

Harvey put down a flat spatula-looking tool and stepped over to her. "It looks worse than it is, Sarah." His voice was assuring.

"I found out I need a permit for this work."

Richie stopped his hammering and came over to where they stood. The two men exchanged a look then focused their gaze on her.

"You mean, now that we've discovered the job's

going to be bigger than we thought?"

She blew out a long breath and turned her head in the direction of the staircase. She lowered her voice. "Well that certainly compounds it, yes. But, I received a complaint from the township committee protesting any renovation without a permit."

"Well that can't be good." Richie said.

Harvey shot him an annoyed look.

Richie shrugged. "What do you want from me? I'm a carpenter, not a lawyer."

Harvey turned his attention to Sarah. "I'm sorry. I should have double-checked but this seemed like such a simple little job. All the work I've done around town has been for private residences. Maybe they're bigger sticklers for inns."

He shook his head. "You know, I had an auto body shop before doing this stuff. When that went bust I started doing odd jobs for folks. I should have known to check with the committee since this is a place of business as well as a residence. I screwed up."

Sarah thought of her first contact with Harvey. He and his buddy Richie had been outside a neighbor's house painting their siding. The neighbor had given him a glowing reference. When she'd heard he had a family to support and a business that had gone under, well she'd hired him on the spot. Little did any of them know that Sarah's renovations would require permission.

"We *all* screwed up, Harvey. Guys, look. For now, let's put the work on hold until I straighten this out. I've already filed for the permits, but now we'll need to provide a new drawing of the work involved."

"They're definitely going to need to know about

this." Harvey pointed to an area of black mold stains on the subflooring. "Or else they may shut us down again."

She gave a sad nod. "Yeah."

"I'll write up the new estimate and we'll get it to town hall as quickly as I can, Sarah. Okay?"

She gave him a smile. "That would be great."

****

Upstairs Sarah found Hannah asleep on top of her bedclothes. The box Harvey found in the basement was on the floor near the bed. The small jewelry chest now sat on her nightstand. The little drawer front that had come off in her hand was set beside it.

Sarah couldn't help but think of Benny's advice about the wood glue to repair the drawer. Why did he have to be such an overall jerk? It just didn't seem fair.

Hannah looked so peaceful sleeping there on her side, her legs curled up at an angle. One hand dangled over the edge of the mattress. Her hair was splayed around her shoulders, strands fanning over her face.

Sarah could not resist the urge to lightly brush her fingertips over the wisps as she'd done more times than she could count when her child had needed mom's reassuring hand. The move gave Sarah a nice view of Hannah's face and that's when she noticed the opal necklace clasped at her neck.

Feeling an odd zing of alarm, Sarah gazed over at the clock on the dresser. It was time to get ready for the tasting event scheduled for that evening. Ian was due to arrive soon. She gave Hannah's shoulder a gentle shake.

"Hannah, come on, honey," Sarah said when the girl didn't stir.

Hannah opened her eyes and volunteered an easy,

groggy smile, the kind Sarah remembered from when her daughter had been a girl and more carefree.

****

Ian arrived early, his usual, always-ahead-of-schedule self. Still in his business attire, he was a dapper sight in a fine-cut navy suit. His white shirt was still crisp even after a full day's work; his paisley-print tie added just the right hint of whimsy to his otherwise staid appearance. He was a walking, talking store-front mannequin. He greeted Sarah politely, kissing her cheek with cool lips.

"Where's our girl?" he asked genially.

"Still fussing." Sarah smiled.

Her daughter and Ian made a striking couple, Hannah with her downy mane and fair skin, he with his angled face and dark hair. What a bride and groom they'll make, she mused, a photographer's dream.

Sarah gave his face another look. Ian had no bad angles. It was as if he'd been made from a cast.

"Whoa," he said as he looked through to the open doors of the sunroom. "What's that all about?"

Harvey and Richie had packed up most of their gear and tarped the area in which they'd been working, but the disturbance to the room was still quite evident.

"The carpenters found a leak. They're almost through fixing it." She surprised herself with the easy lie.

Ian made his way toward the room and Sarah followed, a clench forming in her chest. She was a school girl with the teacher scrutinizing her science fair project with a critical eye.

"It's not as bad as it looks," Sarah said lightly. "Are you, uh, looking forward to tonight's tasting?"

Ian didn't respond. She watched him as he surveyed the space with a scowl so similar to one Gary often planted on his own face that her body started to brace the same way it used to.

Hannah appeared, freshly showered and dressed in a cute, little blue dress. A puff of floral scent preceded her into the room. "Hi," she said, coming up next to Ian.

He turned to her and kissed her temple. "Hi, babe," he said absently. "Look at this, huh?"

"Yeah," she said and sighed. "They promised it won't be a problem time-wise." She cocked her head, angling her gaze to meet his. "What do you think?"

He shook his head slowly. "It doesn't look promising, I'll say that. It's more than a little disconcerting, but I'll admit I have no clue about these things."

The doorbell rang. Even though Sarah knew it had to be Gary and Piper, she was relieved for the diversion from the condition of the sunroom. She hurried to the door.

Gary stood erect with little Tina in his arms, all snug in her denim jacket with the faux leopard collar that matched her mom's.

"Come in," Sarah smiled. "Hope we're all hungry," she added as they came into the foyer.

"Say hi, honeybunch," Piper said as Gary set Tina down.

The little girl looked up shyly at Sarah and tucked her chin. Admittedly she was a pretty child with auburn hair like her mother's, and a pouty mouth all her own.

Sarah bent down to her. "Hello, Miss Tina," She said. "We're all going to a little party tonight to taste the food for Hannah and Ian's wedding. Won't that be fun?"

No reaction. Tina sucked the tips of her index and middle fingers into her mouth. Her steady eyes penetrated Sarah's much like Gary's used to when he wasn't *telling* her he thought she was stupid, but sure as hell thinking it.

Hannah and Ian greeted the new arrivals.

Just when Sarah thought they'd escaped Gary's observance of the sunroom, she felt like she'd been catapulted back to the science fair.

Gary's head snapped in that direction. "What the hell, may I ask, is that?" He strode to the doorway of the sunroom like Heathcliff back from the moors. Unfortunately, everybody else followed.

"That was my reaction, too." Ian sidled up beside Gary, the two tall men making a wall in the doorway. Each stood with the same stance, hands in their trouser pockets, their heads angled to one side like the dog in the old Victrola ads from Sarah's grandma's day.

"Ridiculous," Gary said under his breath.

"You think it'll be ready in time?" Ian asked Gary as if he had anything to do with it.

Gary shook his head. "I don't see how, buddy."

"What do you think we should do?" Ian continued.

Irritation rose in her. Thanks to Mr. Benedetto she had not only learned how to feel anger, but how to express it. And she was about to. Instead she posed, "We don't want to be late."

Hannah, the only one who was listening to her, looked at her watch. "Mom's right," she said to Ian, who did not respond. "Ian," she said louder.

He turned in her direction. "I'm sorry, babe. What

did you say?"

"We have to leave," she said.

Piper chimed in, as if taking the cue. "Gary, come on let's go. Tina, do you have to use the potty?" She crouched in front of her child.

"No poo-poo," the girl said.

"How about pee-pee?"

"No."

Bodily functions established, they filed toward the door. While Sarah grabbed her jacket from the hall closet, she felt a presence beside her. She didn't have to look to see that it was Gary. She could smell his over-zealous application of top-shelf cologne from a mile away.

"I'm putting my foot down this time," he whispered hotly. "We're moving the wedding to my club."

Sarah slipped her arms into her jacket sleeves. Typically, Gary neglected to offer a chivalrous hand. She grabbed her purse, closed the closet door, and stepped around him.

"We're not discussing this now."

This was supposed to be a joyous event. She would not allow his opinion to blemish the moment and she certainly wasn't about to fuel it with a response. But inside she was Mount Vesuvius and this ex-husband of hers was looking like a resident of Pompeii.

From the open front door Piper said, "Gary, Tina wants you to carry her to the car."

"Daddy," the child called, confirming the statement. She reached her little arms out to him.

He acquiesced, leaving Sarah alone in the entryway, the last to leave.

****

Melrose Caterers was dressed for company with linen tablecloths adorning round high-topped tables, the long white fabric flowing long and elegant. Candles twinkled in cut glass holders. Long buffet tables arched in a crescent in the center of the room. Attendants, dressed in white and black, served offerings from expertly shined silver chafing dishes.

Champagne flowed freely, no glass left empty for long. Tina, the only child in attendance, was given a special Shirley Temple cocktail with *three* cherries, at her pouty insistence.

"Unbelievable," Ian said. His mouth closed over a morsel of crab-stuffed mushroom cap. "Wonderful," he punctuated after he swallowed.

"I've had four of the baby lamb chops. Melt in your mouth." Gary sipped his champagne, pulling the whole strawberry into his mouth. "You're driving tonight, babe." He winked at Piper.

So, Ian and Gary both call their women "babe." For some reason the endearment didn't sit well with Sarah. It sounded sexist to her somehow, but what did she know? She'd allowed Gary to call her "Sarah Doodle" for more than two decades.

Tina discovered the dessert table and wandered over to the trays of chocolate-dipped butter cookies. She managed to get herself covered in the sticky coating, the goo dotted in her hair. All this, Sarah noticed, transpired during one of Gary's turns to be watching his little darling.

"You know what, Gary? I'd like to get something to eat, too. When I get back from cleaning her up, you're in charge of Tina. But *actually* keep an eye on her this time."

"Sure, babe."

Piper carried a squawking Tina into the ladies' room to do some repair work.

Hannah and Ian had gone off to sample the filet at the carving station. Sarah was sure if she was left alone at the table with Gary he'd find a way to bring up the goings-on in the sunroom. She went to the one place he couldn't go—the ladies' room, to join his *babe*.

Piper had placed Tina on a bed of paper towels on the sink top and held her steady with one hand while she swabbed the child with a wad of wet paper in her other hand. "Hold still, honeybunch." The squirming girl's only interest was to wrench around and play with the automatic faucet. The girl's shirt sleeve was saturated.

"Can I help?" Sarah offered before she even had a chance to think about it. She reached over and held onto Tina so Piper had two hands free to clean off the chocolate.

"I should have been born an octopus," she said smiling warily. "This little girl can get into everything."

"It's the age," Sarah agreed.

"I don't know how it was when Hannah was growing up, but these days this parenting deal is supposed to be fifty-fifty. Gary didn't get the memo."

Sarah didn't know how to respond. Gary had not been hands-on while Hannah was a toddler. It wasn't until she was fully independent that he'd gotten into the groove of parenthood.

By the time Hannah had hit junior high Gary had turned into an over-involved, pushy father steering the girl in his chosen directions. Sarah eyed Tina and wondered what Gary would be like when *she* was in junior high. After all, by then he'd be in his sixties. *Oh man.*

Piper placed Tina on the floor, having satisfactorily cleaned of her chocolaty mess. She washed her own hands. "Don't touch anything," she ordered. She looked into the mirror, caught Sarah's gaze, and produced a hesitant smile.

"I'm sure you know that Gary won't relent about holding the reception at the club." Her tone rang of warning. "He's convinced it'll be best."

Sarah folded her arms across her chest. "Not going to happen."

Piper tilted her head as she met her gaze. "He's pretty stubborn, as I'm sure you recall."

"The wedding's not moving to his club." Sarah was careful to keep her voice firm, but not impolite.

Piper's mouth had turned into an appreciative smile. "You're not like what Gary says you are."

Sarah stiffened at the words. She didn't want to hear whatever description Gary had given his new wife about what she was or wasn't like. She turned to the mirror, pretending to fuss with her bangs, giving them a flip.

"I'm sorry." Piper touched her arm. "That came out wrong. What I meant was that Gary doesn't give you enough credit. He's sure you'll eventually give in to what he wants." She smiled slyly. "He's wrong, isn't he?"

Sarah returned the smile.

Piper lifted her daughter into her arms. "Let's go find Daddy. He's going to get you some fruit."

"No fruit. Cookies!"

As they left the ladies room, Sarah had a renewed appreciation for Piper. Maybe Gary hadn't married a marionette after all. Seeing the two of them together over the last four years had looked just like that, Piper at his side, silent, letting him do all their talking offering up nothing but a nod of agreement from time to time.

When little Tina had arrived, Piper had always busied herself with changing, burping, and quieting her when she fussed. After four years, apparently Piper had had enough of Gary's sovereignty.

Sarah glanced over at Piper striding across the floor with purposeful steps, Tina bouncing at her diminutive hip. She handed off the child to Gary, leaned close, and whispered something with a stern mouth. To Sarah's errant pleasure, Gary's mouth fell open exposing a mouthful of panko-encrusted shrimp.

Maybe Gary has a chance to become a better husband and father this time around, Sarah couldn't help but think. He'd learned to respect Piper more than he'd ever respected her, but that wasn't of consequence to Sarah now. What mattered was that she would not acquiesce to his desire to overtake Hannah and Ian's wedding. And, for the first time she was totally confident that she meant it.

On the ride back to The Cornelia Ian, having had more champagne than he should have in order to drive, sat in the back seat of Hannah's car. Sarah in the front passenger seat stared out into the dark night and wondered about the two of them.

During the tasting she'd seen how Ian condescended to the wait staff and over-talked the caterer when she tried to explain her viewpoint on aspects of their affair. She'd watched Hannah's face at Ian's behavior. Sarah had found her unreadable, without affect, good or bad. That bothered her.

"The food's going to be fabulous," Sarah offered into the stillness of the car.

"I know," Hannah said softly, eyes on the road ahead of her. "I think we did a good job making our selections."

Ian remained quiet in the back seat. Sarah craned her neck a quarter turn, saw that his head was back against the headrest, eyes closed. She faced forward. "I think Ian's asleep," she whispered.

Hannah peered back. "Yup."

"He seemed to be pleased with the caterer."

"Absolutely," Hannah made a little clicking sound with her tongue. "If he wasn't, trust me, we'd know."

They drove the rest of the way in silence, but the wheels were turning in Sarah's head. Her mind flashed to the way Hannah had thrilled over the finds from the basement, memories of her high school and college days. She remembered her daughter cradling the opal necklace in her hand like a fine treasure, more valuable than any price tag would have said it was.

She went upstairs, leaving Hannah and Ian to take residence for the night in one of the guest suites. They would catch the train into the City tomorrow morning.

She slipped into pajamas and slippers and went into the kitchen to make a pot of chamomile.

Hannah appeared in the doorway. "He's out for the night." She came into the room and took a seat at the small marble table Sarah used as a center island. She had changed into PJ's, a cute tap pant set, very unlike the baggy, old cotton tees she often wore.

"What kind?" Hannah asked motioning her head in the direction of the teapot.

"Chamomile."

"Oh, good." She got up and grabbed herself a mug from the cabinet. "It'll help me conk out. I want to sleep like a rock, no dreams, nothing."

Sarah prepared the tea convinced that there was a message in her daughter's comment. *Maybe though,* she thought, *I'm just looking for a message where there is none. Maybe Hannah's just exhausted.*

The phone rang and Sarah looked over at the wall clock. Ten-thirty. "Hello?"

"Sarah, it's Benny."

She bit her lip. "Hi."

"Is it too late to call?"

"Uh, no, is something wrong?"

"I need to talk with you. Can I come over?"

"Now?" She looked down at her nightclothes.

"It's important."

Her heart stuttered. Considering he'd come into her life simply to damage it, she couldn't fathom why her instinct said yes. "I'll meet you by the front door. Don't ring the bell, though. My almost-son-in-law is asleep downstairs."

After she hung up the phone she flew to her bedroom calling over her shoulder to Hannah. "I have to get dressed."

"Who was that? Is something wrong?"

"No," she tried to keep her voice casual. "Uh, Benny's stopping by."

"It's kind of late isn't it?" There was suspicion in her daughter's tone, and Sarah hated it.

Now that the truth had been revealed about the

permit issue, would Hannah start second-guessing her? This was Benny's fault, too. Why the hell had she said yes?

Sarah peeked her head out from the doorway of her room. "I have no idea what he wants to talk to me about. But, it's not *that* late."

She went back in to her closet, pulled out her warm-up suit, and yanked off her pajamas. She tugged on the suit, then trotted into her bathroom, switching on the light above the mirror. She looked ghastly.

She'd already washed off the little bit of makeup she'd been wearing. Her face was white like an undercooked pancake. The smattering of freckles resembled cinnamon sprinkled in an unappetizing way. She dabbed on a slick of lip gloss and ran a comb through her hair.

In the mirror she saw Hannah come into the room and lean against the bathroom's door-jam. Her arms were folded, her eyes assessing. "He seems nice." Her words dangled like a worm from a hook.

Sarah put her brush down and turned to face her daughter. "Okay, stop right there, my dear. First you're trying to match me up with poor Norman the mailman, and now you're *fishing* around about Benny. Go drink your chamomile."

"Let me just make this little observation, Mother." The girl eyed her strategically, leaning closer. "I saw the way you two looked at each other. He watches you, and you watch him. Mom, I know for whatever reason, you're dead set against dating anybody, but you have to admit you've noticed him. And," she flashed a winning smile, "that, to me, is a good sign."

Sarah snapped off the light and stepped around her

167

daughter.

"No comment?"

"It doesn't deserve one. He's just an acquaintance. Nobody."

"Okay," Hannah let the word drag off her tongue. "You put on lipstick for him. Just another observation." She tilted her teacup to her lips. "I'm going to bed. Talk to you in the morning, Mom."

After Hannah had retreated downstairs to the room she would share with Ian for the night, Sarah slipped on her sneakers and padded down to the foyer to wait for Benny. She did her best to ignore the remnants of Hannah's words.

She peered out the side panes of the front door. The beveling distorted the view into a wavy blur, turning the scene outside into a Monet. In a couple of minutes Benny's shadowy figure approached. As she watched him walk up the sidewalk her heart quickened with each step.

Even in the distortion of the glass she could tell that his shirt fit him well and, again, the man was in faded jeans. Her heart shimmied as he ascended the porch stairs.

Hannah's words filtered back into the front of her mind and she pushed them away.

As she opened the door she heard a familiar crumpling sound and felt the door tug against what she knew had to be wedged beneath the door. Another note.

She bent to pull it into her hands hearing it tear in the release. When she stood again her eyes found Benny's dark gaze. She displayed the wrinkled envelope. "Another one."

"To match mine." He produced a note of his own.

Chapter Fourteen

Sarah whispered a barely audible, but clearly stern "Be quiet." She motioned Benny inside.

He followed her up the staircase to her apartment, finding it ridiculous that he suddenly felt like a school kid sneaking into his girlfriend's house while her parents slept. Maybe it had something to do with his eyes seeking to focus on the sight of her backside as she maneuvered the stairs.

The gray sweats fit snugly, revealing the appealing contour of her body. Thankfully, she'd climbed fast, like his heartbeats.

The wallpapered living room walls and the cozy furniture positioned around the wooden trunk substituting for a table made a nice, homey space. It felt lived in, real, honest.

He followed her into the smallish kitchen with a single large window on one wall. She had hung a stained glass light-catcher in front of the pane; a floral pattern that he guessed looked pretty nice in sunlight.

"How about some chamomile?" she asked, pouring a bit more into the mug she already had.

Why not? "Sure, thanks." He looked at her fully. Her sweat suit's zipper was down enough in front to reveal a hint of the contour of her breasts. *Oh man, stop.* He looked away.

The wrought iron stool set at the little marble

island squeaked when he lowered his weight onto it and he wondered if it was meant to hold a man. She sat opposite him.

He cast his eyes around the entirely feminine kitchen. The yellow and white checked wallpaper, broad white-painted molding, and pots of ivy on the sill all created a welcoming effect.

And yet, he felt like an intruder. He closed his eyes against everything and took a breath. "Here's the note I found tonight on my front stoop when I got back from my jog." He put the note on the marble table, smoothed out the page, and angled it in her direction.

Her gaze fell to the text and she recited it aloud. "Please don't involve yourself in what's not your business."

"A *polite* little coward, huh?" Benny commented, refolding the note.

Sarah opened her own note, her long, tapered fingers slightly trembling in the task. She unfolded the page, the same paper on which his had been written. She read silently, her intent eyes scanning from left to right as she absorbed the message. She looked up with questioning eyes and handed him the paper.

"Friday night. I'll explain," he recited.

"Now what?" she asked.

"I think we should contact the police." Benny said. "At least that way they can keep an eye on the place in case this guy's nuts enough to come here."

"I don't like this," she said.

"Me neither. Not one bit."

****

The next morning, Sarah was still shaky. The idea of Benny getting a note, too, was disturbing.

She wondered if her trembling fingers, as she buttoned her shirt now, might have something to do with Benny himself. She shook the thought and filled her lungs with a deep, cleansing breath.

It was no use pondering what-ifs. Maybe in another place and another time she'd have given the idea of Benny a realistic thought, but for now she had a job to do.

She finished dressing, grabbed a hard-cooked egg from the bowl in the refrigerator, and headed downstairs. Hannah and Ian had already left for the City and she was just as glad not to have to make small talk.

Locking the door behind her, she double-checked it before heading back to town hall to talk with the police.

She and Benny had agreed to meet at ten. He was right on time, and for a change he was not in blue jeans. His black training suit, with the white piping running down the side of the legs and the arms of the jacket, fit him well. She felt dismayed in the truth that it wasn't simply his jeans she'd noticed. Apparently, it was the man.

"How'd you sleep?" he asked.

Her face flushed, making her feel stupid, pathetic really. His question had nothing to do with her dreaming of him—a sultry, shadowy memory she hadn't allowed herself to rehash. Until now.

She reached up and squeezed the bridge of her nose as though the pinch could magically erase the images floating in her head like a swipe over chalk on a blackboard.

"Sarah?" He stepped close. His cologne wafted to her nose. That wooing scent snaked around, and choked her resolve to not look him the eye.

"You okay?"

Sarah cleared her throat. "Yes, yes, fine." She shook her head and gave her bangs that whack she'd come to use as a poke to her sensibility. "Just anxious to speak to someone about this." She held up her latest note.

They were seated again in front of Officer Carr. He studied the two new notes, Benny's and hers, looking from one to the other. "Any ideas yet on who's behind this?"

"No," they said in unison and shared a look. Benny gave her a little grin and her stomach cha-cha-ed.

Okay, I might have a psycho on my hands, yet I'm sitting here thinking about how appealing it is that his eye tooth crowds over the one next to it. She flipped her bangs. Twice.

The officer fingered the photocopies he'd previously made. "Somebody's seriously not happy about this wedding taking place and your inn's preparation for it. We're still waiting on the forensics. But, even my naked eye can see the handwriting is identical to the others."

He looked at Sarah. "Unfortunately, there's nothing I can do besides send a patrol car to keep an eye on your inn. Not park there, mind you, but he'll be in the vicinity at intervals."

He waited for a reaction but Sarah had none. It was as if she was in a dream or in a TV show episode, the kind that usually ended with a corpse, a shootout, or some other lousy outcome.

"We don't have the manpower to station somebody for hours at a time. But, we'll be a presence." He smiled. "How far away is the wedding again?"

"Now? Four weeks," she said. She shot Benny a look. "Permits allowing." A sinking glob of reality zoomed to her belly.

"You haven't received your permit yet, Mrs. Grayson?"

She glanced over for Benny's reaction. His head remained facing forward and she saw his Adam's apple bob up, then down.

"Not yet. I'm a bit panicked, as I'm sure you can understand. The carpenters are anxious to do their work but it's on hold for now until I have a permit in my hand."

Officer Carr nodded. After making photocopies of each of the notes, he added them to his file and handed the originals back to them. "We'll be in touch as soon as we get the handwriting analysis back. But, I would ask that you both contact us if you receive additional notes or if anything else occurs. Meanwhile, we'll continue to surveil Tidewater Way."

"Is somebody keeping an eye on Clyde Stone?" Benny asked.

The officer's eyebrow quirked. "He's not suspected of anything."

"Yet."

****

Outside the building, hands shoved in his jacket pockets, Benny stared at the ground. The sad fact was that he couldn't look at Sarah.

He knew the bothersome notes had nothing at all to do with him. But the truth was that he and his idiot brother had caused her additional anguish—grief he had come to decide was unnecessary and unfair.

Who were he and Sal to impose their beliefs on the

town? Whether Ronan's Harbor had party-happy inns riddled all over the landscape was none of their business. He should have stayed out of it. He kicked a pebble, sent it clacking over a storm drain. He should have done lots of things.

A ringing sound jarred his thoughts and he finally looked up at Sarah. She reached into her purse, withdrew her phone, flipped it open, and said "Hello" into the device.

She was silent for a long moment. Benny watched her eyes dart back and forth, not focusing on anything. She pulled her lips in on themselves then let them spring free. The sight dually stirred him—concern comingled with a spark of arousal. He blew out a breath to push it away.

"I'll be right there," she said. "Do you hear me? Stay put. I'm coming now." She closed the phone and looked up at him. Her amber-toned eyes were painted with worry.

"What's wrong?"

"It's Gigi," she said to him. Her hand clutched at her chest. "I have to go get her in Margate." She fisted the fabric of her jacket into a bunch. "I need to go home and get my car."

Her eyes were big and round. For the first time he noticed the amber irises were peppered with golden flecks to match those damned freckles on her nose.

"She's scaring me," Sarah added, almost to herself. Her words trembled. "Really scaring me."

Without thinking Benny grabbed her elbow, startling her. He could feel her arm stiffen. "Come on, my house is closer. I'll drive you."

****

Sarah didn't have the time to ponder why she was in the passenger seat of Benny Benedetto's black Jeep. All she really could do was watch the little screen of his navigation system. She silently willed the little arrow to move faster as it travelled along the straight blue line that represented the Garden State Parkway.

"So Sarah, do you know what this is about?"

"Not for certain," she said softly. "But I have an idea."

This reeks of Mickey Nolan. Gigi hadn't even sounded like herself. She thought back to the first sounds she'd heard when she'd picked up the call. For a split second she'd worried that the gravelly rasp had been a crank call, something linked to the notes.

Her head ached. *What the hell was going on?* Suddenly, it seemed like nothing was as it had been and everything that was supposed to happen, wasn't. Were they really on their way to the southern Jersey town of Margate or was it true, after all, that the world was flat and they were actually racing to its edge?

Benny gripped the steering wheel at ten and two. His mouth was set, his jawbone distinct, eyes intent on the road. Her mouth went dry.

His appearance struck her as that of a movie criminal or gangster with his dark broodiness. His broad frame filled the car seat. Sensing her gaze, like the bloodhound she knew he was, he turned to her.

"Okay?" he asked. A softness had come to his eyes, powerfully evident in the brevity of their shared glance. Something genuine beamed in them and that, she knew, was the reason she sat beside him now as they went to retrieve her best friend.

This man was the biggest pain in the ass she'd ever

known but, damn it, she trusted him. She closed her eyes. Gigi wasn't the only one that needed help. Apparently, wrong-guy syndrome was contagious.

They took exit thirty-six off the freeway following the signs to the Margate Bridge. Sarah offered to pay the toll but Benny shook his head and pointed to the EZ Pass gadget affixed to his windshield. His navigation system directed them down Ventnor Avenue where they turned onto the road toward the bay.

"What did we ever do without these direction gadgets, huh?"

"Compasses." His voice was low, a near whisper.

"Never could figure out how they worked," she said, then clarified. "I was a scout troop drop out."

He ignored her nervous attempt at levity. "They're easy enough." His eyes continued to watch the road ahead of him as he spoke. "You hold a compass up to your chest so that the needle points to magnetic north. They call that *true north.*"

His knowledge of the antiquated device turned her on. He could recite the phone book and her ridiculous senses would hear a sonnet. She kept her mouth shut as he continued.

"You have to align the needle and the little arrow, it's usually red. Then you twist the base until it points in the direction you want to move toward."

"If I relied on a compass to find my way here we'd be in Wyoming before we found Margate."

"It sounds more difficult than it is."

"Were you a Boy Scout?"

"No." He chuckled. "Do I seem like a scout to you?"

A Rottweiler. A cowboy maybe. But, no. This was

no Boy Scout.

"Uh, not really. I guess it's your compass knowledge."

"My father showed me how. I inherited his antique compass."

Up ahead, on the left, the sign for the Osprey Inn came into view. "There it is!" She pointed her finger and Benny switched on his blinker.

****

Benny pulled his truck into a head-on parking space in front of the motel. The stucco façade had seen better days, but at least the place wasn't a dive. It had clean, newish blue and white striped awnings and freshly painted doors and trim.

He turned to Sarah. "Need me to go with you?"

Sarah shook her head. "I'd better go alone."

"I'll be right here if you need, um, anything." The word "me" wouldn't form on his lips, the taste too foreign.

Her mouth curved into a small smile as she closed the door, turned, and walked hurriedly toward the hallway.

Benny switched on the radio and reclined his seat. He hoped some soft music would distract his thoughts, or at least relax the ongoing tightness in his chest that was the new norm since the moment Sarah Grayson entered his life.

He rooted around the glove box for something to munch on but found nothing, admonishing himself for not replacing the bag of pretzels he always kept on hand. He looked at the clock on the dash. It was well beyond lunch hour. His belly was empty.

He sat upright and punched a button on the

navigation screen deciding there had to be plenty of available eateries nearby, even in the off-season. He thought of Sarah's comment about the value of such a device and his lengthy reply about the use of a compass. *Where had that come from?*

He looked at the clock again. She'd been gone a while. He made the mental note to give Sarah ten more minutes and then he was going to find her. Why hadn't he gotten her cell phone number? That was a no-brainer for someone who'd been a cop for half his life. But, Sarah Grayson did a good job at scrambling his brain. Besides he was too hungry, and on the verge of ornery, to think clearly. Ten minutes tops, and that's all he'd give her.

****

Sarah sat on one bed, Gigi on the other. For the last half hour her main function had been to feed Gigi a continuous stream of tissues. Gigi was on a roll, going from sobbing, broken, jilted lover to rabid drama queen. Sarah knew better than to interject anything until the woman ran out of steam. So, she waited and doled tissues from the box she held on her lap.

"You know what I'm going to do?" Gigi asked, tossing yet another tissue onto the floor. "I'm going to hop on a plane to Vegas. Yup, I am. Non-friggin-stop."

Sarah knew Gigi would do no such thing, but she didn't comment. She pulled another tissue from the box and waited until Gigi reached out a hand to beckon for one.

"I think it's time I met this sometimes-wife of his, don't you?" She sniffed. "I mean, after all, it's been *years.*"

She started to cry again, her mouth pulled down

forming a "u" of lips on her face. A squeaky sob escaped her. "Years," she repeated, quieter this time, her tone absent of the rage it had held a moment ago.

"How many years has Mickey Dolan been telling me his marriage is over? Huh?" She turned to Sarah and punched the mattress with both hands as though imploring her for an answer.

She remained silent knowing Gigi would spew it. "Seven goddam years, that's how many. I believed him every freaking time. Can you believe that? I'm sitting here alone, packed and ready. And, he's taken the wife to Vegas to 'give it another shot.'"

Her laugh was more like a growl. "I'm pathetic. I gave that bastard the best years of my life."

That was enough. Sarah got up and joined Gigi where she sat, carrying the box of tissues with her. They sat side by side on the faded boldly floral bedspread. "Number one, the best years of your life start today, pal, okay?"

"Yeah right," she said and snorted. "If this is the beginning of the best then I'm screwed."

"Gigi, knock it off." Sarah's voice came out more harshly than she'd intended. Her atypical unsympathetic sound surprised both of them, and for a moment they just stared at each other.

Sarah knew that if she recoiled at this point she'd lose Gigi to the sea of self-pity again. She sat up straighter, cleared her throat and kept her face stern. "From this moment on, any time you give to thinking or talking about Mickey Nolan, even if it's in plotting on how to get him back for hurting you, is a delay in the start of the best years of your life. You got that? He's had seven years. So, how many more days, hours, or even minutes does he get? It's your choice."

"You're supposed to be smoothing my hair and offering to go to the vending machine for chocolate." Gigi sniffed.

"Not this time," Sarah was emphatic. It felt good, even though she was really just winging it.

Gigi pulled her own tissue from the box and swabbed it over her swollen, red, wet face. "What time is it?" she asked from behind the tissue shrouding her eyes like a veil.

Sarah looked at her watch. "Two-ten."

"Tell me when it's two-eleven."

Gigi lowered the tissue from her face and met Sarah's gaze. She was still a mess of smeared makeup but Sarah finally saw evidence of her best friend's features there amidst the Picasso painting of her face.

"Why?" Sarah asked, feeling a trickle of relief.

Gigi wiped her nose with an exaggerated swipe of the tissue. "I want to remember exactly when the best years of my life started."

Sarah checked again. "Right now."

Chapter Fifteen

While Gigi used the bathroom to tidy her appearance, Sarah rejoined Benny outside. Thoughtfully, by using his GPS, he'd found a diner that was open for business. She was starved.

She briefly filled Benny in on Gigi's situation. While the words tumbled from her mouth, she finally allowed her frustration to surface. "He's a poisonous snake," she spat. "And, I swear, if she goes near that louse again I'll chop her legs off."

Benny laughed heartily. It was the first time she'd heard the sound come from him. She found it pleasant—a deep resonant tone that put a light in his eyes and transformed his expression into one of affable appeal. The moment zapped her breath, rendering her speechless.

"Well, that'll save her from having to buy shoes," he said. His ridiculous response to her equally absurd comment released her tension. She couldn't help but chuckle.

In the briefest of moments, the levity vanished as they sat in the closed space within Benny's Jeep. But Sarah did not miss the message in his eyes, the momentary knowing that something new had transpired between them. It was an acknowledgement of a connection that she absolutely could not, and did not, want. But there was no denying its existence. Not anymore.

Thankfully, Gigi emerged from the motel. She had done a good job of putting herself back together. Her hair was in order and lipstick in place.

"Thanks for bringing Sarah to my rescue," Gigi said into the open window of the vehicle. Her breath smelled of minty toothpaste.

"Want some lunch?" Benny asked.

"I could eat," she said. "Want me to follow you?"

"Come with us," Benny said. "I'll bring you back here after the diner."

Gigi nodded at the suggestion. She went to her car and popped the trunk. As she did, Sarah turned to Benny. "Thanks, I don't want her driving right now."

"I figured that."

"I'll go back home with her in her car later. Keep her company," Sarah said.

"Good idea," Benny said.

"Thanks for, you know, doing this." Sarah was feeling shy now that an invisible truth had been released. It was as if a third occupant had already squeezed into the vehicle, crowding them. She focused her gaze ahead through the windshield. She didn't trust herself to look at him right now.

"Hey, it was evident I needed to do something. Plus I've learned that if I get you any more pissed at me, you might chop my legs off. Handy to know."

****

They ordered eggs and hot coffee, and Sarah was pleased to see that Gigi dug right into her meal.

The waitress came by and refilled their mugs, leaving the check on the table. Sarah reached for it at the same time as Benny did. Their fingers touched, radiating a taser-like warning to her senses. She pulled her hand back.

"Please, let me do this," Sarah said, reaching into her purse for her wallet. "It's the least I can do."

"Not necessary." He stood from his chair, marched over to the front counter, and paid the check.

After he stepped away, Gigi leaned forward in her chair and crooked her finger. Reluctantly Sarah hunched forward.

"I didn't want to ask in front of him, how is it exactly that you two decided to be pals?"

"We're not pals," Sarah whispered. She checked to make sure he was still at the front counter. "He was there when you called. I was a nervous wreck and he volunteered to drive. End of story."

Gigi poked her spoon at Sarah like a conductor's baton. "Not buying it. There's a story all right. And this ain't the end."

"Ready, ladies?" Benny asked when he returned tableside.

Sarah shot Gigi a look as she slid from her chair.

The drive back to the Osprey Inn was thankfully a quick one. Sarah felt claustrophobic. The walls of the Jeep seemed to close in, squashing her in her seat, forcing her to notice the man next to her. The sight of his thigh pressed against the leather was unavoidable. The movement of his chest as he breathed was a metronome to which her own heart beat.

Gigi thanked Benny again and tried to convince Sarah she was fine to drive back to Ronan's Harbor alone.

"I'm coming with you."

"Fine, mother." Gigi sounded much like her old

self. "Thanks, Benny."

If it weren't for the weariness on her face an outsider would never guess the woman had just had her heart ripped from her chest. Gigi went to her car.

Sarah touched her hand to the door handle while hesitantly allowing herself to look at Benny. She hated the effect he had on her now. Since seeing the friendly face he'd donned earlier, that was all she could see now. It was as though she wore trick eyeglasses, ones that turned an enemy into a friend. This was bad.

"Thanks again," she said, doing her best to sound aloof.

"No problem," he replied, equally unemotional.

She bolted from the vehicle, swinging the door closed behind her without looking back.

****

On the ride home to Ronan's Harbor, an old song on the car radio set Gigi off again. Sarah watched her friend reach up to swat at a tear.

Sarah hit a button on the radio to change the station. "Want me to drive for a while?" She tried to keep the question casual.

"Sarah, I'm *not* a basket case."

"I know, but…"

"I'm fine." Gigi offered a feeble grin. "See?"

"Want to spend the night at my place?"

"Thanks honey," Gigi said. "I really do appreciate it. Don't get me wrong, but I'll be okay. I promise."

"If…"

"If I find myself *not* all right, I'll call you or come right over." Gigi turned to her. "Deal?"

"Deal."

"Okay, let's change the subject. Let's talk about

your new pal."

Sarah groaned. "I explained this to you already. Nothing's changed. Benny and I are not 'pals.'"

"That's not what I see."

"You're seeing *and* talking nonsense."

"I'm through with nonsense, Sarah. I'm reformed. Remember? Since two-eleven."

Sarah smiled. "Yes, I remember."

"I think it's your turn to check your own time clock, my dear." Gigi gave her a quick challenging glance before turning back to face the highway.

Sarah didn't respond. Her betraying, trick eyeballs found the side mirror with the reflection of the black Jeep following behind them. She could see Benny's face behind the wheel.

When they reached Ronan's Harbor, Benny's truck was gone from view. Sarah bid good-bye to Gigi, making her promise again that if she needed, she'd call.

Sarah entered The Cornelia and headed up the staircase. She wasn't up three steps when she heard a knock. She turned toward the door thinking it sure hadn't taken Gigi long to figure out she needed company after all.

Sarah opened the door to find a tall man in a dark suit staring at her.

"Can I help you?" She closed the door a few inches as though a sudden wind had caused her do so.

"Sarah Grayson?"

"Yes."

"Hello," the man said and extended a hand. "If you have a minute I'd like to speak with you. My name is Clyde Stone."

Clyde Stone! Her mind reeled with indecision. In

all likelihood this was the creep who'd written those notes. What was his agenda? Should she let him in? Go out onto the porch with him? Slam the door?

She remembered that one of the cops told Benny that Clyde Stone was a black belt in karate, adept enough to send one of his muggers to the hospital. She swallowed hard. What if he was really a psycho?

She'd taken a women's self-defense class at the recreation center with some of her garden club members. She tried to remember what she was supposed to do if someone grabbed her. All she could think of was "the collapse move" that would turn her into a ragdoll—enough of a dead weight to hopefully topple the attacker and put the victim in a position to kick the attacker in the groin.

She eyed Clyde Stone. Tall and lanky, narrow shouldered, black-rimmed glasses. Not too scary-looking, but still.

"I won't take too much of your time," he said. "I'd like to discuss purchasing your inn."

Anger shot through her, dispelling the thoughts of self defense. Her Cornelia Inn needed defending and she was all it had.

She jutted the front door open with a forceful arm and stood tall in the doorway. "You're wasting your time. It's not for sale."

Clyde Stone stepped forward suddenly and grabbed her by the shoulders with both hands. Adrenaline coursed through her system, charging to her brain. Instantly she envisioned the demonstrator at the women's defense class and saw herself practicing the moves with her partner. She let herself fall limp, collapsing backwards onto the hand-hooked rug in the foyer. Clyde Stone toppled into the room with her.

"Oh my God," he said, pulling himself up onto his knees.

Eyes closed and lying prone, just one thing chanted in her head. *Kick him, kick him…*

"Shit, lady," he said leaning forward enough so that she could feel his breath on her face. "Did you pass out or something? Crap, you have epilepsy or narcolepsy or one of those things?" He poked her arm with one spastic finger. "Wake up, lady."

He didn't sound menacing, that was for sure. He sounded scared. Was it a trick? Did he like his victims alert? It was now or never, she shot her eyes open and kicked at him aiming for his balls. Instead, her loafer flew from her foot and hit him in the head.

"Ow, what the hell?" he shouted, putting a hand to his head. "What are you, nuts?"

"Leave now," she boomed. "How dare you touch me? I could charge you with assault."

"Assault?" He barked the word. "I tripped over that stupid mat out there. I could sue you for damages."

She sat up straighter. He didn't move, but continued to stare at her, with one hand still at his forehead. "I'll count to three, then I'm yelling like a banshee."

"Hold on. Let me help you up," he said, reaching for her hand.

"One…"

"Listen, Mrs. Grayson, I think you might want to hear what I know about your inn."

"Two…"

"It's going to be condemned."

Chapter Sixteen

Sarah stood in her foyer staring at Clyde Stone, who also had risen from the floor. He pressed one hand to his head and in the other he held her shoe.

"What are you talking about?" she demanded.

"I believe this belongs to you." He jutted the brown leather loafer in her direction.

He removed the hand from his head where a reddening welt had begun to show. Sarah swallowed the instinctive guilt that pinched at her but she couldn't help feeling the need to justify her rash move.

"You can't show up at my door and suddenly come at me like that."

"Come at you? I fell. And then you assaulted me."

"You're lucky I didn't shoot you."

"You have a gun?"

His voice was so filled with terror that she couldn't help but snort in his face. "I might," she bluffed. "But, you better start explaining about using the word *condemned*."

"Have you seen the condition of your foundation?"

"What about it?"

"It's decayed, crumbling out from under your inn. I'm surprised the town hasn't shut you down before now."

Harvey and Richie hadn't mentioned anything about the foundation when they'd first come to give her an estimate. But that wasn't the only thing they didn't know to mention.

She swallowed hard realizing that though Harvey and Richie had performed plenty of small jobs for some of her friends, that didn't qualify them to tackle her inn. At the time it seemed like the right choice.

Harvey's mother had been a member of the garden club and she'd taught Sarah everything she knew about tulips. Her son had lost his service station, and needed work.

Clyde Stone interrupted her thoughts. "Look, I happen to know that most homeowners' insurance coverage excludes some 'perils,' as they call them. Crumbling old foundations are one such peril. I also can tell you that fixing that foundation is going to involve extensive work. And lots of money and time. Lots."

"You've done your homework on my inn, haven't you?"

"Watch," he said and withdrew a marble from his pocket. He bent low and rolled it across the wooden floor. The little glass globe scooted to the end of the foyer, slowed, then reversed direction and rolled lazily back toward them.

"The floor's pitched. If you don't fix the foundation the whole place could fall. I'm sure you don't want to take the lives of your guests into your hands."

He paused as though waiting for his information to sink into her every pore. "I'm prepared to make you a fair cash offer for the place. More than fair, all things considered."

She opened her mouth to speak, but nothing came out. Her mind reeled with the wedding plans, and the upcoming season that provided her livelihood. What the hell was she supposed to do if this guy was right?

"Mr. Stone, I think this conversation is over."

He extended a business card toward here. "I'm in town for a few more days. If you come to realize that I'm right, which I hope you do, please contact me."

And he was gone.

Sarah stood alone in the foyer. She cast her gaze around at the furnishings, the wall art, the draperies. She went to the banister, ran her hand up over the smooth mahogany.

She looked down at the rug she'd purchased from an Amish woman in Pennsylvania, the tufts a riot of color. Her eyes filled with tears, blurring the scene. She blinked them away and her gaze riveted to the marble, still on the floor.

She pulled on a jacket and went outside. She needed to see the foundation for herself. A strong wind had brewed, whipping her hair harshly. She trod along the perimeter of the structure, running her fingers over the obvious cracks, the missing mortar in places between rocks that left gap-toothed-looking holes in the façade.

A chalky substance covered her fingers, remnants she was sure of the disintegration that had occurred without her even being aware. She closed her eyes, wiping the powder off her fingers by swiping them across the back pockets of her jeans.

She pulled the jacket tight across her body as the wind pressed at her back. She strode through the yard to the front door.

Inside, she paused. She wondered what to do now? Where to turn? Her eyes found the portrait of Cornelia

DeGraff in her splendid butter-yellow gown. *Our house is crumbling out from under us, Cornelia."*

Sarah went to the phone. She knew not to bother Gigi with this news, not after the day the girl had had. Sarah wouldn't dare call Hannah and send her kid into a tailspin.

Her mouth was dry and her throat scratched when she swallowed. She dialed Benny's cell phone number, surprising herself that she knew it by heart.

The call went to voicemail. When she heard the beep, her tongue had tied and her mind had no idea how to relay what she needed to tell him. She hit the end button and put the phone back in its cradle.

****

Arms loaded with food and a six-pack of beer, at the convenience store, Benny heard the cell phone ringing in his pocket. He waited until he was able to lay everything down on the counter at the register before he reached for the no-longer-ringing phone.

There was no message, but he saw that the call had come from Sarah. A funny pain jabbed at his insides, a kind of poke at his heart.

His mind went right back to the thoughts he'd been trying to squash all day. Sarah Grayson. Exasperating, pigheaded, and irrational Sarah Grayson.

And yet there was no denying the feelings that had brewed in him. He wanted her. He wanted to kiss that pink mouth, run his fingertips over her face, count the freckles, and kiss each one. His thoughts were pitiful, and he groaned audibly.

"Sir?"

He startled alert to find the young clerk at the register peering at him as if he were about to keel over.

"I'm sorry," he laughed and gave his head a shake. He reached for his wallet. "What do I owe you?"

"Thirty-two fifty."

He withdrew a pair of twenties and handed them to the young man who slipped them into his tray and fished out the proper change.

"Having a party?" he asked as he handed bills and change to Benny.

"What?" Benny looked into one of the bags. What else would the guy think? A family-sized bag of tortilla chips, a can of bean dip, and all the rest of the makings for his famous seven-layer Mexican dip. Let alone the beer.

"Something like that," Benny said. He pulled his purchases into his hands. "Have a good night."

He hadn't intended to buy so much. It would be a long walk back to his place with all this stuff. Thoughts of Sarah had propelled his need to arm himself for what he was sure would prove to be a long night ahead. He'd dig out a couple of cop-chase DVD's he'd packed somewhere. They, along with his refreshments, ought to do the trick. No time to think about a woman he had no right to want.

But, she'd called. Questions filtered into his thoughts as he made his way home. What had she wanted? Maybe she was in trouble. God only knew what she was capable of getting herself into.

He shook his head. *Not my problem.*

Or, what if she was feeling the same thing he was? He remembered the way her eyes clung to his, those golden flecks keeping him from looking away. Was this an opportunity? Would it be yet another wrong choice to ignore it?

He thought of the compass, his father's relic that all these years he'd detested. The thorn that pricked his ego, that had made his heart bleed with knowing that the old man had thought so little of him.

At first when he'd seen the hand-tooled wooden case the lawyer had placed in front of him on that day he and Sal sat in the man's office, he'd thought it might be a treasure of some kind. After lifting the lid, the old brass object all but laughed at him. Was his father's message true? Would he always be a loser? Destined to be lost and in need of a device to give him direction?

He readjusted his packages, bracing himself against the gusts of wind that blew into his face. He saw The Cornelia Inn up ahead, the lights already on inside. Sarah was home.

He did not need a compass tonight.

Chapter Seventeen

The doorbell sounded, jarring Sarah. *What now?* She trotted down the staircase to the front door. She knew who stood outside the moment she saw his silhouette through the beveled glass.

Her nervous system, she decided, was a mess. The news about her house, the wedding plans, Hannah's quirkiness, and then there was Benny Benedetto. How much could she take?

If she had half a brain, she'd ignore the front door and charge right back up to her apartment and go to bed early with earplugs in place.

The half of her brain she no longer possessed opened the door. The wind was strong enough now to do all the work. Benny stood hunkered down into his black jacket, laden with packages.

"I, uh, stopped on my way home from the store."

They stared at each other for a long moment. Finally, she spoke. "Come in. You want to put those down?"

He placed his bags and the six-pack on the floor. "It's really kicking up out there." He rubbed his hands together. Nice, masculine hands.

"Yes, something's brewing." She folded her arms across her chest. Again they shared a long gaze.

"I came by because I saw you had called."

"Yes, I did," she said. "Clyde Stone came by for a

visit."

"What?" Benny's eyes grew, the dark orbs beaming with intensity. "Sarah, he could be some kind of wacko. You talked to him?"

"Yes," she said, letting out a whoosh of air. "After I hit him in the head with my shoe."

"Why? What'd he do to you?"

Before she had time to process it, Benny had rushed to her and grabbed her upper arms into his firm hands. However, he had not tripped over the front mat. And she would not hit Benny with a shoe.

"It was a misunderstanding," she said softly. She was acutely aware of Benny's nearness. His face was sharp, eyes alert. "He tripped over that mat out on the porch and fell forward. I thought he was attacking me."

Benny let his hands fall. His face softened and something new shone in his onyx eyes. Amusement? A trace of a smile played over his lips. "So you threw a shoe at him?"

"Actually, no. I was aiming for his crotch." Now *she* couldn't help the grin that claimed her mouth.

"And you got his head instead. That's some kick. Shit, how long are those legs of yours?"

"Yeah, very funny. Benny, he came here with an offer to buy the place. He said it's ready to fall down and if I'm smart I'll let him buy it."

"Don't listen to him. We figured that's what he was up to when the cops found that list in his wallet. He say anything about writing those notes?"

She shook her head.

"I hope you told him to pound salt."

"I did, basically. But he's right about the foundation disintegrating. I saw with my own eyes."

"You didn't know anything about that until now? What about those guys doing the work for you? They never mentioned that?"

"Nope."

"What I want to know is how does this Stone guy know so damned much? Did he trespass onto your property and inspect your foundation? Everything about this stinks."

"I don't know. He said insurance doesn't cover decaying foundations. Apparently, he's got the funds to make the inn safe."

"You're not considering his offer?"

"No, but I'm scared, Benny. I don't have the money to do the repairs. How am I supposed to keep an inn going if it's not safe? Maybe it's time for a new reality check."

"We don't know a thing about this guy. We can't believe a word he says."

She pulled the business card out from her pocket and extended it toward him. "I don't know. He could be legit."

His eyes scanned the text. "Wait a second. It says here he's the president of the Metropolitan Karate Institute."

"Well, the police did say he was a black belt, right?"

"Yeah, they did." As though a light bulb flashed on in his head, scorching his brain, Benny pulled out his cell phone and flipped the screen a few times. He tapped a finger and flipped some more.

"What are you doing?"

"I'm checking something." His eyes were intent on the screen. She watched his finger's rapid movements as he shuffled through electronic screens.

"Damn it to hell."

"What?"

"Sarah," he looked up at her. "There's something I need to do. I'll explain when I get back. It won't be until later, though."

He reached for the door, it flew open and an icy gust whipped into the room.

"And please, don't talk to this guy again until I come back."

Sarah watched him retreat down the sidewalk. He moved too quickly and the wind was too loud for her to even attempt calling after him.

She stood in her foyer with her arms clenched across her chest and his bags of groceries at her feet.

****

Benny struggled with the wind on his race home. The force of air pushed against him, but adrenaline pumped strong and nothing would hold him back. *I knew it.* There was no way this was a coincidence.

Benny now pictured that photo hanging up on Sal's self-aggrandizing wall. The karate school where he'd earned his black belt had given Sal a new buddy…named Clyde Stone. He recalled in detail now the photo of Sal in his dress blues shaking his teacher's hand, the benefactor of some donation, both of them smiling in kinship into the lens.

Damn it, Sal was going to come clean about whatever the hell he was up to. If not Benny might need to choke it out of him.

He went inside the cottage, grabbed a bottle of water from the fridge and shoved an apple into his jacket pocket. He turned around and went right back out, locking the door behind him.

He climbed into the Jeep and headed toward the main thoroughfare. If the traffic was right, he'd make it to Sal's office around seven-thirty, right around shift change.

The Parkway was slick from a fast and furious bout of rain. Although the rain had subsided, an angry wind howled through the windows of his vehicle. It only served to fuel Benny's frustration.

He wasn't just pissed at Sal. He was pretty mad at himself for being stupid enough to get into this predicament.

Periodically a strong gust would rock his truck, especially when he ascended the crest of the Raritan River Bridge. Cars slowed and traffic clogged the roadway, reducing Benny's speed to less than thirty miles per hour. At this rate, it would take him all night to get to Glendale. It didn't matter. He wouldn't be stopped.

He crawled along, switching lanes like a squad car chasing a criminal. He snorted into the empty cab of his vehicle. "Oh, I'll bet my ass I'm chasing a crook. Hands down."

An inventory began to form in his head, a mental list of all the times he'd had to cover for Mr. Bigshot over the years. The first time Benny remembered was when they were kids and Sal had gotten caught lifting a Playboy from the drugstore. Sal had lied right to their old man's face and Benny had been coerced to confirm it.

But that had been just the beginning. There'd been times Sal cheated on girlfriends and made Benny cover for his whereabouts, convincing him to lie and say his brother was sick in bed.

He'd overlooked the way Sal's good grades proved to be the product of his paying some brainiac kid to do his reports for him. Benny shook his head as he drove.

When he had called Sal a fraud to his face, his brother had laughed at him and spewed his life-long motto. The words rang in Benny's head now. "I'm just doing what works for numero uno."

Inside the precinct a young officer sat at the front desk. He looked up expectantly when Benny approached, no recognition in his eyes.

Before the man could get a word out, Benny's question barked from his lips. "Sal Benedetto still here?"

"Your name, sir?"

"I'm his brother, Benny. He here?"

The officer gave him the once-over with his new-cop eyes while reaching for the handset of the desk phone. He mumbled into the speaker and nodded his head a few times before putting the phone down.

"Down the hall, second door on…"

"Yeah. I know." Benny stormed past him and maneuvered the corridor.

Sal stood at his desk, front and center of the backdrop of his wall of framed bullshit. Benny didn't meet his eyes, but rather scanned the frames. In the spot where he'd seen the photo from the local rag now hung a freeze-frame photo of Sal's kids screaming with glee as they plunged down the log flume ride at an amusement park.

"What's up?" Sal asked. Sal had done his best to sound nonchalant, but Benny wasn't fooled. He saw the flash of worry in his lying eyeballs. Benny knew it well.

"New addition to your wall?" Benny pointed to the shot of his nephews and niece.

Sal didn't even turn in the direction of the photo. He continued to look straight at Benny. "Yeah."

"Where's the one that used to be there?"

Sal shrugged his shoulders like it was no big deal. "It broke."

"You can stop the crap right there, Sal."

Sal sat down and sighed aloud. "Sit down Benny," he said, pointing a fat finger to his guest chair. "It's been a long day. Just come out with it."

Benny remained standing. "You first. Tell me about Clyde Stone."

"Not sure what you mean, brother."

"Okay." Rage stoked inside Benny's gut, bubbling through his system. "I'll clarify it for you. Clyde Stone is not some *nobody* that you couldn't be bothered getting one of your guys to look into. Is he?"

Sal didn't react, just continued to look tired and bored.

Benny stepped closer to the desk. "Clyde Stone is an associate of yours. As a matter of fact, his karate school is where you got your black belt, the same school that donated money to your PBA."

"And?" Sal almost yawned with boredom and Benny had all he could do not to slug him one.

"And he wants to snatch The Cornelia Inn out from under Sarah Grayson. For Christ's sake, Sal! She's a nice lady that just wants to live her life and run her goddammed inn. Until you came along and friggin' dragged me into this with you."

"My turn?" Sal asked, unfazed.

Benny's mouth clenched so tight his jaw ached.

"Yes, Clyde Stone and I are associates, Benny. And he's going to be a very rich man, very soon. He's opened up an opportunity for me—for us, if you'll just calm down and let me explain."

"Whatever it is, I'm not interested."

Sal started to laugh. "Not interested in a piece of a multi-million-dollar townhouse community in one of the sweetest little spots along the Jersey coast?"

Sal waved his hands at him. "Benny, Christ, think about this. You'll see Clyde's got it sewn up if you'll take your eyes off the broad with the piece-of-shit bed-and-breakfast. He's going to turn that whole strip into a ritzy resort town. Think The Hamptons, little brother. We can be in on the ground floor of his project. Do you have any idea what that could mean for us?"

"What the fuck, Sal? We filed complaints against Sarah's plan to expand a small part of her facility so she could throw her only kid a nice wedding, because it would 'upset the town's peace.' Isn't that how you put it, Sal? Leave little Ronan's Harbor as it? And now you're telling me it's been part of a scheme that'll demolish half the town?"

"Not demolish. *Improve.* Trust me on this, for crissakes. When are you going to stop thinking small, Benny? Clyde's got the zoning guy down there—who, by the way, owed me a favor—in on it."

He paused to plaster an effusive grin across his face. "This is a done deal if you'll just shut up and let the big boys deal with the logistics." Sal spewed a caustic chortle. "Maybe you could just go bake us a celebration cake, or something."

Forty-eight years worth of pent-up frustration raced through Benny, whirling through his veins like a tornado stirring up every memory he had of Sal's underhandedness.

A sudden calmness moved through Benny's system, enveloping him like the sight of a safe harbor on his horizon. He knew without question the refuge bore the name Ronan. And, wrapped within that visceral knowledge was the image of the woman that loved the little town. Sarah.

"I'm out."

"Benny, be serious…"

"I'll contact an attorney in the morning. Buy me out."

"I can't."

"What do you mean you *can't?*"

"Every cent I own is tied up with Clyde."

"Then it goes on the market first thing in the morning. We sell, we split it, we're done."

"No way."

"Tell you what, Captain. Either this is exactly what we do or I'll go right to your Chief and let him know about the little "favor" you're cashing in on in Ronan's Harbor—the favor that will negatively affect the lives of everyone in that town."

"By 'everyone in town' you mean that chick you're looking to nail."

"You can't rile me, Sal. Not anymore."

Sal bolted from his chair. Obviously he knew Benny wasn't kidding. His brother had never threatened to expose Sal before, no matter what the hell he'd done. Ever.

Right now all Benny wanted was to make things right. How it played out with Sal and Clyde's rotten deal didn't concern him in the least.

He turned to leave.

"Benny," Sal implored. "I'm your brother. We're blood. Why are you doing this?"

Benny faced him squarely. "I'll tell you in language you'll understand. I'm just doing what works for numero uno."

He went through the door and closed it tightly behind him. He had things to do.

Chapter Eighteen

Sarah put Benny's shopping bags on the main kitchen's counter and switched on the lights, needing somehow to avoid the dark. For truly, that's where she was in every aspect of her being—in the dark.

After slipping the perishables into the fridge, she looked around the room. The square, functional area was the very heart of her inn. Here is where Cornelia DeGraff's staff had fixed meals and prepared celebrations.

It had been where she and her seasonal helpers made breakfasts for her guests. During those times the kitchen brimmed with succulent aromas of breakfast sausages, quiche, and rich coffee. She breathed in now, the scents absent. Would those smells ever return, or was her inn doomed?

Benny's image floated through her mind. She'd come to accept this as commonplace now. She liked him.

What did it matter that he'd been the one to step in and halt her plans? Maybe he'd actually helped save the wellbeing of Hannah and Ian's wedding guests. The foundation might have crumbled right out from under the reception, risking everyone's safety.

She made her way into the hallway and went into the sunroom. She switched on a table lamp bathing the area in low, golden light. The sheeting over the furniture had an eeriness that gave her a chill. Ghosts of her dream loomed at her now, aloof and intangible.

One shrouded mound was the stack of boxes packed with wedding supplies she'd accumulated in the weeks since the planning had begun. She slowly removed the draping and dropped the dingy sheet into a pile on the wooden floor. She sat down on the bunched fabric and pulled a carton close, nestling the box in the crook of her outstretched legs.

She opened the flaps exposing square glass vases stacked on top of each other, cushioned by sheets of bubble wrap. She lifted one into her hands. She recalled the day she, Hannah, and Gigi had gone to the floral wholesaler and selected the vases. Hannah's bright-eyed approval appeared in her thoughts.

Hannah. It was time to tell her daughter about the condition of the inn. And, it was time for Sarah to admit that the likelihood of a wedding reception taking place here was about nil.

She placed the vase back in the box, refolding the flaps over it. She checked her watch. It was after ten already, too late to call. The news would only disturb her sleep.

In the morning she would contact Hannah and then, dear God, she'd call Gary—so he could work on the arrangements of moving the wedding to his club. He'd gloat, she was sure, but right now even that idea mustered no animosity.

The wind continued to howl through the old windows, whistling a sad tune. She pulled her sweater closer around her frame as she shut the light.

Then she heard it—a noise that wasn't the wind blowing against the house. It sounded more like a series of clicks followed by a rattling, like a door on a hinge.

She closed her eyes and listened again. The only sounds she heard were the thumps of her own heartbeats racing in her chest.

She left the sunroom and made her way toward the staircase, cowering low. Lamps in the entry and in the living room's window cast soft light. She was too frightened to attempt turning them off.

What if someone was out there? Her eyes darted to the parlor windows, their panes exposed by the pulled-back lace curtains. All she could see beyond the glass was nighttime's inky blackness. Could someone see her inside moving about the rooms? A cold shudder danced over her skin.

She needed her cell phone. Realizing she left it on the main kitchen's counter, she crept down the hallway. The stove's hood light was on, as was her nightly habit. It gave her enough light to spot her phone. Crouched low, like a soldier in an ambush, she edged to the island.

The outside noises sounded again. This time she heard a banging followed by a hard-hitting sound. *Holy shit! Who's out there?*

Sarah scooted her folded self close enough to grab her phone. She slid to her knees behind the wall of the island, tucking herself between it and the refrigerator. Her heart raced against the whirling thoughts in her head. Was she making a big deal out of nothing? It *was* windy tonight.

Maybe the sounds were from a shutter that had come off its hinges. Or perhaps a tree limb had fallen close to the house. Her instincts told her it was something more.

She wasn't taking any chances. Not these days. Her collection of anonymous notes told her this was a potential problem. She dialed Benny's number cringing at the loudness of each digit's tone when her finger tapped it. She waited, breathless, for him to answer. *Pick up, pick up, pick up.*

****

Benny was back in his Jeep just ten miles before his exit off the Parkway. In the morning he was going to town hall to blow the whistle on that little toad of a zoning officer. Then he hoped he could convince the mayor to lift the red tape and grant Sarah her approvals. Vindication filled his empty belly, satisfying him.

His first priority tonight was what gave his senses a zing. He needed to see Sarah, tell her what he knew, and make her a promise. Benny never made promises, but this was one he could offer with confidence. He would do everything he could to undo the shitty mess she was in due to him.

There was one more part to tonight's plan. He was going to kiss her until they both needed air.

His cell phone rang, the bold sound emanating from his dashboard Bluetooth device. He clicked the button on his steering wheel, engaging the call.

"Benny." Her voice was a raspy whisper filled with such urgency that it stabbed him in the center of his chest.

"Sarah, is everything all right?"

"No," she said. He could hear her breathing. "I think someone's outside."

"Call the police."

"If it's the guy that's been writing the notes, when he sees their lights he'll vanish again. I really need to be done with this once and for all. It has to stop. I can't live like this. But, I'm scared. Really, really scared."

"Sarah, don't be foolish. Who cares if the guy runs chicken shit when he sees a squad car pull up? Call them. I'll be right over. I'm about five minutes away."

He steered off the exit and took the local road toward Ronan's Harbor, crossing the still-wet surface of the bridge. He navigated the streets onto Ocean Avenue and down Dolphin.

When he turned onto Tidewater Way he saw flashing lights dancing in the darkness ahead, ricocheting in a series of colors across the wet roadway. He pressed the brake pedal as he approached what turned out to be two cruisers in front of a massive, fallen old tree. Its trunk and branches reached nearly the breadth of the street.

An officer in a black rain coat stood from his task of placing flares in a row. He held up a hand as the vehicle came near. Benny lowered the driver's side window when the officer came around the vehicle.

"Sir, you'll have to go down Dolphin. Tidewater's closed," the officer said.

Benny craned his neck. There were no flashing lights down the block near The Cornelia Inn and there was no sign of a cruiser hovering near there either. *Damn it to hell,* he said silently. *That stubborn woman didn't call them.*

He eyed the officer and weighed informing him of Sarah's concerns. Maybe it had turned out to be nothing after all. Or maybe she was sitting alone in her house with nothing but a goddammed garden trowel to protect her.

He took a deep breath and let it expel from his

chest. He'd better investigate it himself first. The boys in blue would be on the street for a while and he'd be able to summon them quickly enough if it turned out something was indeed up. For the moment, he'd respect Sarah's decision to keep them out of it.

"Sir?" the cop asked.

Benny snapped to the officer's attention. He gestured to the tree. "That's a big one, huh?" Benny asked. He tried to sound like an interested bystander rather than a man with a girdle of concern clenched around his torso.

"Yeah, you'll need to access Dolphin."

Normally that would have been fine news since that was the direction of his cottage. But, he needed to get to Sarah. What he wanted to do, should do, was tell the officer that Sarah suspected a possible intruder on her property. But, he knew he wouldn't.

"I need to visit a friend at Four Tidewater."

The officer shook his head. "The utility truck is on its way. It took down the phone lines. They'll have this remedied soon enough but for now, sir, I'd suggest you go home and stay dry until that happens."

Benny stared through the wet windshield. The rain had picked up again, coming down in hard pings on the hood of his vehicle. It would be a bitch to walk to her house in this mess. But he was in too deep now. "Okay if I walk it?"

"Buddy, is it that important you visit somebody tonight?"

A vision of Sarah trotting down the boardwalk wearing some fool rubber galoshes on her feet, wielding the midget shovel popped into his head. "Yeah, it is."

The officer tilted his head as though he'd heard something pretty preposterous. This, Benny decided, wasn't too far from the truth.

"Okay, you can hoof it if you want. Knock yourself out. But you'll have to move your vehicle out of the way." He motioned to where Tidewater intersected with Dolphin Road.

Benny thanked him and steered his truck to the side street. In a minute's time a cloud had apparently burst open and the rain poured down in buckets. *Damn it to hell.*

He snapped on the overhead light in his Jeep's interior and looked around for something to use as a shield. He always kept an old sweatshirt in the back. Where the hell was it now that he needed it?

He looked under the seats and into the storage area in the back. There was the black plastic garbage bag filled with old linens he was supposed to bring to the town dumpster.

He climbed over the seat, grabbed the heavy sack, and dumped the articles into a pile onto the seat. He took the empty garbage bag into his grasp and poked a hole in the bottom seam creating a makeshift poncho. He found a Mets hat among the items he'd dumped out and even though it would probably saturate before he managed to take a couple of steps it was better than nothing. He donned the poncho-bag and slammed the cap onto his head.

He ran down the wet macadam as the rain pelted him. His feet sunk into the sogginess as he jumped onto a strip of lawn to circumvent the downed limbs. His footfalls made a squishing sound. Water slapped back at his pant legs with each step.

Ahead The Cornelia was dimly lit, the front porch light casting a cone of yellow over the front doorway. He gave the grounds a quick once-over as he trotted up the walk and up the steps. Nothing appeared amiss.

However, the night was very dark and anyone could be hiding behind a shrub or in the back of the house. The first thing he needed to do was find Sarah to make sure she was all right.

He rapped on the glass panel of the door. "Sarah, it's me, Benny," he said.

No response.

He knocked again, this time with enough force to risk breaking the glass. "Sarah," he shouted now.

He peered inside but all he could make out in the wavy distortion of the door's pane was the empty foyer. He'd give it one more shot before he kicked in the damned door.

A figure emerged from the hall beyond the foyer. He squinted to make out the short rounded being as it approached tentatively. *Who the hell is that?*

It was Sarah, crouched to half her height. She crept toward the door in her balled-up state, her legs jabbing out like a bottle dancer at a Jewish wedding. *For crying out loud.*

When she recognized that it was Benny at the door she jerked upright and nearly dove to the door. She yanked it open.

"Benny!" shot from her mouth like a sob of relief.

She surprised him by throwing her arms around his shoulders and pressed herself to him without regard to his current state of Hefty-bag wetness.

They entered the inn together, their footing off-kilter, and they nearly toppled to the entryway's floor.

"What are you wearing?" she asked, standing at arm's length. A smile broke out across her face. "Is that a garbage bag?"

"Yes, it is," he said. "I had to walk here from up the block. There's a huge tree down blocking the road."

He studied her face, sharing a long eye-lock. Neither uttered a word, but communication zoomed between them.

Finally, her lips parted. "Thank you for coming."

"I'm guessing you didn't call the police, did you?" he asked.

She shook her head.

He was about to protest her decision, when he heard a slamming sound.

"There it is again," she said sotto voce.

"Sounds like it's coming from out back."

She nodded. "Somebody's out there. I'm sure of it. And, I just know it's the note-writer."

"Let me call the police," he said.

"No. The note did say he'd be here tonight. If he runs from the police, I'm back to square one. I can't take it anymore. This guy needs to think it's clear to be here and talk to me. I just hope he didn't see you arrive, you know, dressed like the 'Man from Glad' and everything."

"Sarah, listen to yourself. You're rationalizing a stranger's presence. You can't solve this."

"I have to."

"What would you have done if I didn't get here?"

"I'm just glad you did. This is going to stop tonight."

He recognized the determination in her voice, stronger than the hint of a sob bubbling in her throat.

He checked his watch. "It's eleven-thirty. We wait one-half hour. At midnight it's no longer Friday night. Agreed?"

She let out a deep sigh. "Okay. But, we can't let him know you're here. He could be looking inside the windows right now."

He was at a loss for words. Apparently she had a strategy and for thirty goddammed minutes he'd play along.

Chapter Nineteen

Sarah led the way into the kitchen, again crouched like Quasimodo while Benny followed sans black plastic bag.

She could tell what he was thinking. He thought she was an idiot hiding in the space between the refrigerator and the island. Maybe she was an imbecile to hold herself hostage laying in wait for a stranger to appear and explain himself. She *was* at her wits' end.

Her inn was crumbling around her, much like her life. But the one thing she could do, the only piece of power she had, was to face down the person making matters worse.

"Have a seat," she said in a low voice.

She plopped down onto a large throw rug. Benny followed suit making a soft grunt that sounded more like a scoff.

She offered him a tortilla chip from an open bag. "Chip? She held up an opened jar. "Salsa?"

"Are those my groceries?"

"Yes," she bit into one. "Sorry. I didn't have dinner. Have one but don't crunch too loud. Take small bites."

"Where's my beer?"

"In the fridge but you can't open it now. The light will give us away."

He reached into the bag and fished out a chip,

snapping off an end with gnashed teeth.

He was quite a sight in the semi-darkness, in socks with his outstretched legs in those signature jeans, darkened by dampness from the knee down.

She'd be even more nuts to offer to throw them in her dryer for him. Hell, bad enough he was here alone with her in the dark, his thigh just an inch or two away from hers. No way was she suggesting he free himself of that denim.

"So, now we wait?" He raised his shoulders, let them fall.

She raised her chin to the amusement in his voice. She sat up straighter as they both leaned against the cabinetry, their shoulders nearly touching. "We do."

He released a breath.

"Did you realize you forgot your groceries after you left?"

"Yes." He repositioned himself to face her. "Sarah, I have something to tell you."

His intent stare riveted her as she listened to the story of his visit with his brother, awestruck by the fact that he and Clyde Stone were partnered with Nick Pallis. She *knew* that zoning officer was no good ever since she'd first seen him unabashedly allowing his dog to pee on her tulips.

"I'm going to town hall first thing in the morning to blow the whistle on this. And, I'll do everything I can to get you the permits you need."

She felt a tear sting her eyes. A solution. Under normal circumstances she'd be elated on all levels. But, right now, that news just made her sadder. The Cornelia was crumbling at its foundation, as was she.

Tears fell from her eyes and she didn't even bother

to brush them away. They were real and it was time for them.

Before she knew it, Benny's arms were around her and she let him hold her. The feel of his big embrace, the solidity of his chest, the scent that no amount of rain could ever wash away, all worked together like an elixir.

She closed her eyes and breathed him in. She could almost hear the melody of Pete Bailey's music from that first night at the Pier House.

A loud bang sounded and they broke apart.

"I'm going out there," he said. He struggled to stand up from their cramped hideout.

"No, Benny, don't," she implored, grabbing at one of his arms. "You're going to scare him away."

"Enough is enough," he said. He took the flashlight she had beside her on the rug and darted from the kitchen down the hallway toward the front door.

She followed him. "Benny, it's only been a few minutes. We agreed to wait until midnight."

"Sorry." He shoved his feet into his sneakers, bent down, and tied his laces like he was assaulting them.

"Then I'm coming with you," she said.

"Sarah, for God's sake, wait here."

"I will not." She ran to the coat closet to retrieve her gardening boots. She tugged them on and turned to go with him. He was already gone and the black garbage bag was missing, too.

She carefully navigated the slick stairs in her boots while rain pelted her skin like needle pricks. She immediately saw the footprints in the sodden ground. She traced them across the front of the house and around the side. Benny had the flashlight and she struggled to see where she was going in the darkness.

Her heart pounded. *Where is he?* When she reached the back corner of the house, she paused and peered around the building, straining her eyes.

Benny was standing with his flashlight's beam pointed at the front of the shed where she stored summer supplies. The door to the shed had broken off from its hinges and lay nearby on the wet grass.

The light shone into the interior of the enclosure and as Sarah approached she caught glimpses of the old familiar items. The shiny metal handlebars of one of the bicycles she kept for guests' usage, two stacked Adirondack chairs that would grace the front porch in a couple of weeks.

"What do you think? Was he in here?" she shouted over the thrum of rain.

"Still is," Benny said without moving.

Breath lodged in her lungs, she stared deeper inside the shed following the beam of light to the back wall. Behind the dainty wrought iron table that belonged in her garden stood a solitary figure of a man. Her heart stalled in her chest as she let her eyes rest on his face. *Dear God!*

Chapter Twenty

Jeremy Hudson stood frozen with his back pressed against the rough wooden wall, his hands raised in the air as if caught in a police raid. He was bug-eyed with fear as though Benny aimed a revolver at him rather than a flashlight beam. In his hand, held aloft, was a familiar-looking envelope.

Confusion and anger danced through her senses as she registered the identity of the intruder. "Jeremy?"

"You know this clown?" Benny asked, keeping the beam right on Jeremy's face.

"Yes, I do," she said. "For God's sake, Jeremy, what the hell are you doing?"

"I screwed this all up," he said. With one eye squinted against the light glaring at him he reminded Sarah of Popeye.

"I was hoping to come here tonight to straighten it all out." His comment was directed at Sarah but then he turned his gaze to Benny. "Dude, are you wearing a garbage bag?"

"What's it to you? What the hell are you doing hiding in this shed?"

"I came here to explain everything to Mrs. Grayson. When I first arrived I saw two cop cars coming down the block. I panicked. I kept seeing flashing lights."

"Apparently there's a fallen tree," Sarah said.

"They're on the street taking care of that."

"I…I didn't know. I thought you called the cops on me."

"So you decided to break the door off her shed?" Benny fired his words like bullets.

"No, I wanted to just wait it out. I was desperate to straighten out this whole mess. The rain was coming down so wicked, I broke into the shed and I guess I screwed up the latch. The wind kept blowing the door so hard until it finally snapped off."

Sarah and Benny exchanged a look.

"Who is this idiot?"

Sarah let out the air that had taken residence in her lungs. "He was Hannah's first boyfriend."

"The one with the opal necklace?" Benny sounded incredulous.

"You know about that?" Jeremy asked. He, too, was incredulous.

"Jeremy, please." Sarah made to silence him before he managed to totally piss Benny off. "Benny. This isn't a criminal. Let's go inside and have Jeremy explain what this is all about. Okay?"

"It's your call, Sarah." Benny waved the flashlight like a billy club. "Come out of there and follow Sarah. I'll be right behind you."

****

Inside the kitchen, Benny removed his dripping plastic covering and tossed it into the large sink. He was still soaked, as were she and Jeremy.

Sarah, in bare feet with her pants rolled up to the knee, went into the Henry Clay suite to retrieve bath towels. She doled them out to the men before wrapping one around her chilly wet shoulders. She used a corner of the terry bath sheet to blot her saturated hair. She rubbed it as dry as she could. She was still shivering.

"I'm putting on a pot of tea," she said.

"Screw the tea," Benny said. "Let me have one of those beers."

Sarah closed the cabinet door she'd opened to retrieve mugs, deciding that Benny's idea was better. She pulled the six-pack from the fridge and placed it on the island.

Benny handed one to Sarah. She twisted the top and took a long swig. This was definitely what the moment called for.

"I'm really sorry," Jeremy said.

"Jeremy, I don't understand. Why on earth would you try to threaten us? Have you lost your mind?"

"Mrs. Grayson, please believe me…I didn't even realize how the notes must have sounded. I just figured you'd know somehow what I meant."

"Well, actually, unless what you meant was to scare me and interfere with my plans, then no, I don't have a clue as to what you could possibly have wanted."

"I'm still in love with Hannah."

Her body jerked, causing the towel enveloping her to slip to the floor. "What?"

Jeremy shook his head. "I thought you'd figure it out. That night at my shop when you bought the stationery I thought that was like your acknowledgement. I'm so sorry. Not about loving Hannah, of course…just the notes."

"Now I've heard everything." Benny reached for another beer. He tossed it to Jeremy. Although he flinched when it came at him, and the bottle wobbled in his hands, Jeremy caught it.

"Thanks, man," he muttered softly. The beige satin-bordered bath towel draped his head like a shroud.

Benny ceremoniously folded his towel on one of the bar stools and sat on it. He took a long pull of his beer. "Kid, let me tell you right now, I'm not leaving. So whatever you've got to say to Sarah about this bullshit you can start talking now."

"Jeremy, is that for me?" Sarah pointed to the misshapen, damp envelope he'd placed on the counter beside him.

"Yes. It's my explanation. I was going to leave it in case you weren't home, before…you know, I had to hide."

"Well, why don't you just tell me now?"

Jeremy pushed the towel from his head and it rested on his shoulders. He took a sip from the beer bottle.

"I'm still in love with Hannah. And, I think she still loves me."

"Cripes," Benny said.

"What? Since when? She's getting married in less than a month."

"She doesn't love that dude."

"How can you even say that?"

"We, uh, well…I was in New York not long ago."

"You were?" Something inside her twisted around and cinched into a knot.

"We spent some time together. We had dinner, that's all. But, it was enough."

"When was this?" The hinge of Sarah's slacked jaw ached. *What the hell was he saying?*

"In hindsight I see that the words I wrote to you

could have been misconstrued."

Benny harrumphed.

"My coworker pointed that out to me when I told her about what I'd said in my notes."

"You mean that girl that was in your shop the night Mrs. Allen and I were there?"

"Mara, yes. After you left I confessed it all to her. I told her how it was my plan to explain everything to you right then and there, but I couldn't get you alone for a minute. Mrs. Allen likes to talk."

A wry smile formed on Sarah's face. This was just so bizarre. She sipped the beer again, surprised at how much she enjoyed it.

"Look, kid," Benny said. "Why didn't you just say what you meant?"

Jeremy shrugged. "I thought for sure Mrs. Grayson would know what it was about." He turned his attention to Sarah. "You remember when Hannah was about to leave for college, and she broke off our relationship? I knew it wasn't you that convinced her to break up."

Sarah turned to Benny. "My ex-husband wanted Hannah to go off to school *unencumbered*."

"Do you remember what you said to me that day?" Jeremy asked.

"No." She wracked her brain for the memory. She did recall the day. But, she'd been consumed with her baby girl going off to be an adult, beginning her life and the future that she deserved.

Jeremy had helped carry Hannah's boxes to the minivan, his shoulders slumped with resignation. Silent and dazed, like two robots, each of them had gone back and forth into the house to retrieve her belongings.

When they had been about ready to leave, Hannah

and Jeremy stood facing each other. Sarah now remembered the lurch of her own heart when they'd folded into a desperate embrace.

Gary, barking orders to hurry, had done his best to end the moment with as much finality as the swing of an axe.

The two kids with tear-filled eyes had whispered softly to each other. Jeremy had unabashedly caressed Hannah's hair in spite of her father's obnoxious rants for her to get in the car because traffic would become a nightmare soon.

Hannah had climbed into the back seat and Jeremy gently closed the door, leaving his hand a moment to linger on the handle. He had turned to Sarah to say goodbye.

The words came to Sarah now as if written in ink on a sheet of shell-themed stationery. Before she could say them aloud, Jeremy spoke.

"After you told me that our time apart didn't have to mean forever, you said something else."

"The same wind that extinguishes a spark can also stoke a fire." The words escaped from her lips in a whisper.

Jeremy smiled. His eyes brimmed with tears. "Yes."

Her eyes floated to Benny's. Their gaze locked on old words of reassurance remembered by a man with an unwavering heart. Sarah swallowed hard. Who knew that random wisdom could serve as a boomerang?

"I love her." Jeremy said again. It was a simple statement, but powerful to Sarah's ears.

"Jeremy," she said. Her throat ached. "Hannah's getting married. I really didn't expect this at all. I mean, honestly that night in your shop I had the feeling you and your coworker were…"

"Mara?" He laughed. "Um, she's gay."

"She is?"

"Yeah. As a matter of fact she thought Mrs. Allen was hot. You know, for someone, uh, older."

Benny grabbed another beer. "And *that* calls for number two."

"Jeremy this is crazy."

"Sometimes the truth is crazy."

Silence befell them. Her eyes found Benny's again. They shared a forceful stare before Benny quickly pulled his eyes away and chugged his beer. Sarah took a second bottle into her hand and gave the last one to Jeremy.

Jeremy took a long swig before turning his attention to Benny. "I only left you a note because any time I tried to explain to Mrs. Grayson you seemed to be around. I've made a big fat mess out of this."

Sarah's head filled with more than Jeremy and Hannah's parting moments. Her mind flashed with snippets of the two kids' obvious camaraderie, the ease of their interactions, their connectedness. And, too, she recalled their palpable attraction.

At the time she'd worried about their physical involvement, hoping they'd behaved responsibly. But, there'd been no denying the magnetism between Jeremy and Hannah.

She'd known it at a level of her being the same way she'd known she and her husband did not share that, and never had.

She thought of Hannah and Ian. Did they share that same kind of love? If they did, she didn't see it.

Actually, wasn't it just recently she'd noticed a detachment in her daughter? Stoicism in Ian? Would what they shared have the power to sustain itself over time? Did they have the spark needed to withstand any wind? What stoked them?

She'd drained her second beer. The affect was a combination of the warmth of nostalgia and something else that had begun on a dance floor with Benny Benedetto. She let her eyes filter to him. His eyes were already on her, waiting.

"Jeremy, your approach in all this wasn't great," she said.

"Sucked, is more like it." Benny downed the rest of his beer.

"I know. I'm so sorry."

She held up her hands. "Okay, stop apologizing. That aside, I am concerned about how this will affect Hannah's life. She's scheduled to get married in a few weeks."

She swallowed hard. "I mean, you had dinner *one* night. You might be setting yourself up for major disappointment."

Benny surprised her by asking, "Do you think she's totally happy, Sarah? I mean, I was here when she found that necklace."

Jeremy gave a broad grin and Sarah felt a jab in her heart. Beer also had a way of bringing honesty to her surface.

Hannah deserved honesty from her. And, she deserved it from Jeremy, no matter the outcome. It sure as hell wasn't her job to keep anything else from her daughter.

"I think you need to talk with Hannah."

A still-soggy Jeremy gave her a hug and muttered a thank you. Then he walked around to Benny and offered his hand, which Benny tentatively took into a handshake.

"And, please, kid, do us all a favor. Tell her in person. Skip the notes," Benny said.

And Jeremy was gone through the door, into the night, a gust of wind blowing into the room in his wake.

Alone with each other and nothing left to drink, no one else to focus on, Sarah and Benny found each other's gazes. The burst of air that engulfed them did not chill her but rather acted as a bellows to the flame she could no longer deny.

She reached for the used towels, bundling them into her arms in a desperate attempt to escape into busyness.

Zealousness had become her solace over the years. Her garden out back was testament to that. In springtime the Rembrandt Tulips would be ablaze with their yellow and red stripes. The bed of Esthers, pretty and pink with their silvery tips would glisten in the coming sunshine. A garden of respite from what she'd lacked.

But, tonight nothing could chase away the feelings that whirled in the air, sprouting in abundance.

Benny stepped around the island and came close. He had collected beer bottles into his fists, holding them by their necks.

"Where do these go?" he asked softly.

She pointed to the recycle bin. "Thank you."

Benny placed the bottles into the receptacle then rinsed his hands at the sink drying them on a towel. Sarah watched and continued to hold the bunched towels in her hands like a terry bouquet. She needed to think, to break the spell that hovered over her.

"What do you think will happen now?" she asked, knowing the question was lame. How could Benny know?

He searched her face, his countenance soft, his eyes bathing her as if drinking her in.

She had no idea what repercussions Jeremy's declaration would bring. But, she did know about the man standing just inches from her. Her heart, swollen with emotion, bursting with need, slammed rhythmically in her chest.

This was crazy. Everything was crazy right down to Jeremy Hudson and this whole night.

"I think what will happen is what's supposed to."

"Benny, the wedding's right around the corner. This could become a fiasco."

"I learned a long time ago, that just wanting something to work out doesn't mean it will."

She thought of all the time, the wasted days of her life, she'd spent trying and wanting her world to be what it wasn't. She'd tried to be the woman Gary wanted her to be, to have the strong, united marriage she yearned for.

She opened her mouth to speak, but the only thing that came from her lips was a sad sigh.

"You know what?" he said in a gentle, soothing tone. "Let's shut the lights down here, make sure the doors are locked, and then you can let me fix you some tea upstairs while you get a nice warm shower. I'll send you off to beddy-bye, we'll call it a night, and I'll head on home."

Have Benny join her upstairs in the solitude of her

little apartment? Was that a good idea? She swallowed hard. She'd lost the ability to judge. But she was all too acutely aware of what she wanted.

"Come on up."

Chapter Twenty-One

Upstairs, Sarah showed Benny around the kitchen so he could start the tea. She felt his eyes on her as she stepped up onto a small wooden stool and reached for the tea kettle from a shelf. She hopped down and found their proximity dangerously close.

She thrust the kettle at him. "If you'll excuse me, I'll get out of these soaking clothes." A flush of heat climbed to her face. "Thanks for getting the tea started."

She turned away and headed toward the short hallway to her room. "The teabags are in the cabinet to the left of the window," she called over her shoulder.

Behind her closed door Sarah tugged off her damp, uncooperative pants while her mind reeled.

What would Hannah do with the news Jeremy would deliver? Was there some truth in what Jeremy said about the possibility of Hannah still loving him?

Sarah remembered how she'd found Hannah asleep on her bed wearing the opal necklace. She closed her eyes and took a deep, cleansing breath. All she'd ever wanted was for Hannah to be genuinely happy. The question was what did that mean now?

Whatever Hannah's definition of happiness turned out to be was up to her. Sarah wet her parched lips. Yes, *her* job now was to let it go, stop worrying, trust her kid, and let Hannah do whatever felt right.

Happiness deserved a chance and that started with the truth.

Her eyes focused on the closed door that shielded her from the rooms beyond and the man that was out there preparing tea. She swallowed hard. Could she follow her own advice?

After a quick shower she stood at her grandmother's mirror for a quick assessment. Her drying hair had turned into a fluffy brown puff, looking like a brown chrysanthemum blossom. She collected the mass into a bunch and stuffed it into a rubber band.

She leaned in close to the glass and stared deeply into her eyes. Something was different. She blinked before opening them wide. Yes. It was there. Her own truth shone back at her like tiny pin dots of light. Her heart welled in her chest. Happiness deserved a chance.

****

Benny stood at the sink fiddling with the top of the kettle Sarah had handed him before disappearing down the hallway. He tried to keep from imagining what she was doing behind her closed door. But, his mind went there.

He liked that messy, caught-in-the-rain look she had tonight. The wetness in her hair made it curl around her face, framing it in a halo of softness. Her face, free of any makeup, boasted its appealing freckles.

Benny opened the cabinet in search of teabags and struck gold. Behind the tin marked "Blackberry Blend," was a short squat bottle of blackberry brandy.

He grabbed a small saucepot from the drainer, abandoning the kettle. He made a concoction of tea, brandy and water, one that would warm their chilled skin. Inside his body was already a furnace of want.

Sarah came into the room wearing pale gray sweatpants and a matching pullover sweatshirt. She'd pulled her hair into a low ponytail that rested at her neck. He couldn't help but notice the little ringlets that had escaped the fastener, appealingly decorating her hairline.

With hands shoved inside the kangaroo-looking pouch on the front of her shirt, Sarah came to where Benny stood hovering over the saucepot on the stove. She smelled fresh and clean like laundry off a clothesline.

"That's different," she said.

"Hope it's okay I used a pot. I needed it to create this blend."

She peered in as he stirred the contents. The slow circular action released a pungent, fruity aroma. The combination of the succulent scents and her nearness nearly buckled his knees.

"Smells delish. What's in it?" she asked, standing dangerously close.

"Try it first, then I'll tell you."

"That's how we're going to play it, huh?" she asked. She took a tall tin canister from the counter and brought it with her to the small kitchen table.

He poured measures of his mixture into two waiting mugs and joined her. She had opened the canister and placed a round blond cookie on a napkin at each of their places at the table.

"What's this?"

"Try it first, then I'll tell you."

There was a small Mona-Lisa kind of smile on her lips, a flirty little grin that had the identical effect of a gulp of his toddy.

Sarah brought her mug to her lips and took a sip. She muttered a muffled moan as she pulled the cup away. "You found the brandy." She sipped again. "Very good."

There was something different about her, Benny decided. She was more relaxed in spite of the events of the evening. In spite of being rattled by the late-night appearance of her daughter's first love.

Hell, that on top of the fact that Clyde Stone had swooped in with talk of her building falling down, and then his revelations about Clyde and Sal's scheme.

She deserved brandy to accent her tea. She deserved more than that.

He bit into the cookie, a tasty almond-flavored round. "Good. Did you make these?"

"You think you're the only baker in Ronan's Harbor?" She tilted her head, assessing eyes on him. "Did you always like to bake?"

He could have just given her his typical shrug— that understated gesture he'd used all his life—but not tonight, and not to her. "Always," he heard himself say. "Since I was little."

"You come from a line of bakers?"

He watched her take a nibble of her cookie as her gaze remained intent on him.

"My mother was one of those natural bakers. She didn't need cookbooks or anything. It was only when I started showing an interest that she started writing recipes down. I still have them."

That little smile was back on her face. "Must have been a fun household." Her tone was light, but the eyes still focused on him, beaming with sincerity.

Benny couldn't help but respond in kind. "Well,

not when it came to my liking to bake. The men in my family saw it as a sign of weakness." He didn't fool her with his hollow-sounding laugh.

The brightness in her eyes dimmed, but the orbs remained intent on him. She didn't reply to his comment, but he saw the way she pulled her lips in on themselves.

"We were all cops from my grandfather on down. It was like an unwritten law or something. Benedetto men went into law enforcement. And, well, let's just say my turning into a real baker wasn't worth the aggravation."

"So, you went into law enforcement."

"Twenty-five years."

"But you didn't give up on baking."

"For a long time I did. Life got busy. I got married, worked a lot of overtime, the marriage went kaput. You know how it is. But, baking's always been there in my head, you know?"

"I do." She cocked her head. "When did you get back into it?"

"After I retired. It's amazing how it came right back to me. It's like riding a bike, no hands on the handlebars, arms stretched out in the breeze." He suddenly felt uncomfortable, as if he'd said too much. He shrugged. "Something like that, anyway."

He hoped the softness in her gaze was not laced with pity, but rather understanding. It surprised him how much he wanted that.

"I know. My sanity has been this inn." She stared into her mug, both hands wrapped around it. "When Gary and I called it quits, I had no idea how on earth to do this." She looked up and gave a little grin. "I mean, what did I know about running an inn all by myself?"

Sarah shrugged. "And now? Maybe not as much as I should know."

"Sarah, I'm sorry for your having to go through all this," Benny said, meaning it. "And, I apologize for my part in it. But, I have a plan."

She smiled at him. "Well, that makes one of us. I'm all ears."

"First thing on the agenda is meeting with the mayor, letting him in on what's going on. Hopefully he'll get those permits signed for you."

"Unfortunately, that won't change the fact that the foundation is about to give out and I can't afford to fix it."

"It's quite probable that Clyde Stone was exaggerating."

She gave him a nod. "I'll call my insurance company as soon as the office opens."

"So, you do have a plan."

Her look was sly. "Well, what do you know?"

He lifted his mug in salute. "In the morning then."

"It's already morning," she said.

He consulted his watch. *Shit, it was almost two.* He got up from the table. "Well, then I guess it's time to say good night."

She followed him to the sink where they each placed their mugs side by side. They shared another long glance.

"You going to be okay?" he asked softly. He looked down into her eyes.

"Yes," she said. She pulled her lower lip into her mouth, then let it spring free as though the effort would summon courage.

He felt his heart squeeze.

Her eyes smoky and hooded, she finally released a whisper, "Benny, I was wondering. Is there anything else involved in that plan of yours?" She took a miniscule step closer.

"Yes." He released a breath. "I'm pretty sure there is."

"How sure?"

"Damned sure." Benny pulled her close, their bodies melding instantly, their lips locking in a deep kiss.

Her arms lifted up over his shoulders and she wrapped them around his neck. She massaged a hand at the back of his head, her fingers delicate, yet firm. Their mouths moved back and forth rhythmically in a kiss that tasted both new and at the same time familiar—like long-lost lovers finally reunited.

The kiss broke but not their hold on each other. Their embrace only deepened and he could feel the length of her body against his. He whispered what was in his heart. "I've wanted to do that for so long."

"Me, too," she said.

He felt her warm breath on his neck. He pulled back so that he could see her face. Her eyes shone with emotion and it took his breath away. How in hell was he going to leave her now?

"I…" He tried to breathe. "I should go."

Sarah shook her head no.

****

In her whole life the only time she'd done this—led a man into her room by the hand—was in a fantasy. Reality, she was learning, was better. But pretty scary, too.

She gave his chest a gentle push with one finger, just a touch really, one that certainly wouldn't have enough force to move a sheet of paper let alone a man. But, that was all it took. He slowly collapsed back onto the quilted coverlet.

She stood in front of him, their eyes bound to each other. A jumble of emotions careened in her chest, in her belly, in her blood. Nerves, anticipation, surprise at her own behavior. It was all those things and it was the message her blood rushed around inside her, but mostly it was an electrical charge that obliterated any reserve. The throb of freedom that pulsed through her settled somewhere deep.

She tugged the sweatshirt over her head as she realized she'd never done that for an audience. Ever. The effort felt clumsy and the hood caught on her ponytail yanking her hair by the root. The garment was off and on the floor and with it was the elastic that had tied back her hair.

She couldn't even begin to imagine what the wavy brown mess looked like. She quickly gave it a shake with both hands, an apology for its appearance sitting on her tongue like a gumdrop.

"I love your hair," he said, raising up on an elbow and resting his head on a hand.

"You do?" She wanted to tell him he didn't have to say that, but the look on his face was so true, she believed he meant it. It baffled her.

"Yeah, it's"—he searched for a word—"springy."

That made her laugh and she plopped herself down next to him on the bed. If she turned just so, she knew she'd be able to see her image in the cheval mirror across the room. Absolutely no way. One look at herself in a bra—albeit her best one with the tiny satin bow between her breasts—and her hair bushed out like an overgrown hedge and she'd lose her nerve.

Benny reached up and touched her hair, a delicate hand that erased the thought. His fingers caressed the strands. "In the light it looks like it's laced with gold. But you knew that."

No, she didn't know that, but she didn't say so. She had no breath with which to speak.

He let his hand slide away from her hair, and placed a finger under her chin. "Come closer."

She leaned in, her heart slamming into her ribs, beating like a drum, a really happy drum.

"Your eyes are my favorite part of you, though. They look like amber with warm flecks of color."

An ache formed in her throat. She could tell this was not just flattery. This was unabashed honesty.

It touched her so deeply it was an effort for her not to cry. "Thank you," she managed in a low, barely audible whisper that rode gently on an escaped breath.

He beckoned her with the guidance of that finger at her chin, slowly bringing her mouth to meet his. It was a gentle, soft kiss, a touch of their lips that lasted just long enough for her to want more.

She pressed to his mouth reclaiming the courage that had begun its life here in *this* room on *this* night because of *this* man. He tasted of the brandy from the toddy he'd made for them. It was a sweet, succulent flavor and she savored it.

Benny rolled back, pulling her onto him, as their kiss deepened. His hands ran over the skin of her back, gentle touches feeding her desire like magic. His fingers found the hook of her bra and released it. She helped him free her of it, all the while their kiss still intact.

Finally, her lungs screamed for air, and she broke the kiss. She stared down at him in the dimness of the room, his eyes beacons of emotion. They each breathed heavily, gulping air.

She had the urge to tell him how much she'd been thinking about him over the days and weeks. How the sight of him in his jeans had clung to her senses since the beginning. How the memory of their dance, that random kiss in the dark, came back to her every night as she lay in this very bed.

In the silence of her room there'd been no one to judge, no one to say it was wrong or silly. But, all she could say, the only word that would form on her lips and escape from her was his name. "Benny."

She didn't tell him how she felt, but, dear God, she showed him. She did.

Chapter Twenty-Two

Sunshine filtered in through her curtains, a bright promise for the day ahead.

Sarah sneaked a glance at the man asleep on his side next to her, the blankets low on his torso. In the light of day she saw the fading tan line on his upper arm. The muscle, a strong bulge under the skin, called to her for a touch. She wanted to feel him again. Now.

Sarah covered herself with the bedding, holding the blanket up to her chin with both hands. This was mad. She was mad. She looked at him again, then back up at the ceiling. Crazy was underrated.

What would happen now? She closed her mind to the thought. She shouldn't speculate, an unfortunate habit she needed to break. She'd spent so much of her life projecting what would come rather than enjoying what was. She peeked at him again. Oh, she was enjoying now, all right.

His eyes opened and a lazy grin formed on his face. "Good morning."

"Good morning."

"You chilly?" he asked, lifting up on one elbow.

"No, why?"

"You've got the blankets up to your chin."

She looked down at herself and then back at him. "Well, maybe a little."

He reached out a hand to brush a few strands of

hair from her forehead. "It's officially morning. We have a plan."

"Yes, we do."

He scooted closer, pulling his side of the blanket up to his chin, too. She could feel his nakedness against hers. Her body zinged with anticipation, apparently having a plan of its own.

They turned to face each other, eyes locked above the highly placed bedclothes.

"Want to know what I'm thinking?"

She bit her lip and nodded her head.

"I know we said we'd tackle our plan first thing in the morning…"

"And it is morning…" she said.

"But, I'm thinking maybe we could modify the plan."

She breathed, allowing her racing heart to be her guide. She reached for him. "So, let's start modifying."

****

Forty-five minutes later, while Benny showered, Sarah made coffee.

She liked the way this felt; liked having a man—*that man*—in her bed, in her shower, in her kitchen. This was so dangerous, allowing herself to lower the guard that she'd nailed in place long ago. Hell, *that* guard had been blown to smithereens.

The English muffins popped up from the toaster as Benny entered the room. His black hair—still wet and shiny—was slicked back on his head, his face clean-shaven. It didn't appear that her old razor had nicked him.

"Coffee?" she asked.

"Yes, indeed." He accepted the mug she extended

to him and took a sip. "Good."

"Milk and sugar's on the table."

He waved a hand. "This is great."

Sarah noted everything about him now that she was allowing herself to like him, to enjoy him. While they sat at the small table going over their itinerary for the day she couldn't focus.

He even drank his coffee in a manly, virile way. She liked that he didn't use the mug's handle but rather wrapped his fingers around the vessel possessively.

She couldn't admonish her adolescent thoughts. If she didn't stop herself she might be asking to wear his ID bracelet—if he had one—to go steady.

They readied themselves and descended the stairs to the front door of the inn. Standing together at the entrance, each ready to tackle their separate missions, Benny kissed her.

His cell phone rang as he was about to leave. He stopped to pull the device from his pocket, talked into it, his eyes darted to her, and then away.

His expression morphed into something that pricked at her ease. Concern trickled into her veins. She was amazed at the automatic response she had, as though an invisible thread linked their senses.

Benny closed his phone after a few half-sentence responses to whatever was being said on the opposite end of the line.

"That was my brother." His voice was low, his mouth a seam on his face.

"Is there a problem?" *Another one?*

He laughed suddenly, but there was no smile in his eyes. "No, actually. Sal found a buyer for the house."

"I didn't realize…" she managed to say before

falling silent. *Hadn't realized what,* she thought? *That it isn't time for happily ever after in Ronan's Harbor?* How many times had the man said he couldn't wait to get out of this town? Plenty.

"Yeah." He raked a hand through his now-dry hair. "He, uh, said I've got to be out before summer starts. That was the deal he made."

"Wow. That's…soon."

"Memorial Day."

They stared at each other for a long moment. She did what she could to appear nonchalant, to hide the reality stinging her eyes and aching in the tender, freshly exposed place at the center of her chest.

"I'll call you," he said as he turned to leave.

****

Benny walked to his Jeep without looking back at Four Tidewater Way. He tried not to wonder if she was still standing at the door but he didn't feel her. Something told him she'd closed the big, old wooden door tightly after he left.

He sat in the chilly leather seat, inserted his key into the ignition, and turned it. The engine roared to life. He turned at the corner of Dolphin Drive and took the unavoidable ride past Sarah's inn. He'd been right. She was gone.

His mind churned with thoughts of Sarah and his impending leaving of Ronan's Harbor. He felt oddly pissed off. But, at what? Or whom? Sal? Sarah?

He laughed to nobody. No, he detested that sour feeling he got whenever he disappointed someone. It was a familiar crappy feeling in his gut, like he'd eaten week-old leftover Chinese.

He had known this would happen. *Shit.* He'd told

himself countless times not to get involved with anyone, particularly Sarah Grayson. Not with his uncanny knack for bestowing disappointment. *Now, here we go again,* he thought. *Double shit.*

Inside town hall, he told the lady at the desk that he urgently needed to see the mayor. He knew from his days on the beat that he excelled at appearing intense.

Hell, right now he *was* intense. He owed Sarah this. Sal had manipulated him and every goddammed thing in his path one time too many. Time was up.

That thought switched his mindset and he went right back to the nagging mental image that would not relent. He saw Sarah again, peeking out from under the country quilt looking vulnerable, her pretty freckled face just like a kid's, eyes dewy and soft.

John Reynolds strode down the hall toward him. He offered his hand, and with a congenial voice said, "Good Morning. Benny, right?"

"Yes, John, I apologize for not calling for an appointment. But I do have something I really need to talk with you about."

"Come down to my office." The mayor motioned with his hand and Benny followed him down the corridor.

Benny sat perched on the edge of the guest chair in Reynolds' office. John's eyes were on him the entire time Benny relayed what he'd learned about Clyde Stone's plan and the involvement of Pallis, the zoning guy, as well as his own brother.

"How sure are you about this?" Reynolds asked. His voice was steady, but Benny had been trained to spot nuances in voice. This mayor was pissed.

"Only what my brother confided. But, trust me,

that's the plan."

"I'll get to the bottom of it immediately, Benny. I appreciate your coming to inform me."

He tilted his head as he eyed Benny. "But, I am curious about what prompted you to share this news. After all, withholding this information would have kept your filed complaints locked solid."

"Sarah Grayson doesn't deserve the trouble this has caused her. I'd like you to toss those complaints in the trash where they belong."

"Your brother's name is on those complaints, Benny. Otherwise, I'd put an immediate rush on giving Sarah town approval."

"I believe if you contact him, he'll concur." Benny tendered the mayor a smile as he stood from the chair and extended his hand. "I'd like nothing more than for this to be behind us all."

"You know what I think?" John Reynolds asked, taking Benny's hand. He didn't wait for a response. "I believe you're forming an affection for Ronan's Harbor."

The words sent a clench to his nerves. He felt his knee joints lock. Not possible. He was leaving by Memorial Day.

Benny thanked the mayor for his time and help, then left the way he came.

Back at the cottage, he was glad now that he hadn't bothered to unpack his boxes. Exiting would be that much more efficient, easier.

****

Sarah stood alone in the entryway. Benny was gone but she could still feel him, smell him. She wondered how long the sensations would last.

Her mind was overcrowded with thoughts. His house was sold. He'd be leaving Ronan's Harbor. What did that mean, she wondered? She shook her head at the thought. She knew what that meant. Although she wished she could outwardly react to the news, she felt too numb. There had been too many things thrown at her at once.

She withdrew the marble Clyde Stone had left behind from her pocket and released it from her palm with a snap of her wrist. She watched the mottled glass sphere roll away, stall and meander back to her like a little round boomerang. She sent it sailing across the old wood planks again, playing a kind of game. But, it was no game. It was confirmation of what she already knew and there was no use in delaying the inevitable. She called the insurance company.

The company's representative was able to schedule an appointment the next afternoon. She stood now amidst the debris and clutter of the sunroom where the sheeting hung like Spanish moss over the carpenter's doings.

Harvey and Richie had arrived earlier to continue with their work. She'd explained the news of the foundation's problem she'd learned from Clyde Stone.

In an incredulous tone, Harvey had asked, "And you're just going to believe the guy?" He'd exchanged a look with Richie and she'd seen the message as if they'd spoken it aloud. They thought she was a fool.

"No," she said perhaps too harshly. "I'm not going to *just believe* the place is falling down. But, I've called my insurance company and they're sending a rep here tomorrow."

"Want us to stick around?" he'd asked.

For some reason the offer sent the threat of tears to her eyes. She managed a soft "No, I'll be fine."

The two carpenters left with promises to return if she needed. She couldn't blame Harvey for not seeing the extent of damage to the foundation. He and Richie hadn't been hired to inspect it. She eyed the disarray of their work in progress.

Hell, she owed them thanks for discovering the basement's water damage. Their find had produced Hannah's box of memorabilia that seemed to have pleased her. So much had changed.

Sarah closed her eyes to ward off the beginnings of a headache. She was antsy. Her mental list grew as she found herself among the sheeted mounds in the room. She needed to call Hannah.

And Gary. It was time to let the man know that he'd have his way after all. Despite her previous unwillingness to consider Gary's request to have Hannah's wedding held at his damned country club, it was time to give in. There was no way she'd risk the wellbeing of Hannah and Ian's guests.

She filled her lungs as she dialed Gary's office phone. His long-time secretary furnished polite small talk. Sarah bit her tongue when she heard herself speaking airily like the old days, prior to Gary's new life—playacting as if everything was just ducky.

Gary came on the line. "Is there a problem?" he asked right out.

"Yes," she breathed. "I'd say so."

There was silence on his end. Sarah's fingers, wrapped tightly around the handset, quivered in their grasp. "There may be a problem with the wedding being held at The Cornelia."

"Well, I could have told you that, Sarah Doodle." His voice had changed from a hint of concern to the insufferable pomposity that was the man's signature. "I'll contact my people at the club and—"

"Hold up," she said. "Listen, Gary. Apparently, the inn's foundation might be in poor condition and it would be unsafe to have the wedding here. I'm waiting on the insurance company to make that determination."

"What?" The harsh tone in his voice rang with accusation as if she'd had something to do with the crumbling of the stones holding up her house. "For God's sake…"

"Look Gary, just go ahead with making arrangements at your club, would you? I need to contact Hannah."

She ended the call with a shaky hand. It was true that Gary enraged her, but really the whole set of circumstances pissed her off. All of it.

She dialed Hannah. There was no answer. Sarah left a benign message that indicated she needed a return call.

Sarah got to work, blissful at the mindlessness of the task of packaging supplies for the wedding so that they could be moved to Gary's club for the reception.

The doorbell rang and the door opened before she had a chance to get to it. Gigi entered the sunroom with a look of surprise. "What now?" she asked. "Why are you packing up everything?"

"The wedding's going to be at Gary's club."

"You gave in to him?" Sarah heard the disappointment in her friend's voice.

"Not exactly. Have a seat and I'll fill you in."

Sarah relayed the whole story, everything from

Clyde Stone down to Jeremy Hudson's revelation.

"Holy mackerel. Jeremy Hudson's still pining away for his first love. Well, what do you know? And we thought he was into that girl that works for him."

"No. Apparently, *she's* into you. He said she thought you were *hot.* You've officially cornered the entire market. Just thought I'd pass that along."

Gigi laughed and shook her head, an effusive grin decorating her face. "Oh, this is just too much fun. What else could possibly happen?"

"I slept with Benny."

After a loud whoop and a series of handclaps, a laughing Gigi did a little jig, jumping with delight.

Sarah couldn't help but laugh, too. In spite of the craziness and the upheaval, she *was* glad.

And, she was happy to see her friend looking and sounding so much like herself. Sarah hugged Gigi close. "Gigi, how are *you* holding up?"

Gigi pulled out of the embrace. "You mean how's tricks since I've started living the best years of my life? Well, it's been interesting. Mickey had the nerve to contact me."

Sarah felt a zing of anger spark her blood. "He—"

"Wait." Gigi was still smiling, anticipation dancing in her pretty dark eyes. "It's delicious. He got home from Vegas and immediately called me with his typical apologies and promises. He loves me, he knows that now, he's so miserable without me. You know, the whole spiel."

Sarah felt herself relax, feeding off the vibes Gigi was sending out.

"So, what'd you say?"

"I told him that I hope he finds what he's looking

for, but it certainly is not me; and I hung up. I've ignored all his calls, texts, emails, and even his flowers."

"Mickey seriously sent flowers to the owner of a flower shop?" Sarah asked.

"Yeah," Gigi said.

The pride on her face was so endearing, again Sarah felt tears stinging her eyes. She'd been doing that a lot lately. "I'm so proud of you," Sarah said.

"Thanks, Sar. I'm pretty proud of myself, too. So's Sheldon."

"Who? Sheldon who?" *Oh, Gigi, no.*

"My shrink," she laughed. "I have a shrink now. How's that?"

"Wow," Sarah said.

"And, before you ask, Sheldon doesn't look like a body builder or anything. He looks like Santa Claus."

"Well, that helps," Sarah laughed, each silently acknowledging Gigi's insatiable pheromones.

"Yes," Gigi chided. "The new Gigi's done with being a ho-ho ho."

"Sweetie, you've never been that," Sarah protested. "I'm just glad you're on the right track for yourself."

"Holding out for the real deal someday," Gigi said. "But, for a while, I'm going to be my own real deal."

Sarah thought of Benny. Her feelings were real, but was there any future in what they'd shared? She didn't know. There was so much about her world now that she didn't know.

"So you and Benny," Gigi said, shaking her head. "It was only a matter of time, my dear. Ever since that night at The Pier House."

Sarah couldn't even protest. Before she could say

anything, the front door opened again and Gary charged in. Sarah and Gigi exchanged a glance. *Here we go.*

"This is quite the disaster, I see. But, truthfully, this is a blessing in disguise," he said as he eyed the cartons and the carpenters' hovel. "Realistically, this is no place for a wedding." He gave her one of his patronizing grins. "You can relax now, Sarah Doodle."

Sarah picked up a small carton of unscented votive candles and marched over to Gary. In the few steps it took her to reach him her mind reeled with all the times they'd been through this same scene. All the times—as he'd said afterwards—he'd given her enough rope and then swooped in to take over before she choked on her own failed plans. *Enough*, she thought with each footstep. *Enough.*

She shoved the box of candles at him, pressing it to his chest.

"Here's the thing, Gary. There's nothing I can do about the condition of my inn until I find out the specifics. I managed to convince the insurance company to send an inspector tomorrow. When he makes his assessment I'll deal with the consequences."

She pressed the box closer against his body. "I am confident that you will make sure the changing of our daughter's wedding venue will be a seamless effort. I'll do whatever you'd like to assist in making the occasion as lovely as possible. Now, if you'll excuse me, I've got a few things to do, as you can see."

She straightened her shoulders, lifted her chin. "And, Gary, I'd like you to stop, I mean it, just *stop* referring to me as Sarah Doodle. No more. Do you understand?"

He slowly took the rattling box of votives into his

hands, eyes on her piercingly, his face a stoic plane. "I didn't realize it bothered you."

"That's my fault, then. But, now you know. Okay?"

"Okay." He gave her a slight nod.

The door opened again and this time their daughter blew into the entryway with a suitcase at each hand. Her face was flushed. Her long, usually smooth, hair was windblown and splayed around her shoulders.

She strode closer and stood at the threshold of the sunroom. She dropped the suitcases at her sides.

"The wedding is off."

Chapter Twenty-Three

They all waited in the inn's main kitchen. Silence hung in the air like fog.

Gary sat perched on the edge of a stool; his body rigid, arms folded onto the butcher-block surface as though he were the chairman and this were the boardroom.

Gigi sat quietly examining the napkin she had folded into a little paper fan.

Hannah, in patterned leggings and a long, sloppy sweatshirt, paced. She babbled while marching back and forth like a duck in a shooting gallery. She was making Sarah dizzy.

"Slow down, sweetie, you're wearing out the floorboards," Gigi said.

"Hannah-bear," Gary cooed. "Please clarify. I'm confused. You're not making any sense. You're not marrying Ian because he didn't buy you an opal? Is that really what you said? For heaven's sake, look at that rock on your left hand. Doesn't that trump an opal?"

"Gary, let Hannah speak." Sarah turned to her daughter. "Hannah, where's Ian."

"He's in New York. Oh, and I quit the temp job, too. And then the agency quit me. So, I'm unemployed *and* I'm homeless."

She started to cry, her hands flying to her face. Sarah jumped from her stool and rushed to her.

Gary rose from his stool and joined them. In an instant their crying daughter was enveloped in their arms, the meat of their parent sandwich.

Hannah continued to cry loud heartbreaking sobs; sounds that Sarah guessed were too deep, too guttural to be new. These tears, this anguish, had to have roots and at last this needed to expel. Though it was more of an explosion.

Sarah felt a hand on her arm and looked up to see Gigi's glistening eyes. She mouthed "I love you," and discreetly left through the back door.

"Please stop, baby," Gary said. "You'll make yourself sick."

His face was ashen. In spite of his youthful attire and his nifty haircut, Gary looked his age. His slate-blue eyes were clouded with worry.

Oddly, Sarah's heart lurched. The man was a lot of things, that was for sure, but Gary loved his daughter. There was no denying that.

"Gary," Sarah whispered, "Let's give her some air." She stepped away and gently touched Gary's hand where it held onto Hannah for dear life. "Come on, back up a little."

Gary did as he was told and took a couple of steps away from his child. He stood with his hands by his sides. Sarah realized it was the first time she'd ever seen him look helpless.

"Gary, sit down. I'll get us some tea. Hannah, sit by your father." The two sat like zombies, one sniffling and trembling.

Sarah poured hot tea into three cups. She delivered the steaming tea with a hushed warning to "Be careful, it's hot."

"Okay, Hannah, let's go over this again. I'm gathering that this isn't some whim. This is something you really feel you need to do, correct?"

"Yes, Mom, I do," she said, the words riding on a jagged-sounding sob. "But it still sucks."

"It does," she agreed. "It sucks." Her mind wanted desperately to go right to listing, one of her sanity-saving compulsions.

Instead, her thoughts ricocheted against the walls of her brain. There were calls that would have to be made, cancellations, returned gifts…

"I still don't understand," Gary said, coming to life. "I mean, I thought you and Ian were perfect." Gary's voice became a whisper. "Just perfect."

"Daddy, we haven't *ever* been perfect. Nobody is anyway. Nobody's *perfect*. People are flawed. We all are, Daddy." She caught a sob, swallowed it. "But, Ian and I don't make each other happy. I haven't been happy in a long time."

"And this Jeremy Hudson makes you happy? Is that what you're telling us now?" His voice started to rise. "Out of nowhere, poof, you're throwing away everything for the kid at the beach?"

Hannah jumped from her stool. "You see, Daddy? This is what you do. You condescend, you dictate, you control. Stop. It's *my life.*"

Hannah looked to Sarah. "Mom, I didn't break off my wedding so I can go off with Jeremy. That's not what I'm saying, you get that, right?"

Sarah did know.

But Gary had selective hearing and she was sure that all he heard was that his virtually hand-picked son-in-law candidate was being kicked to the curb for the surf-loving kid operating a sundries store.

"Tell us what you are saying, Hannah." Sarah shot Gary a look. "We're listening."

She watched Hannah take a deliberate, deep breath and let it out with a whoosh. "I have to find out where my head's at, and I need the time and the space to do that. But there are a couple of things I do know for sure."

She waited to see if Gary and Sarah were still with her. Apparently satisfied that that was the case, she continued as if reciting a list of her own. "I'm sure I do not want to marry Ian. I'm sure that there's something unresolved between Jeremy and me. I'm sure I do not want to work in a big city in a big office doing things that don't matter to me. I want to pursue the career that has always meant so much to me—The Seeing Eye."

Over the years Gary had managed to steer his daughter away from the low-budget philanthropy, into the direction of bigger, more glamorous work and it had failed. Sarah now felt at fault for not seeing this more clearly and calling him on it. But, ah, hindsight didn't need glasses to read, and Sarah did.

Sarah was glad that Gary didn't interject. He let Hannah speak. She had an appointment with the local branch of the organization to learn the requirements for becoming a trainer. The girl, in all her anguish over her tough decision, had already begun a plan for herself. Sarah's heart swelled with pride.

When Hannah had gone to the powder room, Sarah cast Gary an assessing eye. A kind of pity washed over her. He looked like a Thanksgiving Day parade balloon that had sprung a leak. All the gusto had drained from him and he sat in a slack bunch of defeat.

"She'll be okay," Sarah offered.

Gary lifted his downcast head and met Sarah's gaze. His mouth bent in an anemic grin. His cell phone sounded and he reached into a pocket for it.

While he was busy, Sarah went to greet Hannah when she reentered the room. "Mom, I'm beat. Mind if I go flop on my bed upstairs?"

"That's a good idea; I'll be up in a little while."

Hannah motioned her head toward Gary. "Daddy going to be okay with all of this?"

"He's fine. Go flop."

Gary had gotten up from the counter stool and was standing as he spoke into cell phone. She saw his mouth curve into a grin. "I know, babe. I know," he said. "Me, too."

The call ended and he turned to Sarah.

"Where'd she go?"

"To take a nap."

Gary nodded dully. "Well, I guess we've got some calls to make, huh?"

"Yes. I'll keep you posted on how she's doing." Sarah walked Gary to the front door.

"Piper says she'll do whatever we need to help handle, you know, all the details."

"That's great," Sarah said. "Be sure to tell her thank you from me."

He looked at her. "I will. Thanks."

"Hannah will get through this, Gary. She's pretty resilient."

"I have no doubt," he said. "She's her mother's daughter."

****

Up in her apartment, Sarah tiptoed to the door of

Hannah's room. It was ajar, the crack open enough for her to see Hannah on her side with a throw over her body asleep. The poor kid said she hadn't slept the night before.

Sarah thought of her own night. There she'd been, blissful in Benny's arms, while her daughter anguished over her own life. A ball of sadness filled her throat. *Oh Hannah.*

Chapter Twenty-Four

Over a pot of hot coffee the next morning, Sarah and Hannah made a list. Piper had called and volunteered to help with some of the cancellations. Periodically, Hannah released a sigh, looked at her mother, and repeated one phrase. "What a mess."

The insurance company's representative arrived just before noon. Dennis Madison, a squat man with a bushy moustache, introduced himself with a clipped, staccato-toned authority. Accompanying Dennis was an independent inspector, who went by the singular name "Whitey." Whitey had been hired by the insurance firm to assess the situation.

The two shuffled back out through the front door and down the stairs to the yard. Sarah watched through the side window, squinting into the wavy glass.

Would they confirm the doom that now resided inside her bones? Would Whitey warn her to pack up her belongings and leave the inn before she and her daughter got hurt? Her mind reeled with movie preview-like scenarios.

She returned to her phone-calling tasks. The daunting ordeal became tedious. Every invitee that she spoke with offered words of wisdom and sympathy. All were kind. But, relaying the vanilla version of their rocky road predicament wore Sarah out.

"My eyeballs are squirrelly," Hannah lamented as

she crossed another item from her list. "The chairs are cancelled and the linens as well."

"I'm starved but I don't have it in me to make us anything," Sarah said. "Right now all I want is a candy bar."

"Tell you what, Mom. I'll take a walk to the deli and get sandwiches. I could use some air."

"Super," she said with a lackluster use of the word. "Oh, and get us a chocolate bar."

"King size big enough, Mom?" Hannah's eyes were sullen and her mouth curved sideways at an apologetic slant.

Sarah had to give the kid credit—she was doing her best to mask the repercussions of her decision. She knew, too, that Hannah's conscientious efforts to bulldoze through their tasks were her kid's way of taking ownership of the aftershock. That knowledge only served to fuel Sarah to dig deeper and help lighten her daughter's load.

She reached up and massaged the tender area above her shoulder blade. The cluster of knots in her muscles was a familiar byproduct dealt by motherhood's determined hand. They'd smooth out eventually and the soreness would fade away. At least Sarah knew that much.

With Hannah gone, Sarah itched to walk and get a bit of a stretch. She threw on her cable-knit work sweater and went outside. It couldn't hurt to check on the insurance agent's doings and get an idea of what this Whitey guy had to say.

She walked parallel to the variegated flowerbed along the old foundation. She could not keep from examining the winter-hardened mound of mulch where her flowers would soon emerge. The timing couldn't have been more precise, the blooms in full glory in time for the wedding. Her heart quickened. Only, now there would be no wedding.

Now the question of the day was whether or not the tulips she'd so strategically placed bulb-by-bulb would awaken to another season of The Cornelia Inn or would they sprout in the foreground of a condemnation notice? She didn't know the answer, but with each step she took, her need for something definitive grew stronger.

She rounded the corner of the building and spotted the men and their clipboards. She braced for the news. "So, any verdict?" Oddly, her voice came out normal, almost friendly, as if the men were deciding on paint color for the shutters.

"We've got more data to gather," Whitey stated. He glanced up at Sarah briefly before holding a camera in front of his eye.

The agent took a step in her direction. "Who was it that told you the foundation was sinking? Your carpenters?"

"No, actually, it was a private citizen looking to purchase the inn. After talking with my carpenters, they concurred. Or at least they agreed with the necessity to investigate the condition, anyway."

"Well, you've got some serious damage going on, Mrs. Grayson, so in that respect whatever led you to make the call was a good thing," Dennis said. His twitching moustache reminded Sarah of a dizzy caterpillar. She was feeling a little dazed herself.

"A good thing," she echoed.

"But, the source of the water will determine more, right Whitey?"

The inspector looked away from his lens. "I'll need to access the crawl space."

Sarah led them to the sunroom where they navigated the clutter. She saw their eyes scanning the disheveled mess.

"My carpenters were, uh, stopped in mid-project," she explained. "Now everything's on hold."

Dennis crouched in front of the basement's hatch. He aimed the beam of a flashlight into the space while Whitey slipped through the passageway.

"How's it look?" Dennis asked.

"Wet. Lots of water."

Sarah turned on her heel and strode out from the sunroom needing to be beyond ear shot of what they were saying. She found herself back in the kitchen staring out the back door's windowpane. The grounds needed a spring cleanup. It was getting near the time when she'd usually call the landscaper to come and work his magic, tidy up the lawn and the shrubbery. She stepped away from the scene.

Hannah returned with the sandwiches just as Sarah ended her call to Melrose Caterers.

"I got tuna subs." Hannah withdrew two cylindrical packages from the bag. "And chips. I need chips today."

She withdrew an extra-large rectangle of chocolate and waved it in the air. "And the brick you ordered. Maybe I'll take a bite of chip then a bite of chocolate...you know, go right straight to hell."

Sarah shook her head but felt the signs of a true smile playing across her lips. "You're *so* my daughter."

She grabbed for the chip bag and tore it open, offering it to Hannah to reach in for the first handful.

Hannah motioned with her head toward the handset Sarah had just placed into its cradle. "Who was that?" she asked with a mouthful of crunch.

"The caterer. She was so wonderful about everything. And genuinely sympathetic."

"I'll pay you back for the deposit, Mom. It'll take a while, I'm afraid. But, I will."

Sarah did not respond, deciding that Hannah simply needed to say the words aloud.

They unwrapped their sandwiches and each took a bite.

"I can't believe I've put you all through this," Hannah said after she swallowed. "If I could undo it, Mom, I would."

"Hannah, look, imagine if you went through with the wedding and then came to realize it wasn't right. So, let's be grateful for that, even if it took you until now to get here."

"You know, Mom," Hannah said with a cock to her head. "You're really handling this way better than I'd have imagined."

"Nonsense."

"You are. I mean, I like it."

A grin broke out across her lips. "And, I'm also liking that you've opened yourself up to the idea of a relationship of your own."

Sarah opened her mouth to protest, but her daughter held up a hand. "Please, I saw two mugs in the upstairs sink, two dishes in the drainer, a few damp towels in the bathroom…"

"Okay, your honor. I plead the fifth."

The sound of their shared chuckles warmed Sarah's heart despite the fact that she didn't really know what was going on with her and Benny.

Their night together had been amazing, and she knew she liked him—more than liked him. But what that all meant, well, there was no way to tell. She only knew the thought of his leaving town, moving away from Ronan's Harbor, made her ache inside.

Dennis Madison called out. Sarah and Hannah rushed to hear the news. They found him standing in the foyer looking over Whitey's shoulder as they both perused the inspector's open notebook.

Dennis lifted his gaze and smiled with another caterpillar-like twitch. "Mrs. Grayson, these are just preliminary remarks, obviously, and we'll have to prepare our final report, but for now I can tell you that the culprit of your damage comes from faulty plumbing."

"Okay…" she said, not knowing whether this was bad or worse news.

"And, that means that your policy will cover the damage. Minus your deductible, naturally."

Without thinking her hands flew to grip his arms. "Really? Oh, thank God, really? I won't lose The Cornelia?"

"Lose it?" Whitey made a face. "No way. It'll take some overhauling and time. But trust me; you'll be able to get your inn in shape."

She couldn't help it. She started to cry. In the flash of that moment, she had allowed her greatest fear to surface. Hannah slipped an arm around her mother and tucked her close.

"I'm sorry," Sarah said as she swatted the tears on her face. "I was just so worried. I'd been told the place was going to be condemned."

The agent patted her arm as if she were a lunatic. But, she was one relieved lunatic. The two men shook Sarah's hand before taking their leave.

"I didn't realize how worried you were," Hannah said. "Why didn't you tell me how bad it could have been?"

"And, add that to your barrel of fun?" Sarah said. "I knew you'd been tense about something. I wanted to spare you more concern."

Hannah reached up and tightened the elastic band holding her hair up in a ponytail. "You should have trusted me to be okay with knowing what was going on."

A smile came to her lips. "Right back at you, kid."

"Point taken," Hannah said, the words rode on a little grin. "I'm going for a walk, Mom. I told Jeremy I'd stop by and let him know how I'm doing."

"Have you had time to process your thoughts about Jeremy?"

Hannah shook her head, bunching her mouth sideways. "I'm too overwhelmed to really sort anything out. But, there's something in here." She placed a hand to her chest. "And it's never really gone away. What that means, I guess time will tell."

"Have talked with Ian?"

"Yes."

"How's he doing?"

Hannah blew out a breath. "Truthfully, in one way he seems relieved, though mad as hell in another."

"Mad?"

"Ian likes to call the shots." She smiled ruefully. "Trust me; he'll be the first one of us to recover."

Hannah double-checked her ponytail before

breezing out the door.

****

It was all in the timing and Benny had always sucked at that. He stood at the ancient stove, hovering over the small, dented pot, stirring the milk and grated coconut with a warped rubber spatula.

He hadn't tried the recipe for more years than he could count. Hell, finding it shoved in that old box of his mother's had been a feat of its own. He'd had plenty of time to abandon the spontaneous cockamamie idea, but no. Once he started to rummage through the cards and clippings, he couldn't stop himself.

The dry ingredients were no problem. He was good with measurement. That's how he lived too, he mused as he scooped flour into a tin cup. Exactitudes. Just what's needed. No more, because *more* guaranteed a flop.

He sighed as he dumped the white powder into a glass bowl. He refilled the cup and dumped that measurement on top of the first, forming a powdery soft mound.

He grasped his old hand mixer. The outdated avocado-green tool was one of the few items that actually belonged to him. He sunk the beaters into the softened butter and pushed the "on" button. This was the tricky part, the one he'd never gotten right. Timing.

Timing is everything, his mother used to say. He thought of her in her floral dress. Her jet black hair tied up in a knot, hand at her hip, eyes locked on her project as she created another culinary masterpiece. Her timing had always been impeccable, only failing her once—she'd died too soon.

Benny liked making quick breads and muffins. He

was good with the cookie recipes handed down from his mom, too. All had become second nature. But in those recipes were margins for error. He could make do with the ingredients of those concoctions and they always turned out pretty damned good. They were easy.

You've got to accept what you're good at. That was *his* motto.

He thought of what he would be doing once the cake was out of the oven. He had to tell Sarah the news about the permits being issued, and yet he was reluctant to see her. He couldn't look into those amber eyes right now knowing that he would soon be walking away.

He'd thought of calling her about the permits, but that was just chicken shit. He breathed in deeply, letting the air expend through his mouth. She deserved a face-to-face visit.

He concentrated, or tried to. He still had the frosting to finish. His mind consistently reverted to thoughts of Sarah—of looking into the eyes of the woman he'd managed to disappoint in record time. *Disappointing women,* he mused with a shake to his head, *accept what you're good at.*

Later, with the cake cooling on racks, Benny knew he'd waited long enough. He changed his ingredient-soiled shirt, ran a comb through his hair, and splashed water on his face.

On his way to her inn Benny tried to practice his words. *But, how do you tell a woman goodbye when you feel like this?* He swore aloud. No more, he vowed. Done.

He reflected on the Key West brochure. He recalled his notion to retire there, maybe bake for a coffee shop, hell maybe even *open* a coffee shop.

That far away no one would know he used to be a cop. They wouldn't know, or care, that he'd had a life before he'd stepped foot onto their shore. It would be so easy.

That had been before Sal convinced him to go in on the Ronan's Harbor beach house partnership. That had been before Sarah Grayson.

His brother was an opportunistic scam artist and that's just what Benny felt like as he pulled his car up in front of The Cornelia Inn. He closed his eyes. He could not erase the memory of last night.

He could still feel Sarah in his arms, the softness of her skin on his fingertips. If he'd had any sense he'd have left before it got to that—but he'd known it would happen, at least at some visceral place—and that had been his crime.

Benny rang the doorbell and waited. Even after variations of what he should say had rolled around in his mind time and again he didn't know exactly what he would utter. The words lodged in his throat.

Sarah opened the door and stood staring at him. She was a vision in a dark green sweater, her hair wavy and soft. She bit her lip.

He felt a pang somewhere just at the glimpse of a tooth pressing down onto the softness of her pink lower lip. She'd nibbled his the night before, had whispered she liked his mouth.

"Hey there," she said. A tentative smile formed on her lips, reaching her eyes. *Those eyes.*

"Hey there," he echoed. He sounded hollow to his own ears, as if his entire chest cavity was empty, void of what belonged inside, a heart.

"Sarah, I've got some things to tell you," he said.

****

A jolt shot through her. Just seeing Benny at her door did that to her now. At the sight of him, an image of their entwined bodies popped into her head and stole her breath.

But, there was something else, some unease. She felt it, and saw it in his dark eyes. She took a step from the threshold and stood beside him on the porch. She softly closed the door behind her.

"Hannah just got back from a walk. She's inside. Can we talk out here?"

"Sure."

She moved to the top step and sat down. Benny sat in place beside her. She didn't look at him, but rather focused her eyes on a patch of dead grass that would need to be reseeded.

"I went to see John Reynolds," he began. "I told him the whole story and he's going to deal with the zoning guy for his involvement in Clyde Stone's plan."

"Good." She turned to him. "Thank you."

"And he's revoking the complaints my brother and I filed. He's going to put a rush on the permits. You shouldn't have any trouble now, Sarah. It's over."

There was no joy in his eyes. She could feel that there was something more. Whatever that was, she was sure she didn't want to hear it.

"Benny, the wedding's off."

"What?"

She explained while he silently listened, his eyes boring into hers.

"Whoa," he said. "How's Hannah?"

"She's kind of shell-shocked at her own decision, I think." Sarah shrugged a shoulder. "We all are."

"Where does the kid with the opal play into this?"

"He's a part of it," Sarah said. "He was the eye-opener, I think. Will she wind up with Jeremy? Who knows? But, my daughter's got plenty of time to figure it all out."

"You're a good mom," he said. His voice was soft and it rang with something that sounded sad.

"Did you hear anything from the insurance company?"

"They were here earlier," Sarah nodded. "The news is good, well kind of. Not sure what's involved yet, but The Cornelia Inn is not going to need a wrecking ball any time soon. Turns out there is a lot of water damage, but it's all fixable. You know, in time, that is."

"Good news, then. And the cost? Did they say if it'll be covered?"

She nodded her head. "Yes, thankfully, my coverage qualifies the repairs. Minus the deductible, but I consider it a godsend."

"So, what next?" Benny's mouth turned into a lopsided grin. "Any clue how long before you'll be back in business?"

She shook her head. She did not know the timetable for when her inn would be fully restored and ready for vacationers again. There was still a host of things she didn't know, including the reason for Benny's mood and the energy he projected.

She hoped silently that it had to do with regret for leaving Ronan's Harbor, perhaps even a change of mind. But, somehow she knew it was not that. No. She dared not even hope.

"Sarah, I…" Benny rested his elbows on his knees as he stared straight out ahead of him as though he could see what he was about to say written on the row of hedges along the front of the property.

Sarah looked there too and saw only the greenery with a few tiny new growths sprouting up from last year's trim. Sarah let her gaze fall to his profile as he continued to stare outward. Perhaps it was the future he looked for, searched for. She was in that club, too.

"Benny, whatever you've got to say…"

He turned to her. The pain in his countenance shot through her like a bullet.

"Last night was"—his Adam's apple rose and then fell as he swallowed—"so nice, great really."

Watching him trip over his words and struggle for them wrenched her. Her hand itched to reach for his. But, she didn't move.

He shook his head as though trying to cast away an image in his mind. "But, I'm not sure it was the smartest thing, you know, for us to do."

His eyes pleaded with her to say something, but she was beyond words. *What does that mean?* She wanted to shout it at him, but she had no breath, no voice. She waited.

"Believe me," he said. His voice suddenly sounded more robust as if he was trying to convince her, or maybe himself, that he was right. "You don't want me to be in your life. I'd make you miserable. It's what I do."

She couldn't stop the tears from filling her eyes, but she'd be damned if she'd let them spill. She pressed her thumb and index finger against her lids and massaged away the evidence of her blasted vulnerability.

"I'm leaving," he continued. "I've got to be out of

the cottage by Memorial Day."

"So you've said," she managed.

"Trust me, Sarah; this is the right thing for you."

Trust him? Ever since Benny Bendetto had crossed her path she should have known not to trust him. She knew that veering off that path had been her own stupidity. She couldn't even blame him. But her heart crackled into tiny pieces anyway.

"Well," she said after a deep breath. "I agree that your leaving is the right thing." The tears refilled her eyes. "For both of us."

His lips parted as though he were about to say more, but just as quickly they closed again. He gave one short nod and then stood. "I should go," he said.

She stood too, on jelly-filled legs. She put a casual hand on the banister. "I've got to get back inside." She motioned her head toward the front door. "Lots of details still to tackle."

"Yeah, I'm sure."

"Goodbye, Benny." She turned away. She didn't care how long it was until Memorial Day. She wouldn't see him again.

She didn't wait for his retreat, but strode on those wobbly legs as though walking an imaginary line painted across the floorboards. She closed the door and heard the latch click. At least she was the first to walk away.

Chapter Twenty-Five

Back at the cottage Benny broke off a piece of the cooled cake and popped it into his mouth.

He'd done it. He'd managed to replicate his mother's recipe. But, he hadn't bothered with the frosting. He'd lost the desire. He pitched the cake into the garbage and closed the lid.

He went into the living room and stared at the storage cartons still sitting in a line along the front wall. The packing tape had been torn free and he'd need to reapply new strips when he left.

He had a couple of drawers full of clothes, his toiletries, some of his other stuff he had taken out, but not a whole hell of a lot. He could be packed up in no time. There was no way in hell he could wait until the end of May. Not a chance. If he left now it would be as if he hadn't even been to Ronan's Harbor in the first place. Gone without a trace.

****

Sarah climbed the stairs to Gigi's loft and rapped hard on the purple-painted door. When her friend answered, bright smile on her face, eyes expectant, Sarah blurted the question she had on her mind. "What time is it?"

"Did your watch battery die, honey?" Gigi asked as Sarah breezed in past her.

"No. I just need a witness," Sarah said. She was out

of breath, and for more reason than the trot it had taken for her to get here. It was the current state of her existence that sucked the air out of her.

"Sit down. You're making me nervous."

Sarah plopped onto the couch.

"Obviously something's up. You breathe, I'll talk. Here's what I already know. The wedding's off. The inn's not a knock-down but it needs some major help. You slept with the Rottweiler and it was—what adjective did you use?—oh, yes, it was *awesome.* Have I got it so far?"

"He's gone."

Gigi sat on the easy chair opposite Sarah. "What do you mean *gone?*"

"He's leaving. Just going away."

"But, what about his house?"

"It's sold. New owners take over on June first."

"And, what about you and him?"

Sarah snorted. "You mean me? There's no *me and him.* And you know what? I'm fine. I really am." Sarah caught herself pounding her fist on her chest as if she was trying to restart her stalled heart. "I'm more than fine. I'm relieved. I am. Glad even."

"You don't sound glad."

"Well I am!" Sarah clapped her mouth shut after shouting. "I'm sorry, Gigi. I just think he's a stupid ass. And, I'm glad to not be in the company of a man like him. I have enough things to worry about these days. Like what am I going to do to earn a living until I can resume business at the inn?"

Gigi blew out a big breath. "Wow."

"Yeah, wow. So, wait, what time is it?" Sarah looked at her friend.

"It's four-forty."

"Good, nice easy number. Four-forty. I like it. Yes. Okay."

Gigi scooted close and locked her gaze onto Sarah's. "Honey, can I just remind you that I'm the screwball in this relationship? We can't both be nuts."

"This is the minute, the very second, that I start over. A, no more bullshit, and B, no more crap. I'm in charge of me and what happens. What do you have to drink around here?"

"White or red?"

"Red."

Gigi left the room and returned quickly with two glasses of red wine. She handed one to Sarah then sat beside her.

Sarah held her glass up toward Gigi's. "Let's toast four-forty and my emancipation from the bonds of the last few months."

"Wait." Gigi lowered her glass. "Let me say something first. Sarah, I know how much you've had to deal with in a very condensed time. It's been a lot of upheaval."

"You think?"

"And…" Gigi said, ignoring Sarah's snarky comment. "And, I've been your friend for a long time. The woman sitting here on my couch is not the Sarah I first met. You're a totally new person."

"You're damned right I am."

"But, that didn't happen at four-forty today, honey. That happened the day you got that first letter. You know what? That letter may have delivered bad news, but it also delivered you to yourself."

Sarah felt a lump form in her throat. She pulled air

into her lungs. Her mouth was dry, the swallow was harsh. She opened her mouth to speak but nothing came out. Gigi touched her knee.

"You've taken all this craziness by the horns and have wrestled it to the ground. You've won every single battle, Sarah. That's what's *awesome*, pal. *That.*"

Gigi took Sarah's hand into her own. "Benny's the first, maybe the only, man that you've cared enough about to be mad at, disappointed over, given yourself to—despite the odds and the circumstances. If you really think it's better that he's gone, then I'll toast that. But, if you're lying to yourself, then do something besides check the time."

"You're wrong." Sarah felt tears again come to her eyes. This time she left them alone. Let them freely spill in their own way and in their own time.

"I'm not."

"Yes you are. About one thing, Gigi. You are wrong."

"Oh yeah? About what?"

"You're not the screwball in this relationship."

"Okay," Gigi said happily. She held up her glass. "Now we can toast."

****

Benny dreaded Sal's response when he told his brother the cottage would be empty until it closed with the new owner. But, that was tough shit. The fine captain had better know better than to argue the point.

For the first time in their lives, Benny was calling the shots. Sal sure as hell wouldn't want his baby brother blowing any more whistles on this fiasco at this stage of the game; so he would like it that Benny was leaving, or he could lump it.

Benny sat on the indented cushion of the old sofa contemplating his next move. An image of Key West popped in his head. He saw himself driving over the long, water-flanked bridges as he approached the island. Could he really do it? Just up and go?

He sighed. Sure he could. Why not? He lived a nice uncluttered existence sans excess baggage. He'd have plenty of dough once the cottage closed. He closed his eyes. Far-fetched or not it was a sweet, uncomplicated plan.

He went into the kitchen for a beer, popped the cap, and took a long pull. His mind went back to where he did not want it to go—Sarah. It would be a long time before he'd forget the look in her eyes when he'd told her he was closing the door to any further relationship with her.

Even if it was for her benefit, and he knew damned well the day would come when she'd be glad for it, it still sucked to see that disappointment taking residence within the flecks of her amber eyes.

He took another long pull of the cold beer and savored the way it cooled his throat.

He spotted the mixer he'd washed and laid out on a towel to dry. He put down the beer and assembled the pieces into its cradle and clamped them into the plastic storage box. He let his gaze cast about the little kitchen. Yeah, it was old, but it had potential for someone who cared enough to see beyond the disrepair. It had "good bones" as his old man used to say about both houses and women.

He opened a carton and looked for a spot for the mixer. He rearranged some of the items in the box. Each time he palmed one to examine he wondered what the hell had possessed him to keep such a thing.

The 1972 Charger model he'd made when he was a teenager because that had been the car he had wanted at the time. The decals were curling from the plastic now, the glue having dried up long ago. He put it back in the box.

He found his mother's burlap-covered photo album with the cut-out felt letters that spelled "Memories." He settled himself onto the sofa to give the album a look-see.

He immediately recognized his mom's loopy, neat handwriting where she'd written on the inside cover. "Holidays," it said. The first quad of photos looked as if it was his parents' first Christmas.

The black-and-white snapshots captured their youth, smiling for the camera that was most likely held up to his grandfather's eye. His childhood living room with the giant-flowered wallpaper and the filmy window curtains were a glimpse into his far-reaching past, one he hadn't thought of in a long time.

Who knew what the old place looked like now since the family had sold it?

The next page was dedicated to brother Sal's christening event. His young, thin parents stood with the raggedy-looking priest from their old parish, their baby swaddled in a cloud of white. The proud couple beamed at the lens.

There were photos of the party that followed, relatives who'd been gone a long time now, but who still looked familiar to Benny as if he'd seen them recently. It was like looking into his past through binoculars.

Several pages in, beyond Easter feasts and sparkly-flamed, candle-lit birthday cakes, was another Christmas. Benny counted the months. He'd been about two-and-a-half when the shot was taken. He remembered the festive bubble lights with their liquid that boiled when they'd gotten hot enough. He'd loved those. Fronds of tinsel feathered each branch like metallic icicles.

In front of the over-dressed tree stood his young and virile old man, in a white sleeveless T-shirt. His thick, muscular arm cradled a toddler to his hip. Benny recognized himself, a cherub's grinning fat face, watery mouth ready to drool.

The old man dangled an object for the baby, mesmerizing a young Benny with the very compass that sat now in his carton of junk. In the photo Benny's chubby little hand was forever frozen in mid-air as it reached for the burnished brass chain that dangled in front of him. His father's face was aglow like the tree behind him, proud-looking even, as he watched his small boy's reaction.

Benny felt his throat scratch in a swallow. He abandoned the trip down memory lane to fetch another beer. He guzzled half the bottle before returning to the living room. He closed the photo album and put it back in the box.

He fished for the compass and brought it over to the couch to inspect. He lifted it out of the old wooden case and dangled it in front of his face like his old man had done all those years ago.

All this time Benny had been sure the bequeathed memento had been another one of his old man's digs at him, a kind of mockery. Benny tilted his head and gave the chain a gentle swing. That was probably the truth.

But, what if it wasn't? Maybe the old man had given him the compass because he remembered the moment of joy he and Benny had shared over it. Could be.

Perhaps it hadn't been a message of Benny's being lost. After all, he'd been the one to lose his own way in life. Nobody and certainly no compass could remedy that.

It had been his own steps he'd taken to get to this place, right here and now. Not Sal's, not his old man's, not the fact that he'd failed to procreate. Benny owned that, and swallowed that knowledge with the rest of his beer.

He let the compass rest in his palm. It was heavy in his grasp, cool against his skin. He wrapped his fingers around it and pressed. An antique device to rescue the lost or to guide those who seek. Benny suddenly realized that he was neither.

He needed to call Sal right now.

****

Hannah was cuddled under a quilt on the living room sofa when her mother returned home. Sarah felt tired, leaden. She lifted Hannah's feet, sat, and placed them onto her lap. She positioned the quilt over herself, as well.

"How was your visit with Mrs. Allen?"

"Good," Sarah muttered. She leaned her head against the cushion and closed her eyes.

"Jeremy said to 'say hi.'"

Sarah opened her eyes and gave her daughter a long look. Hannah shifted herself, sitting up against a pillow she'd stuffed behind her back. Sarah supposed that to any that didn't know her circumstances, Hannah would appear to have her act totally together. Her patrician features exuded confidence.

Sarah's heart skipped. She knew how tough it had been for Hannah to make choices that had plunged her into a state of the unknown. But Hannah had taken that risk, to avoid making a huge mistake, regardless of the big question mark that now hovered over her. Sarah gave the kid credit.

Right now, tucked under the brightly patterned quilt, Hannah seemed relaxed, more relaxed than Sarah had seen her in weeks.

"You look good, Hannah."

The girl gave Sarah an easy smile. "Thanks, Mom." She lifted a tea cup to her lips with both hands and eyed Sarah over the rim. "It would be a shame to waste this tea, Mom. It's delicious." She produced a wry smile. "You can change it to the "Non-Wedding Tea.""

"We can rename it. But, not that."

She shook her head. "So, Hannah, tell me. Are we talking about future plans tonight or are we just vegging?"

Hannah put the cup down and sat up straight. She folded her hands on top of the quilt. "I think we should talk about future plans and I think you should go first."

Sarah laughed. "Well, that's easy. Right now I hurry up and wait."

"Wait for your future?"

"No, wait for the approvals, the repairs, the rigmarole that'll surely be involved. Just thinking about it makes me dizzy."

"Okay, so that's The Cornelia's plan. What's yours?"

Sarah started to speak, then stopped. She'd almost

said that the two were the same thing, but that wasn't completely true. She was more than an innkeeper. Her life was more than The Cornelia. She'd figured that much out in the last few weeks.

If she were honest, she'd admit that it had been Benny that had helped her see that. Longing crowded her brain and pinched at her eyes. She missed him.

"I'm sorry, Mom. Maybe we should just relax tonight."

"You know what, Hannah? One thing I want for myself is to have the same kind of courage you have. I think you might be my hero."

Hannah pulled her lips in on themselves, her lifelong habit saved for warding off tears. "I have my moments when I think I'm less courageous and more just plain crazy."

"No, crazy is when you just accept a current situation even though you know it's not right." The words rang in Sarah's own ears.

She let her eyes focus onto the flames dancing in the fireplace behind Hannah. She saw Benny in those flames, envisioned him packing up and leaving Ronan's Harbor, his face as sullen as it had been when he'd come by the inn.

It dawned on her right then and there that Benny was leaving without hearing the truth from her. Whether it mattered to him or not, he needed to know how she felt. She needed it, too, regardless of the outcome. She owed it to him but she owed it to herself more.

"Is there any more tea?" she asked.

"Yeah, the pot's on the counter." Hannah gestured toward the kitchen.

"Let me get it. We need to make a toast with the brew if we're going to rename it."

Sarah retrieved the pot, poured some into a cup, and refreshed Hannah's measure. She lifted her cup with confidence. "To our futures."

As they enjoyed the pungent blend, each with their private thoughts, Sarah mulled her personal definition of courage. When the cups were empty they agreed Sarah's herbal concoction would bear the moniker of *The Hero's Tea.*

Chapter Twenty-Six

In the morning, Sarah found herself in The Cornelia's parlor idly running a dusting rag over the table surfaces. The old radio on the bookcase was tuned to a station that played big band selections. She immersed herself in the sounds.

In the foyer she heard Sarah and Jeremy talking. He had come by with his dog, Augustine, named after Florida's town of St. Augustine. Jeremy had acquired the pooch from a shelter there when he'd gone surfing one winter. Sarah heard soft, easy chuckles coming from them both.

She made her way over to the spinet piano and ran her rag over the mahogany. From there she could see the couple as Hannah readied herself to join Jeremy and Augustine for their walk. Sarah watched Jeremy help Hannah adjust a fleece headband over her ears.

There was a familiarity between them, a closeness that time had not erased. Did that mean that destiny would find Hannah and Jeremy together permanently? No one knew, but for now, for today, Hannah was happily joining Jeremy and his dog for a walk.

After they'd gone, Sarah moved into the foyer and stood in front of the portrait of Cornelia DeGraff. The wooing sounds of "Moonlight Serenade" wafted in from the parlor.

"Well, Cornelia, our inn's not going anywhere just

yet," she said aloud to the painting. "I'd say this place has your tenacity."

Sarah looked long at the woman's face, the glint in her eyes. That had been one fearless, determined woman. The clock on the mantel chimed ten times. It was the time she'd decided that she would deliver the truth of her feelings to Benny.

She left a note for Hannah on the kitchen counter before donning her jacket and going outside into the cloudy, chilly morning. A breeze nipped at her skin.

She walked down her quiet street hoping she wouldn't run into Hannah and Jeremy. She didn't want to talk with anyone right now. She needed to keep her mind on what she planned to say to Benny.

The thoughts were a tangle in her head at the moment. She couldn't straighten out the sentences into a precise, cohesive statement. She didn't want to just blurt out something stupid.

Could she even define how she felt? Love was so foreign a concept, a feeling, a part of her life that had been long forgotten, stored away like a memento.

Sure she loved, continued to love. She loved her daughter immeasurably, Gigi, her inn, her town. But a man? This man? An ache formed behind her eyes and in her throat. Dear God, the truth was there, beating inside her, matching her footsteps as she approached Benny's cottage.

A soft yellow light glowed over the front door although it was daytime. The gravel driveway was empty and it was more than the chilled air coming in from the ocean that made her shiver. She strode through the gate and went up to the door. She gave a good loud knock once, twice, a third time. It did not open.

She stepped to the far edge of the stoop and peered into the living room, squinting to see through the slats of the blinds. She strained to make out the interior.

Was he gone already? she wondered. Really gone? Could he have just taken off already, packed up and left Ronan's Harbor in his dust? Her heart sank. She'd missed her chance.

How she felt, now that she had let herself feel it, define it, own it, would stay hers alone, locked in her heart.

She turned to go, the wind stinging her eyes, conjuring tears. She touched the corners of her eyes with her index fingers. She'd been ready to come clean, open her heart. Maybe that was a win in itself. She'd come to take the chance and hadn't chickened out. That counted for something.

As she descended the steps, she paused. She stood silent, breath held. Yes, she heard it. The sound of a Jeep, Benny's vehicle as it approached. Suddenly, all her resolve melted through her, like ice in the sun. She was drowning in momentary indecision.

Benny steered his vehicle into the driveway, the gravel groaning under the weight of the tires. The back of his truck was filled to the hilt with storage cartons. So he was making his exit. This was probably just a pit stop of some kind.

Her heart pounded in her chest. *But, he isn't gone yet. There is still time.* She swallowed hard. Did she still have it in her now that she knew he was packed and ready to turn his back on everything here?

Benny hopped out from the Jeep. His footfalls crunched on the gravel as he came over to her, each step announcing his gaining nearness, as if she needed the stony signal.

"Sarah…"

"Hi…" She laughed for no reason. It was an odd sound that did not belong in the air between them. "Did you, uh, forget something?"

"What?"

She gestured to his truck. "You're all packed up. I thought you'd gone."

He smiled then. It was a soft gentle grin that brightened his face and lit up his eyes. "I went to see Sal first thing this morning. I was going to call him last night, but I decided what I had to say needed to be said face-to-face." He took a step closer. "I've decided to buy him out of the cottage."

"But…"

"He's telling the interested buyer that the place is no longer for sale."

She pulled air into her lungs.

"As soon as I got back to town I went to The Cornelia to see you. Hannah and Jeremy were sitting on the front porch and she told me you'd taken a walk."

"I came here."

"I see that."

"So, you didn't leave. But, all those boxes." She pointed to the back of his vehicle.

"They're empty, Sarah. I was bringing the empty cartons to your place in case Hannah needed them since she's going to be moving home."

"Wait," she laughed again but this time it didn't sound like a misplaced noise. "I'm very confused."

"Come inside," he said. "The wind's kicking up out here."

"No, wait, there's something I came to say and I

just might as well say it, Benny. I almost lost my nerve, and when I thought you'd left already, I almost lost my chance. So I just need to say this. Now."

"Okay then." In a near whisper he said, "I'm listening."

"I have lived a long time not feeling what I feel for you now. I thought it would be a crime, a shame, a disservice to both of us if I didn't tell you…I'm pretty sure I love you."

"I see." He stepped closer, so close she could feel his breath warm on her skin. "How sure would you say you are?"

She looked into his eyes. Her heart raced with assuredness. "Damned sure."

Benny reached into his jacket pocket. "I didn't go to your house just to bring you empty boxes. I went to give this to you, Sarah." He withdrew his father's compass and placed it into the palm of her hand.

"Is this your father's compass?" She asked staring at it. She looked back up at him. "You want me to have it?"

"It's not an opal or anything, but it feels right that you should have it."

He paused, swallowing hard. "I'm not lost anymore. I realized that everything, all that I am, all that I want is here in Ronan's Harbor with you. You, Sarah, are my *true north*. If I ever feel lost again all I need to do is look to you."

Sarah flew into his arms and they embraced there on the short, squat patch of sand that was Benny's front yard. The compass still in her fist, she held him tight. Benny was home and she was his.

A word about the author...

Award-winning author M. Kate Quinn draws on her quirky sense of humor, hopelessly romantic nature, highly developed sense of family and friendship, and her love for a good story while writing her novels.

Her Perennials Series began with *SUMMER IRIS* (Wild Rose Press, July 2010), a Golden Quill Award finalist for Best First book. The second, *MOONLIGHT AND VIOLET* (Wild Rose Press, June 2011), won the coveted Golden Leaf Award for Best Contemporary Novel 2011. *BROOKSIDE DAISY* (Wild Rose Press, February 2012), a Golden Leaf Finalist for Best Contemporary Romance 2012, completes the series.

M. Kate Quinn, a lifelong native of New Jersey, makes her home in South Jersey with her husband Harvey and their magnificent Siberian cat, Sammy.